NO SHELTER BUT THE STARS

VIRGINIA BLACK

2024

Bywater Books

Print ISBN: 978-1-61294-279-7

Bywater Books First Edition: January 2024

Printed in the United States of America on acid-free paper.

Cover designer: Ann McMan, TreeHouse Studio

Bywater Books
PO Box 3671
Ann Arbor MI 48106-3671

www.bywaterbooks.com

For Kate, who understands everything,
and for Nico (again), because this one
is as much hers as mine.

PART ONE

CHAPTER ONE

Kyran's screams scrape the back of her throat until her voice cracks.

Althea's command deck is obliterated, the open communications link now static in Kyran's helmet. The silent explosion spills its violent red and yellow brilliance across the vacuum of space.

Benna. *Benna.* Commander of the fleet, regent, protector, cousin—though more like an older sister—and the only one who knew all there was to know about Kyran, who asked the most from her and gave her more than everyone else combined.

Benna is dead. The light from the explosion fills the cockpit of Kyran's single-person fighter and she shivers, but not from the cold.

The Sifani vessel, the only one left from an enemy squad of five, breaks off its attack and flies toward the dark side of the planet Ellod.

The rest of Kyran's squadron is dead, and the command ship *Althea* is undefended. Those pilots were not her friends, yet they have spent much time together and each loss burns in her chest. She pushes her fighter to maximum velocity, eyes on the ship in front of her though all she can see is Benna.

Whoever is on that ship killed the only family she had left. Escape is not an option for them.

Desolate heartbreak wars with a fiery rage. Kyran has never killed anyone, and today she must learn. Her target changes course, flying toward the asteroid belt and the moons beyond.

Kyran's knees brush the console as she leans forward, willing her fighter to move faster in chasing the lone enemy ship through the black, desperate not to let it get away.

She fires her last missile at the veering ship and misses. The ship isn't firing back. Maybe its guns have malfunctioned, not that Kyran cares.

Her fighter's engine seizes then reengages at decreased velocity. Half the console's sensor feeds blink red. The telemetry module—the only way she'll have to navigate back to the fleet—goes dark.

The fleet is no longer in visible range, and her instruments are failing.

"Althea Nine to flight command," she says into her communications link.

Her rage chills when no one answers. At this reduced speed, her dwindling fuel won't get her back to the *Althea*.

The enemy ship's external lights give away its position, and Kyran won't let it escape the justice she intends to deliver. She follows it into the asteroid belt, where the magnetic interference botches the little data provided by her functional sensors. The larger asteroids are avoidable even with her limited control. The smaller ones scrape her hull, smashing against the canopy visor, alarming her already frayed nerves.

Beyond the belt looms one of this planet's three moons. The Sifani vessel slows when it approaches the atmosphere. Kyran doesn't, closing the distance between the two ships. The controls rattle in her hands as the fighter reacts to the moon's gravitational pull. The enemy ship straightens its trajectory and descends.

Kyran curses at her instruments. The fighter is not rated for atmospheric descent and might disintegrate on entry. Her missiles are gone and her guns are spent, leaving only a projectile drone with an electromagnetic pulse.

The tracking system flickers and stabilizes as life support blinks from yellow to red. A sob wracks her chest as Kyran focuses on her target.

Her fingers, slick with sweat, slide against the trigger as she fires the drone. The machine is virtually invisible in space, but it must work because all the lights on the enemy ship go dark in sync. The ship spirals into a rapidly increasing spin.

The moon's gravity sucks the enemy into its well with Kyran's fighter not far behind. A piece of equipment—something shot loose in the battle or rattled in the violent rotation—detaches as the enemy ship dives toward its hopefully inevitable ruin.

She hopes they die screaming.

The scrape and clank of debris hits her fighter, whose velocity is only marginally slowed by atmosphere. Beyond the fighter's canopy, fiery red light gives way to clouds—thick and murky and backlit. The engine noise roars in her ears as the fighter sinks.

The clouds break and jagged rocky terrain comes into view, black and gray and brown crags and valleys.

This is a lifeless rock.

The controls respond only well enough to lift the fighter's nose. The console goes dark. She has no way to decelerate.

The fighter bounces when it hits the ground, scraping overland, each screeching grind ending in a crunch as parts of the ship fall off.

The light outside is slanted, casting long shadows—morning? evening?—and something larger than her ship looms ahead. Kyran grips her harness tighter before her fighter slams into the unknown.

Sharp pain spikes through her and blackness follows.

Kyran blinks grit from her eyes as she monitors the power conduits. Her workstation on the bridge, with its multiple displays, is double the size of the others and patched into all the major subsystems on board. She's had to divert power from other sections of the ship to keep the flight deck operational.

"Commander Dobri." One deck officer whirls in his bolted seat,

his tired eyes glinting with news as he calls to Kyran's cousin, Benna.

Active duty for bridge staff has lasted seventeen hours and counting, and his announcement sparks a flurry of restless movement on the bridge of the commandeered Sifani ship rechristened Althea.

Tall and lean like Kyran, Benna leans over his shoulder to read the screen on his console. Her short auburn hair, in contrast to Kyran's shoulder-length dark blond hair, falls into her face—both of them are overdue for a haircut. Benna tucks an overlong strand behind an ear as she raises her hand for quiet, an unnecessary gesture since no one is talking. All eyes are on her.

"The scouts have reported in. Probe data confirms the planet is habitable."

A weary cheer rises, then fades at Benna's pointed glance.

"Open a fleet-wide channel," Benna says to the communications officer and points to a deck-to-deck section of bulkhead. A moment later, another display flickers and reveals the blue-green planet and its orbiting bodies, including an asteroid belt and three moons.

"Attention, all personnel. The stars of this system match the old records of Ellod, the planet of our proud ancestors. They were driven out by the tyrants of Sifani Prime. We've now received confirmation Ellod will sustain human life.

"Our people have been spread across the galaxy like sparse seeds." She pauses to clear her throat, the emotion cracking her voice. "Now we've come home."

This time, the cheer becomes a roar. Kyran closes her eyes, suppressing the urge to cry.

While many of her people chose not to join the pilgrimage to find Ellod, over six hundred make up their fleet. For years, they have traversed the outskirts of imperial space, scrounging resources to stay alive while they searched. Now, they have found their ancestral home far beyond the core worlds of Sifani Prime, and the true work begins.

This sector encompasses dozens of solar systems, mostly unpopulated and undeveloped by the empire. It is also outside established Sifani security patrol range, according to Benna's network of contacts. On the bulkhead display, multiple data feeds scroll on the periphery of Ellod's image, data sent from an advance squadron of fighters scanning the planet and its environs. In the wake of Benna's fleet-wide announcement, pilot chatter streams from the bridge's audio ports.

"No signs of humanoid life," one pilot says. "Zero contacts. Repeat, zero contacts. Sending surface topology results."

"Getting some electromagnetic interference on the dark hemisphere from the asteroid field." Laz is their best pilot. His baritone crackles over the connection. "Whatever ore and minerals are in the asteroids keep affecting comms. We lost the sensor drones, so all we know about the moons is they have breathable atmosphere."

The fighters' suborbital scans of Ellod reveal expansive oceans between continents large enough to provide a home for their people for generations.

Kyran had hoped to tend to the fleet forever with Benna securely in command. She is pressed between a longing for a home she's never had and a responsibility she's never wanted.

"Princess, a word?" Benna beckons for Kyran to join her.

Kyran prays Benna doesn't want her to make a speech. She stands and clandestinely stretches her legs, wincing at the sound of ripped fabric. One of her over-mended stitches must have come loose.

"Please stop calling me that," she says when she reaches Benna's side, lowering her voice so no one else hears.

"It's good for morale."

"Not as much as my ability to program the water reprocessors."

Althea *is the oldest and largest ship in their contingent. Appropriated from a repair yard on the outskirts of the core systems and repurposed for the Ellodian fleet, all its surfaces have been scraped of every Sifani emblem and designation. The original ship's programming remains, and Kyran is one of the few people in the fleet who both comprehends some of the Sifani language and also possesses the technical understanding of how the equipment functions.*

"A word from you will give them hope," Benna says.

Kyran's weariness prompts the truth. "They get that from you."

As regent, Benna has commanded the fleet since the death of Kyran's parents. If Benna possessed a drop of royal blood, she'd have been crowned years ago.

Kyran wishes she could transfuse her parents' legacy into Benna's veins. She cannot remember her father's face or her mother's laugh. The future they envisioned for the Ellodian people, for Kyran, grows more substantial.

Benna ignores her protests and raises her voice to the bridge crew. "Today marks the twenty-eighth anniversary of Princess Kyran Loyal's birth into the shining light provided by our ancestors."

Kyran freezes, having forgotten the date.

"We stand on the precipice of our journey's end," Benna says. "When we have established a foothold on Ellod, our first order of business will be the coronation of our queen."

As the last descendant of a long-dead monarch, Kyran is of age to claim her birthright, her kingdom a caravan of stolen ships full of rebels to the Sifani empire, guarded by fewer than a dozen fighters.

The mood on the bridge is ecstatic, but each smile feels like a blow. All they have endured is pushed aside as these people—resilient and driven people who have lived with the realities of an uncertain life in space far too long—turn to her for the perfect future they've been promised, as if her sole existence can change their fates.

Benna dips her head in an unspoken invitation for Kyran to speak, which Kyran ignores. Benna applauds instead, and the deck crew joins her.

Before the applause fades, Kyran returns to her station.

Benna concedes and doesn't pursue her. "Beta shift, take a fifteen-minute break. Alpha shift, once they return, you're dismissed until the next rotation. Everyone else, at your leisure. You've earned it."

Kyran follows the crowd to the line in the mess hall, resolving to wait the half hour for a hot meal. A dozen metal tables, all bolted to the deck, are mostly filled with tired men and women leaning over their meals of greenish-brown stew.

A man in front of her groans. "They cut rations again? We've gone from half-full bowls down to cups."

"Makes the grub look like more," a woman says. "Better for morale."

A fighter coordinator behind Kyran tugs on her sleeve.

"I wish your parents could see you now, Kyran," he says, his eyes

wet with tears. He's twice as old as she is, yet as exuberant as a child. "Their spirits will be pleased when you take the throne."

She nods and says nothing. Though Benna is only a few years older, she is more qualified and should continue to lead. When Kyran isn't aiding the bridge crew with the foreign Sifani systems, she spends her time fixing equipment throughout the fleet or working flight support for the fighters. She can't do the real work to help her people from a throne.

Hot food is no longer appealing. The dispenser near the door administers ready-made rations, reduced to one quarter thanks to their limited supplies and extensive journey. Tasteless yet convenient, the block of processed food has no comment on the anniversary of her birth.

The crew quarters in the aft portion of the ship are beyond the flight deck. Kyran glances through glass along the corridor, which provides an open view of diligent crews tending to mismatched fighters and scrambling to keep aged equipment in working condition.

She's consumed her rations by the time she reaches the barracks area. A short trip to a sanitation stall removes the smell of a long work shift from her skin and the grime from her hair.

Kyran stumbles the last few steps to the dormitory. In one dark room, columns of bunks built four-high into the bulkheads offer restless sleep—no personalization and no privacy. Kyran collapses into the first available bed that doesn't require her to climb a ladder.

She has four hours before she's due back on the bridge. She curls her body toward the bulkhead, her back to the room, and ignores the tears that come the moment the false sense of solitude relaxes her limbs.

She falls into a dreamless sleep.

A crackling whispers to her. Kyran opens her eyes, gasping while a foreign rhythmic tap keeps time with the pain pummeling her head.

The harness holds her fast to her seat. Her body aches from the crash, though nothing feels broken. Weak light shines through the cockpit and into her helmet's visor, emphasizing new cracks and one thumb-sized hole.

The console is shattered, and its metal frame is warped from the impact. The tapping is rain, a thin slurry of dirty water and dust.

The odor of burning makes her fumble for the harness straps.

Fire flickers in the mangled engine compartment, flaring despite the rain. What little is left of the ship's fuel must be acting as an accelerant. The fire spreads toward the cockpit.

By the time she pulls the manual eject lever, flames crawl along one side of the ship, sweat coats her skin inside her flight suit, and smoke curls up from somewhere under her legs.

The canopy pops off as designed. She whines as her boots burn her toes, as flames singe one arm of her suit, and she screams with the effort to release the harness. As she lifts herself from the cockpit, her gloves stick to the still-hot hull, and she whimpers as she yanks her hands free. One glove melts into the frame, and she tears her hand from it.

Kyran jumps to the rocky ground, falling to her knees when her legs don't hold. Something small in the cockpit explodes and spits sparks, and she searches for safety.

Loose, fist-sized rock and scree slow her escape in the waning light, forcing her to lean on boulders with sharp edges. The crackling behind her intensifies as she scrabbles across the crags toward a boulder as tall as her shoulders, one that might provide some cover from the rain.

A loud whistle is her only warning. As she turns to assess the damage, an explosion pops her eardrums, and the percussive wave sends her flying off her feet.

All is black again until two pains wake her—one steady and thrumming, the other sharp and searing.

With each heartbeat, the steady throb pumps in her head and chest, arms and body. She raises her head, feels the pull of new stinging aches against spots on her face. More of her visor has broken off in the impact. She hopes none of its debris is anywhere near her eyes.

The sharp and searing pain comes from one leg, along with a tugging that shifts her whole body.

She screams.

Something hideous and repulsive is biting into her calf. The thing is oval-shaped, as long as her arm and low to the ground like an overgrown insect. She pulls her legs back only to kick the thing away. Despite the ache in the rest of her body, she pushes herself upright.

Kyran's never encountered a creature like this in close quarters. Once, when she was ten or eleven, she watched a briefing for a planetary detachment, one that included a warning about the plants and animals the party might encounter on their mission. The images of those beasts terrified her with too many limbs and teeth to be believed, reason enough to avoid terrain where such things existed.

This creature is far worse than those beasts.

When she kicks it again, her boot connects with its hard shell of a back. Pincers larger than her hands protrude from the end closest to her, and its thigh-wide mouth is full of pointed teeth.

She cries out every time it touches her until she manages to climb atop the boulder. The slippery, slanted surface is only wide enough for her to sit. She pulls her feet from the thing's range.

Ill-equipped to climb after her, it keeps trying.

Kyran's tears blur her vision. Trapped, she shifts her weight and winces against the agony. One leg of her flight suit is shredded and blood drips down one calf from the creature's bite.

Thirst scratches at her throat and nausea swirls in her stomach as her head pounds. She slows her breathing, trying to handle her pain so she can consider her options.

The rain increases, adding more dirt to her busted visor. There's not much to see besides more rock, until she peers at her ship and moans in despair.

Smoke pours from the hulking black wreck. The craft's nose is crushed into a protruding rock. The half ration of food and a spare pullover she'd stashed are likely destroyed. The water reservoir from which she drank while inside the ship is either contaminated or evaporated.

She has nothing.

No equipment to contact the fleet. Nothing to sustain her while she waits for rescue, if they can find her at all. Laz had said the interference from the asteroid belt made scanning impossible.

And how would they search for her? Their active fighters were annihilated, and the rest decommissioned. *Althea's* command deck, with the best scanning technology in the fleet, was destroyed.

How long can she last alone?

Sobbing hurts, so she fights against the tears.

The rain eases and on the horizon where the clouds are thinner, the sun sets. The creature scrabbles and snaps below her feet, incapable of climbing any higher.

Kyran shivers in her rain-soaked flight suit. Night falls and she stares into the dwindling flames of her ship. Adrenaline has long since ebbed away, and she keeps falling asleep, then wakes up startled by the creature waiting to devour her.

In the cold dark, she tries to conserve her energy, to remind herself the light will return, to have hope.

A voice in her head suggests all hope is already gone, and a quick, self-inflicted death might be a better fate than whatever awaits her here.

She exiles it.

Three days after the planetary scans are completed, an exploration contingent discovers a temperate climate near the base of one of the southern mountain ranges—a perfect location for the first colony. The larger transports land the next week with much of the population, leaving only skeleton crews on Althea *and the menagerie of forty-two inactive ships of all classes and function orbiting Ellod.*

The alpha shift briefing is sparsely attended since colonization has begun, and Benna is less formal and more relaxed when she catches up to Kyran afterward.

"You'll soon rule on Ellod, Princess."

"Don't call me that," Kyran says, the words a habit in their conversations—and this time, a distraction. She doesn't want to talk about being planet-side. Who knows what kinds of dangers they'll discover on Ellod? Habitable doesn't mean safe.

She pulls her flight suit fastener closed where it's come undone. "I'll catch up with you in the mess hall when I'm back on board."

"Where are you going?" Benna says, confused.

"I'm flying escort in the next rotation." Another ship is scheduled for landfall at the colony, this one containing the last of the younger children.

Benna shakes her head in disapproval. "That fighter you love so much is a relic and needs a complete refit. The telemetry module is malfunctioning and—"

"I'll keep in line with the other ships." Kyran lowers her voice. "Benna, we've received no reports of Sifani activity anywhere near here. Half the fighters are being overhauled. We're understaffed. I can't skip out on basic duties."

"You're too important for—"

"Either I'm an elitist royal, in which case I need to prove I'm not, or I'm a leader of the people and need to do my part. Both choices mean I'm going."

Benna can't stop her, not without attracting attention. "Paired formation until you're back on the ship."

"Understood, Commander." Kyran glances around to make sure no one is watching them and kisses Benna's cheek. "I know you're trying to protect me, as you've always done. I can take care of myself."

"Be careful."

Kyran rolls her eyes as she salutes.

Moments later, Kyran shoves her perennial fatigue aside and folds her long legs into the cramped cockpit of her fighter, the one most modified from manufacture—and all the customization is Kyran's doing. It's not officially designated as hers, but no one else is as familiar with its quirks.

She blows strands of overlong hair from her eyes and pushes more behind her ears and off her neck before she pulls on her helmet. Ignoring the standard start-up flight sequence, she instead executes the step-by-step initialization in an order that makes more sense considering the system's peculiarity. The button that engages and idles the engine doesn't respond until her third attempt. The altimeter gauge is broken although she won't need it.

The other pilots chatter about when they'll be able to land on Ellod's surface. Benna had wanted her to be the first on the ground. Kyran had refused—too much attention and ceremony. Soon, Benna will be put off no longer and will want her to take her rightful place leading their people.

Kyran's fighter is aligned to the transport's bow. The next few hours provide time for her to contemplate their reclaimed home, with its eddying cloud formations and mesmerizing blue oceans. Ellod is breathtaking in its beauty, even if it represents a responsibility Kyran would rather leave to Benna.

Kyran is no leader. She wants to help the colony in other ways, to aid in building something for her people, something permanent and inviolable. She does not want to attempt to substantiate a legacy held together by the thin wires of her people's belief. She prefers working the skeleton crews locking down the rest of the fleet for permanent orbit.

Benna won't let her hide for long.

She turns her eyes from Ellod, and gazes instead at the stars.

Still, the dim light from distant stars isn't enough to keep Kyran awake, and the silence of space only lulls her into deeper relaxation. She bites her cheek and tastes blood, relieved she hasn't fallen asleep on duty.

As they arrive at the deceleration mark, alarms blast from her ship and from the fleet comms.

Multiple signals appear from the system's entry coordinates, the only place stable enough for wormhole generation.

Voices overlap, urgent and fearful, until one calls for order.

"Althea Nine," Benna says, Kyran's call sign, carefully enunciated. "Break formation and return to docking. Althea Four, provide escort.

All other fighters, when the transport is in atmosphere, get back here."

"Who is it?" Kyran says, breaking protocol.

"Return to bay, Kyran." Benna is terse, which means she's frightened. "Now."

"Incoming." Trasper, one of the tactical technicians who coordinates transport movement, speaks with welcome calm. "Five contacts. Repeat, five contacts. Incoming, vector one four and closing."

Kyran gapes at five dots moving at high speed on her tactical display. Only the glint of starlight on a hull in motion snaps her out of her stupor as another fighter pulls in alongside her. She adjusts course and increases speed, Laz's ship in escort position.

Her heartbeat thunders in her ears. The approaching ships move faster than she's flying, and she won't make it back to Althea *before they arrive.*

"Stay tight, Kyran," Laz says.

"Unidentified crafts." A woman's alto speaking crisp Sifani breaks into their comm feed. "Stand down and hold position pending immediate approach."

Translation to the other pilots isn't necessary. The Sifanis have found them.

The enemy ships break their tight formation and close in.

Kyran has never been in combat. She is trapped inside a fighter in open space against armed Sifanis. Her vision clouds until she takes a breath.

"Transport secured." Wills is their most experienced pilot. She sounds much calmer than Kyran feels. "En route."

One of the smaller Sifani ships bisects Kyran's path, blocking her trajectory to the docking bay and forcing her and Laz off course. It's sleek, more modern than their fighters, with more guns.

This could be a bloodbath, and Kyran is still outside the docking bay.

"She's never going to make it." Wills's annoyance is somehow worse than Benna's fear. "I'm going in."

A green dot approaches Kyran's position, and a blur races past to engage the Sifani ships. One red dot blinks and disappears as a bright fireball explodes.

Kyran's heart hammers in triplicate.

The fight is silent yet not as voices overlap on the comm link. The Sifani woman yells in horror. Benna shouts orders. Trasper relays coordinates and tactical information. The fleet pilots talk over each other, calling out maneuvers and coverage.

"We've got this, Nine. No need for you to waste your payload." Laz is encouraging, despite the heat of battle.

By the time Kyran approaches the bay entrance, three of their fighters have been destroyed. They've taken one enemy ship with them, their exceptional skill outmatching greater guns.

One of the enemy ships is four times larger than the others, discernible only when flashes of light reflect from its black hull, shining on its armored plating—so advanced, Kyran doesn't recognize its class or formation.

"How about some coverage?" Wills says, angry. "I can't save her ass all by myself."

"Althea Nine." Benna doesn't identify Kyran by name or title. "We can't use the turrets while you're outside."

This deferential treatment is unwarranted. Kyran is no more valuable than any other member of the crew—at the moment, she's not useful at all. Benna won't attempt to defend the others until Kyran is secure.

"Go," Laz says.

Kyran presses several buttons on the console. The auto-dock won't engage. Flying manually means she must decrease to a crawl. "Althea Nine on manual approach."

On tactical, another fleet ship and one more of the enemy vanish.

The Sifani woman has stopped talking.

Another enemy fighter sweeps across Kyran's periphery into position behind Laz.

"Laz!" Kyran tightens her hands on her fighter's controls and wills his ship to move faster, to change course. "Behind you."

Laz has lost his characteristic calm and shouts into the comm line. "I don't see it!"

A ball of white fire expands in the space where his ship had been. Kyran raises a hand to block the light.

Laz is gone.

The only other remaining Ellodian fighter veers between Kyran and the last of the smaller Sifani craft.

"My life support's blown out." Wills doesn't sound worried, despite the peril of her situation. "I'm not gasping my way to death out here."

On the display, one green dot speeds into a collision course with a red one until both blink and go dark.

Only the larger Sifani ship is left, close enough now to reveal more of its construction. Its wings indicate its versatility—built for both space and atmospheric travel. Multiple guns line its dark hull, and it maneuvers better than the others, executing tight curls and crisp arcs.

Kyran peels her fighter away from the docking path. She fires at the last enemy vessel, the ringing in her ears the only indication she's been screaming.

She misses with guns and has only two missiles as the ship fires on her, then charges past her. It arcs back for another run.

Benna is yelling. Kyran ignores her and fires at her target. The missile makes contact, clipping the ship hard enough to shake it, forcing the ship to pivot, jarred off course.

Its firing trajectory shifts and one of its missiles—instead of coming at Kyran—shoots silently toward Althea.

The command deck explodes.

The temperature drops as daybreak approaches. The creature wanders off, disappearing into the mottled tan and stony brown camouflage of the landscape. Dawn's pale pink light reveals only rocks and sand in every direction. Kyran shivers, making all the aches and pains more piercing. The bite bleeds through the jagged tear in her flight suit.

When she slides from her rugged pedestal to the ground, she winces at the impact and hobbles toward her ship.

What's left of it.

Hunger and thirst aren't helping the pain. She removes her helmet for a clearer view. The fighter crashed into a large boulder, cramming them both into the ground and leaving no gaps she might crawl under. Shelter is a higher priority than water, at least for now.

The cockpit still smokes, the components within either too hot to touch or burnt beyond recognition. The engine is compacted between the cockpit and the boulder and melted into slag. The landing gear is buried or nonexistent. A long line of wreckage stretches as far as she can see.

Something must be salvageable. She limps along the dark line of broken ground and debris warped by either the fiery approach through the atmosphere or the violent impact.

None of these components can be kludged together for anything capable of sending a signal, let alone two-way communication. Everything is burnt, or mangled, or disintegrated. The burns on her hand make it difficult to carry anything, and with her wounded leg she has little leverage.

A scrabbling sound accompanied by a screech gives her a start. About thirty paces away, two obscene creatures grapple and crash, each trying to pinch the other. Neither notices her, a reminder she cannot remain out in the open.

One of the landing struts broke off in mostly one piece, as long as she is tall and more rectangular than cylindrical. It might help fend off the creatures should they return. Kyran limps to the blackened cockpit and strips a charred stretch of harness. She fashions a strap to carry her helmet so she has one hand free, and loops it over her shoulder while she hoists her makeshift spear.

She decides sunrise is east. Due west is a rocky hill that appears larger than the others and may have better cover against the elements. Minding her wounded leg, Kyran takes cautious steps until she builds a limping rhythm. She loses track of time as she fights the absolute certainty of her circumstances and the implications of her injuries. The skin of her cheeks and forehead feels tight and the sun's glare hurts her eyes. When she puts the helmet back on, sweat pours down her face soon after, making it all worse.

The distance is misleading, and when the sun is overhead, the boulders appear no closer. Every shift of the wind sounds like an approaching threat. The vigilance is tiring, but she can't let down her guard. When she rests, stretching out her wounded leg, the flesh around the bite is swollen, puffy and red. Her heartbeat pulses across the tight skin. Sweat slides down her spine though she shivers. She's not hungry anymore, either.

Fever.

Nothing can be done about it.

Staying upright takes more energy than usual. She distracts herself with the terrain, a pointless effort. In every direction, there's nothing save rocks and sand and scree—no vegetation, no sign of anything alive besides those creatures. The dust makes her sneeze.

When she takes another break and squints back the way she's come, the fighter appears closer than the hill. She managed to crash into the largest thing in the entire area.

She stakes the strut in the loose ground, leans into it, and stands. Her calf throbs with the effort.

She is forced to stop for two more breaks over the course of the afternoon and evening. When she gets to the hill, she finds only an outcropping of more boulders.

It's not until she tries to climb one and her boot slips that she notices it's raining again. Her hair drips into her face as she leans over, and her flight suit is slick. A blister has risen on the hand holding the landing strut. Her other hand is still gloved and slides into a puddle no deeper than her thumb in the curve of a larger stone.

She curses at first, irritated that moisture has made its way inside her glove, until her thirst smacks her more fully aware. Unfiltered water is likely contaminated at best and incompatible at worst. If drinking the only available water kills her, so be it.

She ignores the dirt and grime, flattens herself against the rock and cups her other hand through the water. Gritty and metallic, it tastes terrible. She can't help moaning at the feeling of the wet on her dry, parched throat.

When the grittiness makes the water repellant, she continues her climb. Her hunger has returned. With no options, no solution, she ignores it.

Most of the rocks are exposed to the rain. An overhang looms over a crevice in the rock wall high enough off the ground to protect her from any of those horrid creatures, and provides a measure of cover for her head and shoulders. Darkness falls and Kyran curls into an upright ball, clutching her helmet against her chest. Her guts roil with the content of whatever had been in the water, stabbing her from the inside, and she wills herself not to vomit.

How did she survive the crash? And what good does it do her? She has no resources, no weapons, no supplies. If anyone on the command deck survived the Sifani incursion—and her chest seizes at the thought of Benna dead—none of them knows what has happened to her.

Kyran weeps until she falls asleep.

The next morning, she's stiff, tired, and hungry. Her calf has swollen to twice its normal size, the skin tight and hot against her unwounded hand. Her throat is so dry, it burns when she swallows.

The desolate landscape taunts her as she forces herself to stand. She will not die on this damned rock.

Always forward, never back.

Kyran stares at something she didn't see yesterday, the only thing different from its surroundings. She licks her dry lips in surprise, wincing at the burn.

A steady plume of smoke rises beyond the distant hills.

Something—someone—has made a fire.

CHAPTER TWO

The single thin dark line rises persistently from the distant ground, so it isn't a wildfire. The fleet scans from the reconnaissance squadron yielded little information about these moons except breathable atmosphere and no humanoids.

The Sifani ship. They've crashed here as well and survived, and they made a fire.

If she can get close enough, she might be able to kill them. The how of it doesn't matter as much as the why. They murdered Benna, Laz, Trasper and the others. They stranded Kyran away from her people, doomed her to die—

Tears of mourning mingle with her rage and compel her forward despite the pain driving her to rest. She won't last long with only rainwater and no food, but she will make sure she doesn't die alone.

Find the Sifani ship. Kill the crew.

Never mind she's never killed anyone, let alone with her bare hands.

A straight path to her destination on foot doesn't exist. Boulders too hard to climb must be circumvented, adding time, and gashes in the ground spewing noxious fumes push her off course. Gauging distances is difficult—everything in any direction looks the same except for the smoke. The air is dry—different from the reprocessed oxygen on the ships and in the fighters—and heavy, pressing down on her. Is the gravity denser on this moon? Dust burns in her nostrils and her eyes.

Something scuttles nearby when she passes through a gully, never revealing itself. With wavering confidence, she holds the landing strut like a spear. Is it enough to kill one of those things? She blinks away tears, the fear bitter like bile on her tongue. Though it hurts to move faster, she quickens her pace until the gully is behind her.

She rushes until she trips, scraping the palm of one hand on the rocks. After that, she watches where she's walking more closely. At midday, the air temperature drops and the wind intensifies. She pauses to catch her breath, to determine what's different.

A gray-brown haze stretches in front of her, and the rock formations on the horizon, visible not more than ten minutes ago, have disappeared behind the advancing gloom. The sun is now a barely glowing disk in the sky, subdued by the murky cloud rising before her. When the wall of sand hits her, it roars, pushing her back a step. She winces at the shifted weight on her leg.

Sand obliterates visibility and abrades her skin where the tiny cuts and burns from the crash already ache and itch. Putting the helmet back on doesn't help. She needs cover. There's little near her, and now she can't see more than several strides in any direction.

Luck arrives in the shape of a depression in the sand at the base of a rock slope. She pokes it with the strut to make sure no creatures hide in the gap. By the time she crawls into the hole, she is coughing and blinking grit.

The wind and sand rage, too wild to lull her to sleep, too thick for her to breathe deeply. She forces her muscles to relax, to take what rest she can despite the pulsing pain in her leg and her head.

Find the Sifani ship. Kill the crew. Signal the fleet.

The mantra in her head drowns out the storm.

—w— —w— —w—

After what feels like hours, the storm clears. Resting for a while longer would restore some of her strength, but the Sifanis might be her only chance for clean water. Or rations. Or medicine.

Or communications equipment to signal the fleet.

The ominous rumbling moan of some animal calls from a hole in the rocks she'd not seen during the storm. It sounds much bigger than the thing that bit her, and she scrambles out of the hole until the pain of aching muscles and the gaping bite on her leg slow her down.

An uncertain fate against the Sifanis is preferable to being eaten alive by something she cannot see. With cautious steps to keep her weight from falling too heavily on her injured leg, Kyran resumes her course.

The wind is less hectic now, the thick clouds less ominous. The rains return in the late afternoon, and the plume of smoke persists. Twice she slips on wet rock. The second time, a jagged stone cuts through her remaining glove. Now she has a messy cut to join the bleeding bite. The air is moist and warm, and still she shivers. The fever has returned. At least she isn't hallucinating.

Unless she's imagining the smoke.

When she reaches the crest of the next hill of rocks, alarming shapes await in the valley below. The thickset forms have too many misshapen arms, the beasts too large to fight off with the landing strut, even if she weren't outnumbered.

The animals don't move, and embarrassment replaces her fear.

How long has it been since she's seen trees?

Nestled among the ever-present boulders, squat trunks and gnarled branches barren of leaves make a sparse glade. Kyran maneuvers her way through the scrub brush at the base of one to touch the trunk. Its bark is compressed and smooth, darker than the sand, lighter than the rocks.

The trees are a wonder she has no time to enjoy.

When she resumes her march, she kicks something hard, and peers down at an overturned oval shield-like shape. Uncovered and exposed to the light, several grimy finger-width worms burrow into the sand.

The oval is the hollowed-out remnant of a creature like the one who bit her. The shell is shiny with the creature's blood, only the toughest viscera left. Something killed it and ate everything but the shell, which means larger predators.

Kyran spends more time checking the shadows when she trudges forward and climbs over the rocks.

On the other side of the valley, the ground flattens. The stream of rising smoke is much closer, the currents of air more visible.

When the fire is beyond the next ridge, she removes her helmet and stashes it on its strap. She chooses each step with caution, using the spear for leverage.

The rage and hollow mourning return as she inches her head around the final rock between her and the other side.

In a narrow canyon burrowed in the crags, the source of the smoke is a small fire.

Charred by battle and atmospheric entry, the Sifani ship crashed upside-down, one wing along with half the body of the craft buried under rubble. The fading daylight shines on the dark gray of the ship's hull and glints on its metallic and iridescent green markings. The Sifani symbols include a seal whose numbers are easily translated. The letters, however, shape unfamiliar words—not like those on the surveillance images of patrols Benna reviewed with the fleet pilots.

Kyran doesn't want to think about Benna.

Even wrecked, broken, and land-bound, the ship is imposing, its silent guns and unknown contents more of a threat than Kyran's wounds and fever. This is the closest she has ever been to her people's only enemy, to the regime subjugating whole planets to its will.

Nothing stirs except the flames. No one is in sight, and—embarrassed at the afterthought—Kyran looks around to make sure no one else is nearby. If they have sentries, it's too late now to retreat.

As she peers from the safety of the crevice, she is less driven to kill its occupants and more concerned about evading capture.

She flinches when the boarding door opens with a loud creak.

A woman clad in black emerges from the upside-down door and jumps to the ground. Using the boarding door as comparison, the Sifani appears tall and has a length of fabric wrapped around her head and shoulders, hiding her face. She approaches the fire and rotates a stick with chunks of something attached to it mounted over the flames.

An unfamiliar scent makes Kyran's mouth water. Her saliva emphasizes the dryness of her throat and swollen tongue.

Sand in the canyon swirls as the breeze rises. The Sifani tightens the shawl around her head, her back to Kyran.

Kyran raises herself for a better view. A rock beneath her foot slips and a stream of scree tumbles away.

The Sifani turns in Kyran's direction.

Kyran ducks and covers her mouth, hoping the sound of her breathing won't reveal her location. She counts to fifty, then a hundred. What if the Sifani investigates? Or calls for reinforcements?

A creak and slam echo against the rocks. Kyran counts to one hundred again before she dares to peek.

The Sifani has disappeared. The spit from the fire is gone.

Night descends, and no one comes out again. Kyran could sneak closer or move away altogether. What if there are more of them on the ship? What other chance does she have to survive?

Her muscles tighten and ache and spasm with the length of time in much the same position, worsening when the temperature drops. More than once, she falls asleep before terror or hunger or pain or the cold wake her.

When the sky lightens, she finds the courage to move. She creeps along the ridge, searching for a way to approach the ship undetected.

Someone speaks behind her, and Kyran yelps.

The woman from the ship stands a few steps away. With a familiarity suggesting formidable skill, she wields two weapons—a short sword with a matte black blade and a menacing pistol with a full charge indicator.

Kyran is about to die.

Panic, hunger, thirst, fever, pain from her festering wounds, terror at imminent execution—they all work against her. She sinks into what she hopes is a fighting stance.

She can't hold herself upright anymore.

Kyran faints.

CHAPTER THREE

Kyran wakes up tied to the Sifani ship.

Thick black freightage straps, the kind used to secure containers in transit, tie both her wrists to a gun turret. Since the craft is upside-down and half buried, the gun itself is underground and the turret base is as wide as her body.

Dread passes through her on a wave of nausea. She's going to die. She wriggles and wrestles against her constraints, desperate to escape. Without a knife to cut through the strap, her only escape might be to hang herself, which would take immense effort.

Shock freezes Kyran's useless tugging when she notices the bandages on her wounds. Her hand has been wrapped and with better quality bandages than she might have received back in the fleet. Clean skin pokes from the edges of the bandage covering the bite on her leg.

Why would Sifani brutes give aid instead of executing her on sight?

How many of the enemy are there? How did she not notice one of them touching her? Kyran pulls at the restraints until her skin burns.

Spent and weak, licking her dry lips, she stops pulling when a lone figure appears on the far side of the canyon.

It's the same woman wearing the same clothes, her head covered with the patterned gray shawl. She's pushing—rolling—a knee-high boulder over the sandy ground. The mouth of the canyon is ten or fifteen paces wide, and the Sifani crosses the distance to settle the rock at the base of the canyon wall against several others.

Kyran doesn't move, not wanting to attract immediate attention, and her heartbeat pounds in her ears. Her helmet and the landing strut from her crash are nowhere in sight. It had been foolish to try to approach without more surveillance. The possibility of water had drawn her closer and now she's at the mercy of who knows how many—

Logic returns. No one is helping the woman move rocks and no one else is guarding Kyran, which could mean no other crew lurk inside the vessel. This Sifani might be alone.

Better odds of survival give Kyran strength and courage.

"Let me go." Her voice is a dry croak.

The woman whirls in Kyran's direction, sword in hand, but then she sheathes the blade. She ignores Kyran and instead abandons her current task to retrieve a handful of branches from a small stockpile. She adds them to the fire.

Kyran won't be ignored. "Murderer. Untie me."

The Sifani faces Kyran again. She stalks closer, threatening despite her empty hands. Kyran tugs at the straps, kicking out her tied feet.

The woman stops several steps away. An alto voice dripping with disdain speaks a few sentences in Sifani.

Kyran doesn't understand any of the words except the last one, and anger is preferable to breath-stealing terror.

"I'm not a thief," she says in Ellodian. She works what little saliva is in her mouth to spit. The spittle lands in her own lap. "You're a murderer and your people are nothing but tyrants."

All the Sifani words she can think of are about ship systems—labels of machinery, ship's compartments, or computer commands. Nothing that will communicate how much she wants to kill this woman.

"Warning." She doesn't care if she's mispronouncing it though she's frustrated it's not the right word. What is the word for "kill"?

"Death." It's as close as she can get. She receives no response.

Kyran wishes the Sifani would take off the damned shawl so she could see any facial expression.

"Death," she says, louder though her head pounds from dehydration. Energy spent, she sags against the restraints, relieved she doesn't have to hold herself up.

The Sifani returns to her business of stoking the fire, then trims palm-sized wet red clumps she pulls from a sagging bag the size of Kyran's missing helmet. The woman tosses the scraps into the flames and skewers the chunks on a thin branch to prop over the fire.

The aroma of whatever is cooking turns Kyran's already twisted guts into knots.

The woman lifts a container to her mouth to drink, revealing none of her face in the process, and the sound of slugging consumption snaps some strand of Kyran's dignity.

When the Sifani restores the cap to the container, Kyran swallows her pride.

"Water." She winces when she remembers the language barrier and repeats her demand in Sifani instead of Ellodian. The chances this murderer would know her language is minuscule. When Sifani Prime expands territory, its language is forced on its subjects. Why learn the native tongues of the conquered?

Her captor tilts her head in question.

"Water." Kyran opens her mouth and smacks rudely. The motion hurts her head.

The Sifani approaches in slow and measured steps, her water container in one hand. The long wicked-looking black blade appears in the other.

Kyran squirms in futility against her restraints. Why treat her wounds and keep her captive all this time only to murder her now?

"You leave me here all day and now you're going to kill me?" She continues to speak in Ellodian as the terror rises inside her, though she hides it behind a brave front. Every tale of how the Sifanis have brutalized her people, destroying whole cities, executing adults, and incarcerating children—all those memories raise tears obscuring her vision. She sobs as she speaks, the words incongruous with the dread coursing through her body. "If I wasn't tied up, I'd kill you with my bare hands."

Could she? Could she wrap her fingers around this woman's throat and choke the life from her?

The question becomes moot as the woman comes closer. With dark grace, she raises the blade and presses its tip beneath Kyran's chin.

Kyran stifles a whine. Though she trembles and her chest rises and falls with each jagged breath, she stays as motionless as she can. What little self-respect she has left won't let her beg for her life.

The blade is warm on Kyran's skin as the Sifani tilts her chin up with its tip.

"Water," the woman says in Sifani, correcting the mispronunciation as she lifts the container beside Kyran's head.

Kyran is so shocked that the first drops miss her mouth and splash against her cheek. She sputters and swallows as the water streams, trying not to cough it back out.

Several gulps later, the flow stops. The Sifani pulls the blade away, stashes it at her waist, and secures the container.

"No." Kyran bites back a "please."

The Sifani mutters something Kyran doesn't understand. One of the words reminds her of the medical bay back on *Althea*. Her head hurts too much to untangle her muddled thoughts.

Thirst slaked and all the fight scared out of her, Kyran lets her head fall forward. She closes her eyes, relieved by the sound of the Sifani's steps as the woman walks away.

She falls asleep, until a steady drip of rain runs along the crown of her head and pools in her ear.

Kyran curses and shakes her head to the side to drain out the water. Under the shelter of the ship's overturned wing, she is not free from the elements. Something somewhere is broken, allowing water to flow onto her head.

It's dark now. The firepit still smokes, and the ship's boarding door is closed. When Kyran shifts her weight to maneuver herself farther under cover, despite the agonizing cramps in her arms and bound wrists, something on the ground presses into her thigh.

The water container from earlier is propped against the gun turret. A small rounded disc of plastic no bigger than her hand tilts into the sand. A pressed bar of a full nutrition ration falls on the ground.

She grabs it and shoves a soggy corner into her mouth, moaning at the familiar texture on her tongue. How long has it been since she's had a full ration in one sitting?

When the bar is gone, she plucks the sandy crumbs from the ground and eats them, too.

The water container is only a third full. She gulps it down and curses the Sifani for leaving her so little, deliberately ignoring the fact the woman could have left her nothing at all. Or poisoned it.

She's too wet and cold to fall back asleep. Kyran folds her arms around her body, hoping to keep the food down, and thinks only of how to free herself.

The next time Kyran wakes, the Sifani is on the far side of the canyon, beyond the firepit.

The woman is lean and strong.

In the pale light of morning, the Sifani lifts a small boulder, leveraging it against the base of another rock, and sets it in place with a grunt. She repeats the action, and then again, and as the sun rises in the sky a wall slowly grows, sectioning the canyon off into a type of fort. Considering the creatures Kyran saw, not to mention the one she heard, such fortifications are wise.

The woman isn't using any of the debris from the crash, which is wasteful. Armored plating, broken struts, a bent fin—all these materials would make the wall easier to fill in. The Sifani ignores her obvious resources.

When the sun is overhead, the woman stands on the far side of the fire with her back to the flame. She marks out a circle in the sand, two strides across, and kneels, muttering to herself in its center.

The words are measured, like a promise or an oath. Kyran doesn't recognize any beyond "I" and "stars," but she knows ritual when she sees it.

The woman bares one arm and draws her blade.

Kyran gasps when the Sifani cuts a thin line into her own arm, enough to make the blood bead. She raises the sword with both hands outstretched horizontally as high as her head and speaks aloud.

When she finishes, she lowers the blade to wipe it clean against a small cloth pulled from a pocket, rises, and leaves the circle. She stomps out the line, erasing its existence, and retreats to thrust her sword into the fire.

She repeats the entire sequence of actions at sunset. Kyran has never seen anything like this odd ritual, and though she wants the woman dead, she can't bring herself to interrupt when it happens.

No matter how much Kyran protests, the woman doesn't untie the restraints. Kyran searches for the knots holding the straps in place. They are out of sight, somewhere on top of the overturned wing. The only way free would be to cut through the straps, and Kyran lacks the means and the strength to attempt escape.

At dusk, the woman brings Kyran food and water, ignores her cries for release, and disappears inside the ship.

Kyran is left with nothing but the sputtering fire and the wind for company until she falls into another fitful sleep.

Something wakes her.

Defenseless and restrained, she fears one of the creatures is in the canyon. Frozen, she searches every dark shadow of the predawn morning for movement.

A moment later, the branches holding the spit over the smoldering coals collapse. Scree shifts with a hiss, and rocks tumble into the canyon. One bounces over the ship's frame and narrowly misses her head before it crashes to the ground.

The ground moves again.

An earthquake.

The motion intensifies and jars something loose on the ship. The ground shifts again beneath her, and Kyran ducks her head under her bound hands. The ship shakes, rattling the turret. Something creaks apart, and the earthquake lessens to a rumbling vibration.

A jagged shard of metal now protrudes from one side of the turret, sharp enough to cut bone.

The Sifani is still inside the ship. Kyran fits the width of the cargo strap against the sharp edge, and with an urgency bordering on mania, she saws while trying not to make too much noise, trying not to cry out when her skin tears.

The ground stops shaking, and the Sifani doesn't come outside.

The strap is now ragged enough to rip, and after a rough tug Kyran is free. She stands, knocking her head into the wing with a dull thud, then shuffles forward on cramped legs. Her belongings are nowhere in sight, and the container of water from her prisoner's dinner the night before is empty. She doesn't have time to fix either problem.

She limps into a run.

The rocky bluffs of the canyon are too rugged to navigate and too exposed for her to remain unseen from the ship. She sprints for the newly constructed wall and bounds over it into musty sand, then ambles toward the shadows of more rocks, hoping she will find cover.

She doesn't get far before she comes to a dead end. A chittering sound stops her. She spins toward it and moans in horror.

Several creatures like the one that attacked her leg slither in her direction.

She backs against the rock face, unarmed and light-headed. When she tries to scramble up the rocks, she slips. Too weak to grab a boulder to save herself from falling, Kyran crashes on her side in the sand.

They close in, intent on their prey, pincers clicking and threatening torment.

A savage cry from above and behind Kyran stops her racing heart, and the Sifani drops to the ground right in front of her. With her back to Kyran, the woman raises her sword and her pistol.

The Sifani shoots all but one of the creatures in rapid succession, red bursts of burning energy stabbing through their shells and killing them instantly. She holsters her weapon on the outside of one thigh and shifts her grip on her sword.

She kicks one of the dead creatures aside to clear her path to her remaining foe. Down to one immediate threat, she stomps on one pincer and stabs the creature in the mouth. Repeated jabs into its exposed midsection kill it.

By the time Kyran recovers enough to sit upright, the Sifani has lined the corpses up side by side.

She returns to Kyran and towers over her. The shawl has fallen to her shoulders, revealing her shocking beauty. Delicate dark brows and voluminous black hair frame a majestic pale face with symmetric features, regal cheekbones, and a sharp jawline. The golden pink of the newly risen sun glints in green eyes piercing with intelligence.

Blood and gore drip from the sword, the spatters loud on the sand and stone.

Too mesmerized to stand, Kyran stares at her unexpected rescuer. Her fear drowns in the wake of something new, something indescribable. Kyran can't catch her breath and is helpless to move under the woman's glare.

The Sifani raises her sword to point back toward the ship.

"Food and water," she says in crisp, enunciated Sifani. She waves her other arm at the open terrain in the opposite direction. "Death."

She points at Kyran and speaks words Kyran doesn't know. The meaning is clear. Kyran must choose to either attempt to survive on her own with no resources or return to the slim chance of survival in the canyon with her enemy.

The woman turns her back and tends to the carcasses, leaving Kyran to decide. Kyran trembles from another near-death experience and pretends it's a difficult choice.

The Sifani leaves, dragging her gruesome bounty behind her with yet another cargo strap. Kyran banks her hate and her vengeance, and limps after her enemy.

CHAPTER FOUR

In her haste to escape, Kyran has ripped the bandage over the bite, leaving it exposed and leaking blood. It burns with her movement and stings with her sweat.

The Sifani hikes back to the canyon without looking once at Kyran. Following her feels like admitting defeat, conceding Kyran will never be able to kill this woman when she can't save herself.

Back in the canyon, the Sifani stashes her kills and stands assessing the half-collapsed section of the wall. The earthquake knocked several boulders out of place, and considering how long it took to build it, repairs will take hours.

Kyran is unsure what happens next. She has her answer when the Sifani draws her pistol.

The woman says nothing as she secures Kyran to the ship—this time closer to the boarding door and nowhere near the jagged metal of the broken turret. Kyran is still under cover, and her movement more limited than before.

For the rest of the morning, the woman works to restore the wall and completes her task when the sun is at its highest. She stands in the midst of the same cleared space as yesterday, marks out a circle in the sand, and performs her ritual.

This time, Kyran doesn't catch any of the words. She's more interested in the rigid formality of the Sifani's movements, the pride in her stance, the ease with which she handles her blade.

How many times has she performed this act?

Next, the woman tends to the corpses of the monsters from earlier, carving and stripping each creature into growing piles of muscled flesh, entrails, pincers, and shells.

Kyran's horror grows over the course of the afternoon as the grisly work continues, and she fights the urge to vomit when the wind shifts and blows the revolting odor her way. She's no stranger to butchery. Though she's never carried out the duty herself due to her other responsibilities, others in the fleet have sometimes obtained livestock in trade. On those occasions, such meat was the only way to feed hungry Ellodians. Kyran has tasted fresh meat, but this . . . the gruesome slaughter of creatures so far from appetizing as to be repellant, with the clear intention for them to be consumed . . . Kyran studies the Sifani more than what she is doing.

The woman's face remains blank as she works. She is tireless, focused on each task until its completion. The shells are propped in the sand at the edge of the fire, where the flames burn off the blood and remaining viscera. The pincers are tied together and spread out in a line on a flat rock. The meat—and all this work must mean the Sifani is going to eat the flesh of these disgusting creatures—is transferred to an odd bag and carried inside the ship.

When the woman reappears, she pauses before the last pile. Her shoulders rise and fall with the depth of her breathing, and her expression does not change as she sinks her fingers into the offal and pulls out a long strip of entrails.

Kyran looks away and swallows bile.

All her life, she has been told Sifanis are bloodthirsty and cruel. Such indifference to carnage at close range—black blood splashing on the woman's arresting face without generating so much as a twitch—turns Kyran's stomach. Her opponent is far more experienced at killing.

The woman stretches the lines of guts along the edge of the overturned ship's wing, the strips of beastly insides laid to dry in the sun.

The icy fear is back, slithering in the sweat on Kyran's spine.

At sundown, after her ritual, the Sifani gives Kyran a ration bar and a full canteen of water.

"You don't have to tie me up. I'm not going anywhere." Why say such a thing? Wouldn't she try to press her advantage if freed?

The Sifani ignores her.

At nightfall after she banks the fire, the woman unties Kyran's hands and leaves her a sharpened stick. The ties binding Kyran's legs are too substantial for the stick to penetrate, so escape is impossible to accomplish overnight. The implication is clear. Kyran is a prisoner, but the Sifani won't leave her defenseless.

Kyran pretends it isn't a small kindness and grumbles, lacking the energy to give her protest any heat.

The next day, after her morning ritual, the Sifani strides past the canyon wall and disappears.

Kyran tries again to free herself. She doesn't think about whether she'll attack the Sifani or run, or anything after. When was the last time she was forced to sit still this long? Her work in the fleet kept her moving unless she was on the command deck or asleep. She hates sitting with nothing to do besides obsessing over how helpless she is.

Kyran winces as the straps bite into her skin until she sags in defeat. Her scabs itch, and the stench of her perspiring, unwashed body in the oppressive heat irritates her and feeds her shame.

The Sifani doesn't return until midafternoon. She brings firewood and more dead creatures. The wood is stacked near the overturned ship. The carcasses are dragged next to the firepit, where the woman repeats the spectacle of butchery.

She has collected far more meat than one person can consume and when the horrid slaughter is done, she takes the surplus into the ship, which is confusing. Are more Sifani inside? Kyran hasn't heard other people—are they wounded?

How will this affect her fate?

Questions haunt her as her condition improves. The rations restore her energy enough to annoy her with their grittiness. The woman has increased Kyran's water ration to several times a day, and Kyran chugs it all down whenever it's provided.

What if more Sifanis come? What if this woman is holding her hostage until Kyran can be taken into custody?

If she could somehow overpower her captor, Kyran could use the ship to communicate with her own people. Some of the systems must be working since the woman daily cleans all trace of the day's kills from her hands and clothes. The pulse drone may not have wiped out everything.

The next afternoon, after the midday ritual, the woman spends the better part of an hour clearing smaller rocks from a flat area within the canyon wall. She removes her outer layer of clothing, revealing lithe arms and defined shoulders. The series of physical movements she performs suggests another ritual pattern, this one reminiscent of dancing, of graceful forward advances and smooth retreats.

Between the Sifani's experienced martial skill and the kills she's stacking up every day, Kyran decides it's smarter to bide her time before she makes another attempt at freedom. The woman might decide to let her go since she can't keep Kyran prisoner indefinitely.

She suppresses the thought that they might both be stuck here forever.

Two days later, when the Sifani disappears into the bowels of her frigate with the day's catch, Kyran stares at the emblem on the side of the ship. The sword and vines insignia doesn't resemble anything she's ever seen.

Something hits the ground. Kyran searches for the telltale shape of one of the shell-backed creatures—nothing moves in the canyon.

A whoosh and a thud draw her eyes to the sky. No clouds, no sandstorm, nothing . . . until a yellow-red ball of flame with a smoking inky black tail flies across the canyon and collides with the rock wall.

A meteor.

Another appears, followed by a pair, and Kyran leaps to her feet with a cry.

Two more fire into the canyon, so hot and fast they burn through one of the stabilizer fins and crater the ground where they fall.

She's not safe under this wing. The meteors are small yet pock the greater hull of the ship, which means they'll likely cave in her brainpan if one hits her in the head. They don't appear to have punctured the main body of the ship so the safest place for her is inside.

Inside, with the merciless Sifani.

The argument in her head is brief. Kyran hops as best she can to the door, covering her head with her tied arms though it's futile, her eyes on the skies searching for imminent threats.

She hunches her head and bangs on the door with closed fists. "Let me in. Open the cursed door."

A hot piece of detritus grazes her arm, searing her skin. Around her, stones big and small hiss and burn when they hit the sand or clatter on the stone. Her luck won't last long.

Her demands deteriorate into wordless screams. The door opens and she falls inside to safety, her secured feet tripping her and keeping her from catching her footing.

The Sifani stands at the threshold, head covered by her shawl. When Kyran maneuvers her way to her feet, the black blade of the sword pokes into her chest. Kyran considers this a familiar threat compared to the meteors.

"Look," she says, wishing she spoke more Sifani. She gestures outside with her tied hands.

The Sifani lowers the shawl from her face and peers past the boarding door. The gray fabric falls below her chin, and Kyran gets a closer look at her enemy.

The rich green eyes are deeper set than Kyran first noticed. Strands of the Sifani's black wavy hair fall past the covering to the middle of her back. Her nose has a delicate elegant curve, and her skin is unblemished.

She is as beautiful as she is deadly. It takes longer than Kyran likes for her hatred and horror to resurface.

The woman speaks softly in reverent fear, though Kyran

doesn't understand. A meteor crashes into the side of the ship and the Sifani—who has never revealed any trepidation—jumps in fright and slams the door closed.

They pant in the darkness until Kyran's vision adjusts to the minimal light. And there is light—an orange hue blanching the color from the Sifani's eyes. It reflects off the blade once again raised in Kyran's direction.

The woman says something Kyran can't translate but understands nevertheless. With a frown and a sigh, Kyran nods. Unless she wants to go back outside with the meteors—another hit makes them both cringe—she'll have to follow orders.

The Sifani uses her blade to slice through the bindings at Kyran's feet, leaving the trailing end stuck in the closed door. With a prod that doesn't touch Kyran's body, the woman gestures deeper into the ship. Her eyes are more wary than threatening, and Kyran recognizes the truce. She'll be allowed to stay if she doesn't try to do anything foolish—like attempt to overpower her captor.

Kyran steps gingerly along the narrow corridor to an interior doorway and its upside-down boundary. Beyond it lies the path to the cockpit and, at the other end, a cargo bay.

The woman points at a section of the deck. Warily, Kyran sits and shifts her weight until she finds a comfortable enough position to lean against the bulkhead.

The Sifani moves some indiscernible containers from Kyran's reach—not that she can do much with her hands tied—and while she does, Kyran peeks at her surroundings.

The frigate is in far better shape than Kyran's burnt-out fighter, but none of the frigate's systems are active except for the emergency lights. The Sifani has adapted to the upside-down layout, and a makeshift bunk is tucked into the corner of the former ceiling.

The truth is chilling.

The Sifani is as isolated from her people as Kyran is from her own. On the one hand, the Sifani most likely cannot call for reinforcements. On the other, Kyran can't use the system to signal the Ellodians.

They are both stranded and lost, with little chance anyone will ever find either of them. If Kyran—impossibly—finds a way to kill this woman, she will live out the rest of her no-doubt-short life alone. If she escapes and strikes out on her own, the same is true—and she'll have no resources beyond sticks and rocks and life in a cave.

Her only other choice is to accept her enemy as an ally and for them to forge into uncertainty together.

Kyran pushes the immediate image of Benna's face from her mind.

Yet despite the deaths this Sifani has caused, and setting aside her brutal skills, she has saved Kyran's life in more ways than one. Without her, Kyran would have been dead three times over—from dehydration and hunger, from infection of her wounds, from the creatures seconds away from eating her alive.

The woman sits sideways instead of lying down, eyes closed as she leans her head back. Fatigue softens her features, making her appear more approachable, less feral and murderous.

"What's your name?" Kyran surprises herself by speaking.

The Sifani's eyes snap open and she clenches her hand on her pistol, at her side.

Kyran's heart rate spikes. She's spoken in Ellodian again. "Pilot . . . designation," she says in Sifani, pointing at the woman, who frowns and doesn't speak.

Kyran points at herself. "Kyran." Then she points again at her captor. "Designation?"

Another meteor crashes into the hull on the far end of the cockpit, and they both start in surprise. The Sifani lays the pulse pistol beside her within easy reach. With a glance at Kyran, she rests her blade on her lap.

Kyran doesn't lower her eyes.

"Davia," the woman says.

Then she doesn't talk again no matter what Kyran asks her.

Sometime after full dark, the meteor shower slows. Neither of them moves. At some point, the Sifani falls asleep, shoulders sagging, hands taut on her weapons.

For the first time since the crash of her arrival, Kyran relaxes. When she closes her eyes, the slow, even rhythm of the Sifani's breathing lulls her to sleep.

When Kyran wakes, her head is tipped at an odd angle. She is thirsty, her arms and shoulders are stiff from being secured in an awkward position, and her stomach growls. The interior of the ship is warm, and sticky perspiration coats her skin.

Her movement rattles something near her foot, and the Sifani—Davia—twitches awake.

Kyran stills as the weapon capable of burning fist-width holes in scuttling creatures is now raised at her head.

She lifts her bound hands. "Can't do much with my hands tied." She hopes Davia understands though they don't speak the same language.

Davia lowers the pulse pistol. "Water?" she asks, her voice roughened by sleep.

The deepened tone resonates in Kyran's body, an unfamiliar sensation.

"Yes," Kyran says in Sifani, and bites her tongue before she adds a "please" in Ellodian.

Davia maneuvers them outside to the aftermath of the meteor shower. Larger meteors smoke around the periphery of the canyon. One narrowly missed the ship and lies in a crater of its own making, steam rising into the air.

Davia scowls at the damage. Kyran finds the destruction meaningless since the ship wasn't going anywhere anyway.

Despite Kyran's protests, Davia secures her beneath the ship's broken wing—damaged further by the meteors—and brings another full nutrition bar and water without comment. Davia does the chores that occupy her attention, and Kyran ponders what purpose they serve. Davia performs her odd ritual at the usual times.

The afternoon brings rain. At sundown, Davia unties Kyran's hands, tosses her a sharpened stick, and prepares to board the frigate.

"You're not going to leave me out here, are you?"

Davia disappears inside the ship.

"Davia!"

Kyran stops herself from pleading. She searches for a spot that isn't beneath one of the leaking holes or in a puddle of collected runoff.

Hours later, when the rain has soaked through Kyran's torn flight suit, Davia reappears and stares at Kyran for several long unsettling minutes before retying her hands and untying her feet.

Davia directs Kyran to enter the ship.

The day ends much the same way it began, with Kyran attempting to find a comfortable position and Davia poised to shoot her if she so much as twitches.

"You don't have to tie me up," Kyran says the next evening in her own language.

It's not quite full dark. Davia has banked the fire for the night and untied Kyran's feet from her posted incarceration. They're inside the Sifani vessel and Davia waves her pulse pistol in the direction of Kyran's designated spot.

Kyran is too tired after the surprising heat of the day to sleep against the damned wall and wants to stretch out, albeit on the floor.

She opens her hands as much as she can considering the binding and holds them up in what she hopes is a disarming manner. She tries to remember any Sifani words that would help make her point but gives up and strives instead to speak Ellodian in as calm and reassuring a tone as she can manage. "I'm not going to try anything."

And it's true. They won't survive without cooperating. They can't keep treating each other like mortal enemies, either. Back in the fleet, Kyran worked with several people she disliked as the needs of their people were more important. Couldn't the same rules apply here?

Davia ignores her.

New words come to mind. "No target," Kyran says in Sifani.

Davia is taken aback, alarmed, so those words don't convey the meaning Kyran intends.

She tries again. "No . . . danger."

This time, comprehension flashes in Davia's eyes. They stare so long at each other, Kyran starts to itch.

Davia releases the bindings, steps back and eases down to her usual position. She sets the straps close by, out of Kyran's reach.

The simple action speaks volumes. This woman won't kill Kyran in her sleep, having had at least a dozen opportunities so far to do so. No, Kyran is the one with something to prove.

Kyran sits down with exaggerated slowness and stretches her body along the deck while maintaining eye contact.

Davia doesn't so much as blink. She doesn't lower her weapon either.

Kyran rolls over to face the wall, her back to Davia, hoping the action is clear. Hoping Davia understands Kyran isn't a threat.

She doesn't fall asleep right away, and some time passes before Davia rustles in a way suggesting she's relaxed.

Kyran's eyes are closed and she's almost asleep when she hears a delicate snore.

The uneasy truce continues the next day. Kyran isn't tied up like a prisoner, and she isn't left alone. When she moves too quickly toward the firepit, Davia draws her pistol and aims it at her chest.

"No danger," Kyran says, holding her hands open and outstretched between them until Davia holsters the weapon.

"No danger," Kyran says every time she moves in a direction the Sifani doesn't expect, every time Davia draws her weapon. The first few times, Kyran freezes and offers a placating blank expression and a kind tone. By sunset, Kyran is irritated Davia still doesn't trust her.

She chooses to ignore why Davia might feel that way and why she shouldn't trust Davia at all. With some sadness and frustration, Kyran finds her need to kill her enemy is waning.

Boredom leads her to explore the canyon, but the Sifani draws her pistol because Kyran walks too close to the salvage piles, and gestures for her to move rocks onto the wall. All afternoon, Davia shadows Kyran when she approaches the frigate. Davia stays out of arm's reach, her hand close to her holster when she isn't holding her weapon, directing Kyran to perform the menial tasks of stacking the small collection of wood, or clearing the stones from the sand near the firepit.

Kyran feels like prison labor, but then again, she is.

When it's time for the evening meal, Davia brings a plate and a canteen of water and sets them both beside Kyran.

The plate holds only a corner of a ration, less than a quarter of a cube.

Without thinking, Kyran makes a noise of displeasure.

Davia shrugs, then speaks before gesturing toward the meat over the fire.

"Last," is the only word Kyran recognizes, and swallows the lump in her throat at what it means. The only remaining food is meat.

She stares at the cooking flesh. She can starve, or . . .

Davia's brow furrows, an expression Kyran has not yet seen. Davia takes care to separate the most well-cooked meat and cuts it into smaller pieces on Kyran's plate. Kyran doesn't know what to make of the gesture.

She picks up a still-hot morsel and puts it in her mouth before she loses her nerve. Metallic bitterness covers Kyran's tongue when she chews, and she swallows before it gets any worse.

The next morning, Kyran is shocked and dismayed when Davia roasts a few worms over the fire and then quickly consumes them. Their situation is dire, but this—this implies a frightening level of desperation.

When Davia vomits it all up, clutching her arm to her guts

as she sits for the next several hours, Kyran feels sorry for her. She brings Davia a full water canteen without prompting.

"Thank you," Davia murmurs, panting between the tiniest of sips, sincerity shining from her dull eyes.

Kyran nods, uncomfortable with the attention.

The ebb and flow of the repetitive days doesn't change much—until the afternoon it does.

"Can I sit up there?" Kyran asks in Ellodian, pointing at the top of the ship. When she sits in the dirt beside the fire, she constantly checks for worms or worries one of those shelled creatures is sneaking up behind her.

Davia's blank expression means she doesn't understand. Kyran crouches and mimics sitting, then points upward again. A long moment passes before Davia nods.

Kyran climbs atop the broken wing and sits in a spot untouched by meteor scoring. The wind that drove sand into her eyes earlier in the day has died down, leaving a hot, stagnant silence, all pressing in on her, forcing her to choose between the horror of her memories, the uncertainty of her future, and the discomfort of her present.

Always forward, never back provides no respite today. It's too damned quiet—no humming from ships' engines, no bragging banter of fighter pilots or chatter from other deck officers.

No one speaking Ellodian.

Kyran cannot recall a time when she spent so many hours without talking, without focusing on a task of her own design. The boredom and loneliness of her predicament and strangeness of her ill-at-ease existence with Davia drive her to melancholy. She finds some solace in staring at the landscape, as long as she does not look at Ellod.

Ellod . . . is too much to bear.

Davia walks to the same place in the canyon to perform her ritual. Though Kyran has no idea what the ritual means, it now feels rude to observe, an intrusion on something sacred and personal. When Davia begins to draw her circle in the sand, Kyran turns her attention elsewhere, a new habit of offering privacy until the sound of shuffling sand signals the ritual's completion.

Yet today, the sound doesn't come, and some other noise makes her turn.

Davia stands facing the setting sun, and the wind has blown the shawl from her head to her shoulders. A track mars the pattern of dust and dirt on her face, made yet again when a tear falls down her cheek. Davia sinks to her knees.

She sobs. Her whole body shakes with their force.

Kyran can't look away.

Davia chokes out her ritual's words. The speech is stilted by her crying, but her posture doesn't falter. She handles her sword with capable skill as Kyran has seen before. When Davia cuts across the skin of her arm, the action reveals lines of similar scars.

Davia raises the blade to the sky, and her arms tremble. She slices across her arm again and raises the blade, and Kyran doesn't understand enough of the spoken words to glean their meaning. Davia cuts a third time, as if the ritual is meant to call something forth and fails. As she raises the bloodstained blade once more, she speaks one last time until her crying becomes a wail.

The sound is gut-wrenching. Kyran blinks at her own surprising tears and faces forward again.

Isolation and a fight for survival are not the only things she shares with Davia. So too does she share heartbroken desolation at their fate.

That night, Kyran lies on her back in the ship. Should she apologize for observing something so private? Or ignore the whole thing altogether? She can't offer any kind of solace. She is unnerved and irritated to be so.

A deeper ache grips her chest, a question she can't phrase within herself and an answer that eludes her.

She faces the wall and closes her eyes. An immense chasm looms between them. The woman on the other side is as human as she is, and as alone.

CHAPTER FIVE

Two weeks later, another earthquake knocks several boulders loose from the canyon border.

"I can't move the rock," Kyran says in Sifani. "My feet are . . . cold."

Davia stops what she's doing to scrutinize Kyran's feet in confusion. "Your feet?"

Kyran shakes her hands against the morning chill and blows on them to try to warm them with her breath.

Davia's confused expression turns into something like amusement. "Hands. Your hands are cold."

Kyran curses in her own language, embarrassed at having chosen the wrong word again. "Yes, hands," she says in corrected Sifani.

It's been like this for days with her attempts to learn more of Davia's language. So far this morning, she's already pointed to several items and asked Davia for the Sifani word for them.

Davia points at Kyran and wiggles her fingers. "Hand?"

Kyran frowns, confused.

Davia points at herself. "Hand." She points again at Kyran.

She's trying to learn Kyran's language.

Several things race across Kyran's mind. Davia, who is not as bloodthirsty or as cruel as Kyran had feared and hasn't killed her. Davia, whose people have killed so many Ellodians, Kyran has lost count. Davia, who still twitches if Kyran moves too quickly. Davia, who killed Benna.

Kyran will not share what little she has left of Ellod.

She pushes the rocks into place, ignoring the biting chill.

A month after the crash, Kyran stands beside Davia, her dirty hands on the equally dirty hips of her flight suit. "This . . . catches the water and cleans the dirt?"

While most of the frigate's systems are fried, a few features remain. Emergency lighting, water filtration, the charger for Davia's pistol, basic sanitation—all of it aids their survival in some way. Davia is cautious and has fashioned a solar-powered secondary water filtration system outside the aft bay door of the ship in case the shipboard one fails.

"Yes, but this regulator seal is broken." Davia holds the ruined component, both necessary and useless, in her hand. Part of it has been melted off by a glancing blow from a fist-sized meteor.

The black fabricated ring triggers something in Kyran's memories.

"Oh, this is just like the wormhole generator conduits!" She races to the open door of the frigate.

Though the ship is dark this time of day, Kyran braces herself against the bulkheads as she makes her way to the command hub. Her height is an advantage as she stretches upward to reach beyond the edge of an upside-down console.

By the time Davia catches up with her, Kyran has pulled several cables from the open housing.

"What are you doing? Stop . . ."

Kyran is focused on her task and doesn't bother attempting to explain. Davia will understand soon enough.

Kyran finds the strands she's looking for, yanks them from position, and with quick movements born from rebuilding systems like these more times than she can count, she isolates the desired component and disconnects it.

Davia's tone changes to something dark and disapproving,

and her hand is back on her weapon.

"See?" Kyran raises her discovery between them. "It's like the one for your filtration system. You don't need it since the ship won't fly again."

Davia looks angry, flustered, and her hand hasn't moved from her pulse pistol. Despite the language barrier, Kyran has proven her usefulness in time to prevent Davia from drawing the weapon. Davia's anger fades, and something indecipherable takes its place as she appears to take Kyran's measure again.

Kyran has been speaking in Ellodian and remembers to translate. "The same."

Davia stares at her, assessing. Finally, she nods and leads the way back outside the ship.

They work together in silence to install the replacement component. Kyran is pleased to work with her hands again on components she's spent years handling.

"We must make it . . . safe . . . from fire rocks in the sky."

"Meteors," Davia says, not unkindly.

"Meet . . . meteors." Kyran speaks Sifani like a child. It's better than not being able to communicate at all.

Davia doesn't mock her for it, and Kyran is grateful.

One overcast morning, they hike from the canyon to a nearby arid glade in a gully. Scorch marks top several stumps, indicating where Davia felled lumber for their firepit. The trees are dense from the high winds and the dry climate, and the wood burns long as a result, but the consumable resource must be replenished.

Davia aims her pistol at one gnarled tree not much taller than she is, and with two precise low-power shots, she severs the trunk from its base. When it falls to the ground, she points at it and speaks, not that Kyran understands her.

Davia holsters her pistol and gestures with both hands.

Kyran sighs. She's expected to drag this thing back to camp. The only food they have has to be cooked, and the windy evenings are cool. She could have rigged some other means of transporting it overland, if Davia would let her use the available materials from the crash.

As she wrangles the trunk into position, testing for the best way to lug it back to the canyon, she notices a dislodged shrub. Some of its roots point skyward, revealing odd tubular growths. They resemble some plants the fleet used to trade for, supplementing their rations.

She drops the log and ignores Davia's indecipherable inquiry as she kneels in the sandy dirt. Twisting the tuber from its root takes effort, the roots as dense as the scrub brush itself. She grunts as she severs one.

"Eat?"

Davia frowns in thought, then shrugs a shoulder.

They determine the tubers need to be roasted to be edible, and their bland taste doesn't cut the bitterness of the accompanying meat. At least it's something different.

A new rhythm grows, the time broken into a rough schedule defined by mealtimes, by Davia's rituals, by first light and final dark.

By the third month, the weather has become hotter. Kyran wakes to a warm sticky feeling against her skin and a stickier one between her legs. The familiar ache in her abdomen is overdue considering how long she has been stranded on this rock, and the lack of supplies to handle her condition sparks her anger.

Though this is something they likely have in common, she does not want to talk to Davia about it and can't define why. She sacrifices a few strips of her flight suit into a makeshift pad and uses another strand to tie her overlong hair back from her face and off her neck.

Davia is outside—a development conveying a new level of minimal trust—and Kyran is somewhat relieved. Her own body odor reaches her nose, and she frowns, irritated. Sanitation is now limited to bodily functions, and insufficient for complete cleanliness. These close quarters are poorly ventilated, and this corridor of the ship stinks of them.

She stomps through the boarding door to the nearby rain catch and dunks a container into the water reservoir. A hand bath will be better than nothing.

"We must ration the water," Davia says, her voice flat.

Kyran doesn't look at her. "Need to clean."

"We do not know when it will rain again."

"I don't care," Kyran says in Ellodian, too irritated to attempt a translation.

"Kyran, do not—"

Maybe it's the sound of her name, which Davia has never before spoken, giving Kyran chills she doesn't want to decipher. Maybe it's the blood leaking down her thighs. It's all too much.

With a roar, Kyran drops the container. She grabs her landing strut from where it's propped nearby. In the time it takes her to flip it and aim, Davia has already drawn both her weapons.

They stare at each other. Neither of them moves.

Kyran breathes heavily enough to raise more sweat on her skin. She doesn't attack—she's being foolish—but the anger is hard to contain.

She tilts the provisional spear away from Davia, and leaves the unspilled container on the ground when she walks away.

What little peace they'd achieved between them is gone. At the firepit that night, Kyran still doesn't know what to say. They can't keep living like this, hunting and eating the disgusting carcasses of repulsive beasts and growing more unclean by the day. They'll go mad and kill each other.

She chooses to ignore the irony.

When the sun breaks over the horizon the following day, Kyran fills a canteen and grabs her spear.

She leaves the canyon without a word. When she looks back, Davia is watching her.

Kyran picks a new direction, different from her original approach vector and not the path she took when she tried to escape, nor toward the nearby glade where they claim their firewood.

This time, she walks towards the rising sun.

Not far from the canyon, she passes too close to a crevice in the rock. Its depths are blocked from view until she stands at its edge, and nearly slips down its slick, steep stone walls.

The pit is empty save for the shells of a few long-dead creatures. Kyran counts herself lucky and resumes her path at a slower pace.

She explores for hours, doing her best to keep a straight line and her mind clear of turbulent thoughts. When she reaches a new vantage point, she piles fist-sized rocks together to mark her passing.

The sun peaks overhead. She stacks a larger pile of stones and turns back. This trajectory reveals only more canyons, and now she knows for certain.

At sunset, when she gets back to the canyon where the frigate lies dormant, Davia sits near the firepit, tending to her blade and looking surprised at Kyran's arrival. Maybe she wasn't expecting Kyran to return.

Kyran joins Davia by the fire and gingerly picks a piece of meat from the spit. After she blows on it to cool, she chews and swallows it down, and points in the direction she had traveled.

"No water. No trees. Only rocks."

A long moment passes before Davia nods, easing the tension between them.

Kyran repeats her expeditions for the next few days, each time choosing another course so she can learn more about the areas around them. One afternoon, after half a day's walk to the west, she discovers a small forest of gnarled trees, this one denser than the one they visit. Another day, Kyran trips beside one of the gaseous caverns and decides she should be less adventurous while she's on her own, but she persists in her explorations.

Her caution serves her well the next morning when she travels on one of the slant trajectories between the absolute cardinal directions. She finds a nest of the shelled beasts and they don't sense her presence. She returns early to report their location to Davia.

Davia spends the afternoon sharpening her sword.

After a week, Kyran's anger has faded. In retrospect, much of her frustration stemmed from being limited to the canyon and its monotonous maintenance when she is so used to traveling throughout the fleet troubleshooting problems and contributing solutions.

Uncleanliness doesn't help—her filthy suit is long past disgusting. Dried blood—her own and from creatures who have met their demise—splatters one arm, both knees and the area around the tear where the first creature bit her. Dirt from the rocks, mud from the rain, grease from the meat she's eaten, her own sweat—it's all turned the formerly white flight suit a grimy brown matching the dirt on her own skin.

She hasn't asked Davia for any of her clothes, and Davia hasn't offered.

Kyran is so focused on keeping herself upwind of her own stench and watching out for creatures waiting to attack her that she stands at the water's edge before it captures her attention.

The small lake is no farther across than the length of Davia's ship. The water is gray, a reflection of the overhead clouds, and the middle is too deep to provide a view to the bottom. The shallows near her feet are clear.

She pokes into its depths with her spear to make sure some hideous creature isn't lurking to eat her the moment she lets her guard down. With a last long scan of the periphery to verify nothing is sneaking up on her, she drops to her knees, sets down the spear and canteen, and unfastens her flight suit to the waist.

She can't help a smile as she cups handfuls of the water and splashes her face, her hair, her arms and chest and everything from her navel up—everywhere she can reach. She tries not to get her flight suit too wet. Cleaning some of the dirt and sweat from her body is a relief, even without soap.

On the walk back, she doesn't smell much better, but skin rinsed of grit is an improvement, and she's glad to have found a water source. They won't be dependent on unpredictable rainfall for hydration if the ship system fails.

Davia might be pleased at the news. The canyon is empty when Kyran gets back. Kyran busies herself with stoking the fire and clearing sand off the solar panels on the aft end of the ship. Davia must have traveled a greater distance to hunt today—surprising since her distrust of Kyran keeps her closer to the ship.

Kyran could do whatever she'd like since Davia isn't here. She chooses to climb to her preferred seat on the wing of the ship, fatigue settling her restlessness as the shadows lengthen. From this angle, she stares past the canyon wall, a sense of apprehension growing within her. Has she forgotten something?

It's sunset.

Davia never misses her sunset ritual—has paused mid-task to perform it as if prodded by a celestial chronograph.

The sun sinks halfway past the horizon while Kyran sits motionless, searching for a dark figure against the dusk-colored landscape. Davia doesn't appear.

Kyran identifies what she feels as worry. She leaps down from the ship to add some wood to the fire.

A bloodcurdling scream comes from outside the canyon.

Without thought, Kyran charges towards its eerie echoes.

CHAPTER SIX

What light remains of dusk allows Kyran to traverse the terrain and track the screams to their source.

Davia has fallen into the pit Kyran circumvented in her own explorations. Davia scrambles against the pit's slick, smooth stone walls, attempting to gain purchase with one leg so she can leverage herself up. The other leg is taut, its clothing torn and soaked with blood.

Half-buried beneath her in the sand is a shell-backed creature many times the size of the ones they've seen. Its shell is discolored and pock-marked from meteors, dark where its smaller counterparts are bleached by the sun. The largest part of its body is trapped under the rocks.

Kyran bites back a scream at the horror of the thing. The creature's mouth is wide enough to swallow half of Davia's body in one bite. One of its pincers is broken and useless, while the other contracts on Davia's leg. Davia cries out, clinging with one hand to a protruded root sticking out beyond the rim of the pit.

Her other hand holds her pistol. She can't shoot the pincer without risking damage to her own leg, and she can't twist her body for better aim at the creature without letting go of the root.

Tears stream down Davia's face, horror and fear feeding her whimpers and cries.

Davia fires again, a blind shot in the direction of the threat. The animal screeches, and jerks its pincer, exposing the bones in

Davia's leg. Her fingers slip on the root.

How she's still hanging on despite what must be agony is astonishing.

She may be Sifani, but she shouldn't be eaten alive. Kyran throws herself on the ground, flat at the edge of the pit, and reaches for Davia's hand.

"Davia!"

Her eyes wild, Davia appears shocked at Kyran's appearance. Kyran grabs her wrist and tries to pull her up. Her effort only stretches Davia between rescue and death, and Davia's leg pays the price. She screams again, this time more in pain than fear.

Davia shoots again and accomplishes nothing.

"Give me the pistol," Kyran says.

Davia doesn't respond. Kyran has spoken in Ellodian again. She can't think of the words to convey her meaning, though, and Davia doesn't have time.

"Davia," Kyran says again as she beckons at the pistol with her other hand.

Davia's eyes cloud with mistrust, and her hesitation makes Kyran both angry and sad.

"I won't hurt you." She calms her tone, hoping Davia will understand, and says something she's not said before and swore she never would. "Please."

Davia's grunt morphs into another pained cry when the creature tugs again. She stretches her other arm over to Kyran and relinquishes the pistol.

Kyran has never held such a weapon, and her first shot misses. She corrects her aim after shifting her weight, all while trying not to let go of Davia.

The second shot connects, angering the animal. Davia's flesh tears and the sound turns Kyran's stomach.

Kyran stills herself as best as she can despite Davia's shrill screams, and fires again. This shot punctures well enough that the next tug from the creature severs its own pincer. She fires several more times, losing count and not stopping until the creature stops moving.

Kyran drops the weapon and pulls Davia free of the pit before falling on her side, breath fast and heart pounding. A muffled moan snaps her to attention.

Davia's eyes are glazed by what must be excruciating torment, and wariness mixed in with her relief. She glances at the weapon beside Kyran.

The flash of anger through Kyran dissipates so swiftly she trembles with it. Or maybe it's adrenaline. She stares into Davia's eyes as she puts the weapon back in Davia's hand.

Why does Davia's trust matter?

Davia groans again. They need to return to the canyon as quickly as possible, not only because Davia's wound needs tending. The light is fading, and the short journey won't be easy.

Davia can't put any weight on her injured leg. Kyran doesn't blame her. Part of the pincer is still buried in her tattered leg, and Kyran leans over to remove it. Davia stops her and says more words she doesn't understand.

"Water," Davia says, her words breathy and pained.

They find a slow, effective way to walk with Davia leaning on Kyran who carries a reclaimed sack of tubers. Davia bites back any noise. It could be stubbornness, but Kyran senses only a persistence in doing what must be done.

When Davia falters, Kyran keeps her from collapsing to the ground.

"You're going to have to let me carry you," she says, knowing she's not understood. She gives Davia back her sack, and then—moving as slowly as she can so Davia doesn't misinterpret her actions—she sinks to a partial crouch, wraps her arms around Davia's body, and folds her over one shoulder as best she can before rising.

Davia's moans sound like relief.

Checking each step forward, Kyran navigates toward the fire flickering in the distance. It's full dark when they arrive, and Kyran lowers Davia to her usual place by the fire. The pupils of Davia's eyes are dilated, and she's bitten her lip so hard, it bleeds.

Kyran fetches water and what little medical supplies Davia

has on the ship, nowhere near enough to address a wound this severe. Davia cries out as Kyran removes the embedded pincer and tosses it in the fire.

The strips of skin and muscle are impossible to clean and will be difficult to bandage. Davia vomits to one side. She doesn't complain or berate Kyran for her pitiful efforts. The third time Kyran tries to put the tattered remains of Davia's calf back together, Davia grabs her arm.

"Use the fire," she says.

Kyran doesn't understand. Davia draws her blade, thrusts it into the flame and rests the hilt on a rock.

Kyran gapes in horror. "I can't cut your leg off," she says in Ellodian, catches herself and switches to Sifani. "No—no remove . . . feet."

She wants to curse at her inability to communicate.

Davia chokes against retching again and takes a deep bracing breath. "No, use the fire to close the—"

She says more unfamiliar words, and Kyran interprets her meaning. Cauterizing the wound may be the best option considering their limited supplies. The thought of searing Davia's flesh brings a wave of nausea. Kyran sways where she sits.

Davia's face is crumpled by agony. She nods in wordless encouragement. That Davia would think of Kyran's feelings in this situation makes the queasiness worse. Davia senses her fear.

Kyran takes too long preparing for the action—securing Davia's leg so it doesn't move, making sure Davia won't fall over when the pain worsens. She triple-checks the blade for debris and finds none. Davia keeps her sword in prime condition.

After one last look into Davia's eyes—half-closed by the pain and shadowed in the dark—and a deep centering breath, Kyran presses the flat of the blade against one side of the wound, trying not to burn herself.

Davia breathes rapidly, enduring the agony. Eventually she screams. It echoes off the ship and the canyon walls until it dies in Kyran's ears.

Kyran continues, working her way around the leg, searing it

together. By the time she finishes the cauterization, Davia has passed out.

Kyran does the best she can to clean around the wound. The burned flesh is red and streaked with blood where it isn't puffed and swollen.

Davia isn't awake, so Kyran lets the tears in her eyes fall. She doesn't have the equipment or the skill to make anything better.

Davia doesn't regain consciousness and her breathing is labored. Kyran stokes the fire to cast more light across the canyon, then labors to maneuver Davia into a position allowing Kyran to carry her inside the ship.

Once Davia is in her bunk, her leg elevated on an empty water container, Kyran stands, looming nearby in contemplation.

What now?

The clarity is cold when it hits her.

The woman she once thought of as her enemy lies defenseless. Kyran could use Davia's own weapon and kill her now.

The thought barely takes shape before she casts it aside. Could she answer Davia's trust with murder? Would her family forgive her for not exacting vengeance?

What they might have thought doesn't matter now. No one is here to tell Kyran who and how to be.

She focuses on the rhythm of the tasks they perform every night, and it doesn't take her much longer to do them alone. She burns the cleaning materials, more bandages lost to the fire since she fears giving Davia an infection if she tries to wash them without any disinfectant or cleanser.

Davia's sword lies in the dirt, stained with blood.

Kyran burns off the blood in the flames. After she banks the fire, she climbs back into the ship and closes the door.

Kyran rests the blade beside Davia before sitting in her own corner and doesn't think about why she couldn't put the sword anywhere else.

By dawn, Davia hasn't come to her senses.

Her leg is bloated and sickly, and pus leaks from the ghastly wound. Davia is feverish and can't still the rest of her body despite being unconscious.

Kyran has tossed and turned all night, waking every time she hears a vigorous rustle, a moan, a cry from Davia's oblivion. She is as wrung out as Davia looks as she prepares to clean the wound.

All the water in the ship's reserves is gone. Little remains in the secondary catch and is best left for absolute emergencies. This could qualify, but now Kyran knows of another source.

The day is mercifully cool. Kyran travels with as many containers as she can carry to the lake she found before the altercation in the pit. Carrying all the water back to camp hurts and she sweats from exertion. She stops more than once to rest weary limbs, though not for long. What if Davia wakes? What if she thinks Kyran has abandoned her?

When Davia had was trapped by the creature, she didn't cry out for help or call Kyran's name. Did she expect to die alone in that pit? Was it because Davia didn't think Kyran was within earshot or did she think Kyran wouldn't help?

Kyran is bothered by the thought as she plods forward.

She sacrifices one of the containers to the firepit where it will be forever scored and not useful for much else, but at least she'll have sterile water for cleaning the wound and for Davia's bandages. The bandages have depleted Davia's limited supply, which can't be helped.

Kyran is terrified of possible infection and shoves any possibility of Davia dying as far into the back of her mind as she can.

She doesn't want to consider how she might survive alone.

—~— —~— —~—

The blankets of Davia's pallet are soiled. Boiling the bandages for reuse has loosened the weave.

Kyran's search for more bed linens and any fabric she can rip or cut into strips is difficult. Everything is overhead since the ship is upside-down.

She finds little in the way of personal belongings besides more weapons—a silver-bladed longsword and a well-worn staff—and books. Several outfits are stored in a compartment in the crashed-in living quarters. The under-tunics are ideal for bandages. Kyran tests the theory by ripping one into strips, then assesses another with a more selfish eye.

She removes her flight suit and lets it hang from her waist as she pulls the cleaner shirt over her head. Her torso is longer than Davia's, so it falls only to her navel. It's too tight in the shoulders and arms, and a seam parts when she takes it off.

Most of the clothes have stitching or patches matching the sword and vines on the side of the ship. Kyran doesn't try any of those on. She doesn't tear them up, either.

She discovers a hand-sized rectangular frame with two faces on it stashed in a drawer. The image is of a younger Davia with a similarly aged man. A lover? No, the eyes are the same. A sibling. His smile is wide, and Davia's eyes are bright with something like joy.

Kyran shoves it back into the drawer, angry that Davia has a family somewhere, one she must cherish if she has this image. The irritation assuages any guilt at ripping up Davia's clothes without her permission.

At some point, purpose gives way to simple curiosity, and she searches every corner and compartment. The frigate has a laboratory and medical bay tucked into a modified single-stall bunk space. None of the equipment works and the medical supplies have all been used. Storage containers are stacked in one corner, and they appear to be the only things left intact from the crash. Smaller cases aligned inside are labeled with names Kyran recognizes. Rymind 18B. Rymind 11A. Each contains mineral, soil, and water samples, no doubt for later analysis.

This proof—that Davia is yet another imperial Sifani stripping resources from worlds they don't inhabit—doesn't reconcile with the woman who bandaged Kyran's wounds and saved her from a gory death.

Kyran shuts the case, ending her search for the day.

Davia stirs little when Kyran tends to her and changes out the bed linens. Sifani or no, Davia is defenseless and wounded and deserves care, and Kyran does her best to provide it.

With her tasks complete, Kyran leaves the ship to ease the restlessness flared by her discoveries.

Free and unsupervised, she digs through the debris pile looking for usable wreckage. Containers, struts, plating—all broken items no longer useful for their designed function.

Sifanis are so wasteful—much of what lies here can be repurposed.

With no one to dictate otherwise, Kyran sifts through the stacks, and lets her mind wander to the possibilities of what she can build with her own hands.

The next afternoon, Kyran lifts Davia's head and presses a cup of weak broth to Davia's lips. "Drink," she says in Sifani.

After a few sips, Davia makes a mewling sound, warning Kyran too late, and vomits.

It's the second time today Kyran has attempted—and failed—to get something more substantial than water into Davia's body.

She cleans up the mess, cleans up Davia, and waits until she can try again.

Sunset ends her day of chores and tinkering, and Kyran sits by the fire, boiling more broth when an odd scratching catches her attention.

By the time she pinpoints the sound and rushes to investigate, one of the shelled creatures has burrowed under the wall and nearly breached their meager defense. It's stuck beneath a rock, one claw caught between the boulders.

Kyran runs to fetch the landing strut that is part walking stick and part spear, and when she returns, the thing is almost free. She stabs wildly at it with no martial grace or finesse—nothing like Davia might have done. The screeching stops. The mauled and bloody creature dies still trapped.

Kyran covers the corpse with smaller rocks and buries the pile in sand, hands shaking from the encounter.

Three days later, she wishes she'd kept the carcass. Their limited supply of meat is gone. Kyran used the freshest pieces for Davia's broth. More will be needed.

With Davia incapacitated, the hunting falls to Kyran—a distasteful thought. So is starvation. She has an idea where she can find more of the creatures. How many may lie in wait is unclear.

Davia's pistol rests in its charging station, and borrowing it is both presumptuous and necessary. She eyes Davia's blade. Touching it feels wrong—disrespectful, a violation of Davia's person and her obvious dedication.

Kyran sets one of their water canteens beside Davia in case she wakes. Her long hair is matted by her own sweat and fever, yet her flawless face is more captivating when she sleeps.

Kyran finally tears herself away from Davia's side.

"Guess it's my turn to fetch dinner." She speaks in Ellodian, keeping her intonation calm and unthreatening.

Outside, she collects her supplies and a canteen of her own, and leaves the canyon in search of prey.

Hunting is time-consuming and grisly.

The first group of creatures she encounters is too numerous to approach alone. Two hours later, she comes across a smaller pod of half a dozen of them, nestled in a narrow valley, sluggish in the sun. She observes them for some time as she sits in the rocks above them, delaying the inevitable.

If she doesn't kill these things, she and Davia won't eat.

She dispatches two animals with Davia's pistol. The noise of the blasts is enough to drive the rest of them away.

Kyran waits until they're gone before she moves any closer.

One is half-obliterated. Some of its meat hasn't been ruined. The other was killed by one shot to its hideous face. Kyran flips them onto their backs, bleeds and guts them as best as she can onsite, trying not to lose the contents of her own stomach.

When the task is done, she stares at her trembling hands, at the blood and viscera on her fingers, and lets herself cry.

Is she a monster now? She has killed these creatures and ripped their flesh apart with her own hands. How is she different from the enemy she's labeled bloodthirsty? Does it matter if she does it to stay alive, to keep someone else alive?

No answers come. She doesn't move until the tears stop, drying in itchy discomfort on her cheeks.

Kyran secures the corpses together for the hike back, vigilant against pursuit.

Sunset is a few hours away, and the storm moving in from the south gives the sky a red-orange glow. She stops on a bluff to survey the harsh, unforgiving terrain.

This place where they're marooned has a rugged beauty. Kyran breathes it in before she turns her feet toward home, a crashed, crippled enemy ship entombed in a canyon.

Once the meat has been cut up and stored, after she's made Davia's broth and helped to make her more comfortable, once Davia—who was only half conscious for her liquid meal—falls back to sleep, Kyran sits by the firepit.

She's tired, from effort and productivity and purpose. Despite the emotional turmoil of the day, Davia's condition, the adrenaline of the hunt, and the stress of daily life on this rock—she's more relaxed and centered than she's ever been.

Today, the silence is not as oppressive.

No more constant demands on her time or expertise. If it weren't for her injury, Davia wouldn't need her at all. For the most part, Kyran's nightmares have eased. No rushing from one ship to another, one post to another, no trying to stay awake a bit longer.

No more endless pursuit. No more duty, and Davia has never called her Princess since she has no idea who Kyran is—was—to her people. No more talk of legacy and responsibility, no more admonitions from Benna—

She pushes Benna from her mind.

The momentary peace passes, its price remembered.

It's past midday, and Kyran is stuck inside as another meteor shower pummels the canyon.

She's not as worried as she once might have been. If a meteor strikes the ship and kills them, so be it. She can do nothing to stop it, and worrying about it won't change things.

She sits beside Davia, close enough to check the wounded leg, to adjust Davia's position, to bring her sustenance when needed. She wets a strip of cloth and wipes the sweat from Davia's skin.

Davia doesn't seem to mind Kyran's touch. Maybe she's too far gone. She appears cognizant enough to recognize Kyran is the one giving her water or broth or tending to her wounds.

Kyran lingers over the task of wiping Davia's brow and chooses not to acknowledge her confusing protectiveness of the woman who is no longer her captor.

Davia sleeps as the day falls to night. The storm passes, replaced by the *pik-pok* of rain on the ship.

Kyran stands and stretches against the strain in her back. The rain catch on the ship's stern is probably secure—best to be certain nothing knocked it loose. Outside, the steady trickle of water into the filter is as expected. With any luck and barring any catastrophes, she won't have to walk to the lake for a few days.

After Kyran has settled in her bunk, Davia shifts and cries out. She doesn't wake, and the faint light glints off tear tracks on her cheek.

Kyran weighs her options. If she wakes Davia, the dreams will be over. The discomfort and the pain will not. If Kyran doesn't wake her, the torment of whatever haunts Davia will continue.

Taking care of her wounds is one thing. Emotional comfort is another. Though they've become allies of a sort, they're not friends. Forced companions at best.

She does nothing.

Davia sighs, suggesting the nightmare has passed. "Kyran," she whispers in her sleep.

Kyran rests one hand over her pounding heart, wide awake now. An ache rises in her to hear it again—her name in Davia's softest voice.

CHAPTER SEVEN

Hour by hour, day by day, Davia improves. She sleeps more than not. Her moments of lucidity become more frequent.

The time they spend talking increases since Davia can't yet move much. Kyran encourages Davia to teach her more Sifani, and with nothing but time on their hands whenever Kyran isn't hunting or performing chores around the canyon, Kyran's understanding of the language grows.

Over the weeks of convalescence, Kyran never talks about where they're from, about what brought them here. Today, the heaviness of the past presses like gravity as she considers her lack of training to treat wounds like the one Davia has.

Davia is half-propped up in her bunk. Kyran sits near the open door while the breeze clears the stale air from the ship.

"What is that?" Davia says, her still-tired voice stronger. "It's not a spear."

"No." Without looking up, Kyran continues her work of trimming and carving a wrist-thick branch. "This . . . under your arm and . . . and by your leg."

She lifts the soon-to-be crutch upright. Davia frowns in confusion until Kyran stands to demonstrate. Kyran spends most of the afternoon sanding the rough edges smooth with a piece of broken filter.

"Thank you," Davia says.

Her gratitude is unnerving.

Kyran helps Davia through the door. Outside, the light is

stronger than it's been in days, and it emphasizes the changes Kyran has made. She nervously awaits Davia's assessment.

Davia's dark brows rise in surprise, not anger. "You've been busy."

Stone stairs now lie between the boarding door and the canyon floor, the gaps filled with dried mud. The meteor holes on the wing have been covered by collected shells and warped plating. A rough table now stands under the wing with several contraptions scattered across it, and beneath Kyran's customary seat on the wing's topside are bracketed scaffolding and a ladder. Much of the improvised creations are constructed of scrap obtained from the debris pile.

Davia has more questions in her eyes, an expression Kyran has come to associate with avoiding their respective pasts.

"Hungry?" Kyran asks to change the subject, and with a wan flat smile, Davia nods.

One morning days later, Davia stirs first, waking Kyran.

The sky is barely light when Davia shuffles across the canyon. With slow, careful hops, she etches the circle in the sand and lowers herself to a facsimile of her regular position, her injured leg outstretched as she kneels unsteadily with the other.

Davia hisses through her clenched teeth until the pain eases enough for her to continue. Her eyes close in meditation for a long time before she speaks.

The first phrase begins "I have," and then the next few words are lost. For the first time, Kyran understands more of what Davia says.

". . . I have no shelter but the stars and no home but where I kneel. My heart is . . ."

The rest of what she says remains a mystery.

Kyran's eyes fill with tears, and it's not only sympathy at Davia's pain. She is awed by the strength and fortitude of this woman who is supposed to be her enemy. Here, marooned at the end of the universe, Davia vibrates with purpose despite her condition.

As she has done countless times before, Davia draws her sword across her arm until it's wet with her blood. Kyran is tired of Davia bleeding. She has cleaned up enough of it to last her a lifetime.

Davia holds her sword outstretched longer than usual. Kyran wonders if she's doing it to prove she can, which is a moot effort. Once Davia wipes her blade against the dark fabric of her thigh and sheathes it, she tries and fails several times to stand up.

Kyran is at her side before she falls over. "Let me help."

Davia has regained some color and no longer appears sickly. She is leaner and more angular—wilder everywhere on her body.

Davia glances at Kyran with something like gratitude mixed with the annoyance of needing assistance and something else Kyran can't decipher. It makes Kyran apprehensive, more aware of their proximity than she was when tending to Davia's care. She looks away, then wishes she could look back.

The heat of Davia's body presses against Kyran's skin, and her hair flies wild and brushes Kyran's cheeks. She fights the urge to touch it, to twist it between her fingers to test its thickness and softness.

The moment passes as she helps Davia sit by the firepit.

Kyran stokes the wood and as she has so many times before, wonders what the ritual means. Her curiosity grows at midday and at sunset, and by the evening meal, she can't hold it inside any longer.

"What does it mean?"

Davia sips from a canteen and pauses at Kyran's question. She wipes the back of one hand across her mouth. "What?"

Kyran searches for a word to describe the . . . praying? A ritual? She waves a hand in the general direction of Davia's reserved space. "That—the way you—every day, you . . ."

She falters.

"Ah." Davia's eyebrows rise and fall in understanding. "The kim venu."

She resettles more comfortably in her seat.

"My mother died when I was very young." Davia peers into the fire, but her gaze is directed somewhere far away. "My father was . . . powerful politically. I had no interest in state affairs. Yet few paths available to me met his approval."

Davia sits like a statue, unmoving. The firelight flickers in her eyes, and the shifting light and shadow on her skin emphasize her beauty. Kyran doesn't dare move, afraid Davia will stop talking.

She also fears Davia will continue and force the reciprocity of Kyran sharing her own past.

The encroaching darkness is deeper this night, a safer place for secrets.

"I wanted to pursue the sciences and the secular arts of my mother's people. My father allowed me to study at the monastery on Duveri."

The name means nothing to Kyran. But she understands it must hold some significance and prestige.

"Father insisted on using his influence for my application. I would have preferred acceptance on my own merits—"

She stops as if she's revealed too much, swallows, takes a deep breath, and speaks again.

"I studied mathematics, physics, engineering, and system intelligence. These were challenging and satisfying subjects. I also found . . . solace . . . in the monastery's martial studies."

She pauses to explain any unfamiliar Sifani words, then continues. "The ritual you see is one taught at the higher levels of the art. When I finished my schooling and received the titles and appellations of my advancement, I had established myself well enough to earn my father's favor. We did not speak often. He was always busy with one crisis or another and paid little attention to my studies as long as I performed to his satisfaction. I hoped to secure a position worthy of his approval."

Something in her wary tone warns Kyran the story is approaching a dark turn.

"Those he thought were his allies plotted against him. An

assassin murdered him in his bed." She wipes a tear without shame and says nothing more.

The night's only sound is the crack and hiss of the embers. Not even the wind interrupts.

Kyran pays her respects by remaining silent in witness to Davia's pain.

After several months, the rhythm of their days lends a kind of resolved peace. The swelling of Davia's leg went down weeks ago, and what remains of her ordeal is a gnarled, ugly hand-width scar wrapped around her calf. Her leg can hold her weight, though she moves faster with the crutch.

The inevitable occurs and their menstrual cycles sync.

They've yet to exchange words this morning as Davia maneuvers through the boarding door first. Kyran follows and shuts the door.

"Leave it open," Davia says.

"Too much sand."

"The air is stale."

The air is beyond stale—it stinks with their body odor, made worse by the heat. Given a choice between the irritation of sand in everything and the stench, Kyran chooses the stench.

"You open it," Kyran says, then instantly regrets her snappish tone. Opening and closing the door is an unspoken challenge for Davia, whose ease of motion is still limited.

With an angry set to her jaw, Davia steps forward to do as Kyran has directed. Kyran lifts a hand to stop her.

Kyran opens the door, already irritated at the sand she'll have to shake from her blankets later.

She decides to hunt earlier in the day to avoid the afternoon heat, though her guts feel heavy and she wishes to hit something. She craves food with flavor, not gamy meat and roots tasting of dirt no matter how much she cleans and prepares them. She yearns for soap and hot water, and other things that would only come with rescue.

No one is coming to save her from this damned rock—her life is here and now. She shoves any hope for rescue down and channels her anger and frustration into new courage, getting close to her prey to stab it with a newly crafted wooden spear, menacing off two smaller creatures before they can attempt to attack her.

Kyran returns to the canyon with her kill. She meets Davia at the table under the wing and splays the carcass on its surface without speaking.

Davia has taken over much of the meat preparation since Kyran does all the hunting. She divides the meat into three piles—fresh chunks for the spit, thicker portions to be cut into strips for preserving, and odds and ends for soup.

Davia pushes the first several slices across the table toward Kyran, who stands closer to a rudimentary drying rack.

Kyran speaks without thinking. "You cut the meat too thick."

It's her first complaint directed at Davia, who pauses her methodical slicing.

Kyran lifts a slice when Davia frowns. "See? The edges will get too tough, and the middle will be too chewy. Cut them thinner."

Too late, she realizes she's given an order.

Davia's next slice is so thin, the meat is translucent.

Kyran sighs. "This is just going to turn into rope. We'll be digesting it for weeks."

The knife clunks when Davia drops it on the table. "Are terrorists so particular? Were you some sort of professional food preparer to have such exacting standards?"

Fuming, Kyran says nothing.

The tension thickens between them with the expectation that Kyran say something about who she is and where she's from.

After a silent dinner, after Davia's kim venu, they sit by a fire they don't need. The heat of the day hasn't eased and it's far too warm to go to bed. The ship will be stuffy for hours, making sleep impossible.

Davia is not as companionable as she's been of late. At least she doesn't hold the promise of violence.

Kyran surprises herself by speaking.

"My name is Kyran Loyal." Davia wouldn't understand the significance of her surname, so there's no harm in sharing it. "I was born planet-side during autumn in the northern hemisphere of Mila, a planet beyond the borders of the Sifani Prime empire."

She pokes a spear at the fire. The flames leap, casting shadows on the canyon walls.

"We stayed there until I was two, then traveled to Berendum on the edge of the territories for a while." Here with Davia is the longest she's been on a planet in decades. "After that, for the next ten years or so, we moved around a lot."

She remembers little about those years except her parents. All the space stations were the same to her as a child.

"I never spent much time with my parents. My mother in particular was active in the movement to overthrow Sifani rule of the occupied worlds." Kyran clears her throat, nervous about revealing so much. "Althea believed those planets should have the right to govern themselves since they hadn't been granted formal citizenship, that a greater alliance was possible, and she was vocal about it. It made her one of the foremost targets for those in favor of the existing regime."

She waits for Davia to interject, to defend her government and its rulers.

"How did you end up so far away from the core systems?" Davia asks instead.

"Long, long ago, we were driven from this planet." Kyran gestures at Ellod though she doesn't look at it herself. "By war, by famine, by Sifani invasion. We escaped and traveled beyond the old boundaries of the empire, and found a new world to make our home. Later, that planet was conquered in the Landin expansion."

Every king tested their mettle by invading new worlds.

"By the time I was born, we'd long been a nomadic people, searching the stars for the original Ellod."

Kyran can't sit still, shifting her weight, poking at the fire. All this is in the past, all events she doesn't want to talk about, and yet she cannot stop. She never thought she'd share any of it with her enemy. What does it matter now? Escape is impossible, rescue beyond unlikely.

She finally gazes at the planet, a sphere of green and blue in the night sky.

"We came to rebuild, and I was to lead my people, to deliver on my parents' plan."

She can't help muttering her own commentary. "One person can't change the course of an entire people—people who've spent years scratching and scrabbling in the ass-end of the galaxy."

Kyran doesn't mention how unqualified she felt for the task, regardless of the training she had received or how many people had pledged to follow her. She has never believed another queen is the best thing for her people. How could her claim of a crown change the truth? They had nothing as long as the Sifani queen and her empire hunted them. Kyran could better serve her people in other ways.

Except now she won't serve them at all, and none of this matters anymore.

"What happened to your parents?" Davia's murmur is little more than a whisper pulling Kyran from her dark thoughts.

This is the part she wants to tell the least.

"When I was fourteen, they were captured by the Old King's troops. They were the figureheads of the rebellion, so they were transported back to Meteus for trial."

Kyran's voice turns flat. She tosses a pebble into the fire, eager to be done. "When the old Sifane died, the queen ordered the execution of all incarcerated dissidents in his honor. My parents were among them."

Davia's gasp doesn't surprise her. The story is shocking to those who haven't heard it before. Benna makes—*made*— Kyran recount it at every fleet gathering to remind her people of what they'd lost, of the brutality they'd suffered.

Kyran is somewhat inured to their potency, having spoken

these words so many times, and nothing can make the loss worse. It's already the most painful thing she's ever experienced, her isolation here included.

The wounds have long since scarred over enough for her to function. She spent her remaining adolescence angry and alone. Benna had seen to her studies of Ellodian history, made sure she understood every aspect of her parents' vision, and years passed before Kyran treated her with anything like compassion or affection.

Whether Kyran was interested in her preordained path was never discussed.

Instead, Kyran had fantasized about running away to the heart of Sifani Prime, joining the Sifani armed forces and working up the ranks. She had envisioned a future where she joined the elite guard and secured a posting close enough to kill those responsible for her parents' deaths.

Those dreams were an angry adolescent's fantasies. She had often considered how impossible such dreams were, and she has never been as far from them as she sits now—on a desolate moon so distant from her once solitary goal she might as well never spare it another thought.

And yet the vision is as powerful as ever.

"Your empire has stolen my culture from my people, your queen has taken everything from me and my family, and if I could, I would—"

She can't bring herself to say the words, though the threat lies in the air. Davia is quiet, more silent than usual. Maybe speaking open treason—even here where Kyran can't be arrested or incarcerated—is too much for their tepid truce to bear.

Davia's eyes hold horror, not judgment, and then something piercing and hard.

Kyran hasn't felt marrow-deep cold since her first night of exposure in the rain. Davia's unyielding gaze is like ice on her skin despite the heat. It reminds her of the people Davia killed in the battle that drove them here.

She mourns the lost peace between them when Davia's eyes

shutter in a way that blocks all her emotions. Davia stands and leans on her crutch before she speaks.

"I am Davia Sifane," she says, distant and cool. "The Old King was my father."

Shocked and unable to move, Kyran can only stare as Davia disappears inside the ship.

PART TWO

CHAPTER EIGHT

Davia is five years old, and someone shakes her awake. "Wake up, girl."

The voice doesn't belong to her madi.

The windows are dark in the room she shares with her mother. Across the room, the other bed is empty, linens undisturbed. Davia is pulled from her bed, and she cannot free herself to go back to sleep.

"Come quickly," the woman says, and now Davia recognizes her. She is the cranky one—tall and slender like Davia's mother. Her long black hair shimmers and her eyes are as brown as her skin. She is beautiful like all the women here in the golden rooms, but always frowning and displeased about something. She isn't cruel, like some of the other women who spend their days in the garden with Davia's mother. She isn't kind either.

"Where's Madi?" Davia asks. Why hasn't her mother come to wake Davia herself?

"She doesn't know?" Another woman asks, tears in her voice, sniffling as she pulls Davia's clothes from a carved wooden chest and stuffs them into a cloth sack without care for neatness.

The cranky one's expression softens in sadness. "Someone will speak to her about Jora when she gets where she's going."

"Where am I going?" Are they sending her to be with other children? She has been the only one in these rooms with her madi all her life.

The crying one pats her shoulder. "Where Ethelyn can't—"

"Where you'll be safe," the first woman says.

One tugs pants on her legs while the other ties the sack to Davia's back. They pull her towards the door.

Two men wait on the other side of the threshold. They are a matching pair—towering and broad-shouldered, their armor and weapons frightening. The women push her forward.

One of the men clutches Davia by the shoulder, and she does not speak. No one speaks when soldiers come. Everyone waits in silence until they escort someone away.

Most of the time, the person comes back.

Did they take her madi? Are they taking Davia to her now?

They say nothing, not to Davia and not to the women as they leave.

The men walk her through the great room full of lounging pillows and potted plants, past the enormous fireplace taller than Davia. When she is allowed to visit, this is a lively place where her madi and the others read and play music and sew. Now the room is empty and dark save for the light from a few lamps.

They pass through the great room's elaborately carved door, beyond which Davia has never seen, and two more soldiers join them. Davia runs, barefoot, trying to keep up so the soldiers will not be angry at her.

At first, this part of the building is no different from the rooms she knows—floors of black tile, walls decorated with tapestries, windows too high for Davia to see through.

They walk a long time, and Davia almost falls asleep as she is pulled along by the men above her. When they pass through an archway covered in gold and jewels, she wants to stop and stare—to reach out to touch. The soldiers guide her into a hall twice as wide as those where she lives.

Does she still live there?

The windows are closer to the floor here. The sky has lightened and the first rays of sunshine touch the tops of the buildings.

All the structures are connected, their walls painted the same brilliant green, their towers topped with gold, like in the stories her madi told her.

Madi never said they live in a palace.

Davia is eleven, and excited to see her brother.

"Anin!"

After two weeks of nothing to do besides study and endure forced deportment lessons for a court she is not allowed to attend, and no one for company besides the latest rotation of governesses and instructors—replaced often to weed out traitors who might attempt to kill her—Davia trembles with anticipation.

"Davia, you've grown so tall," he says as he bends to embrace her.

He lies and Davia loves him for it. The doctors say she is small for her age.

They share a father. Anin's mother—High King Anahd's wife, Ethelyn—gave birth mere days before Davia was born, and they have been raised in separate parts of the palace. Anin convinced their father to allow him to visit Davia.

Anin has the stately bearing of a man, dressed in the formal royal Sifani colors of white and silver with green jeweled accents, his hair trimmed close to his head like a soldier.

She tugs at his hand and leads him across her suite to her desk. "Come see."

Davia showers him with tales of her studies and gripes about the staff. She demonstrates the scientific experiments she has conducted to emulate his education. Her work is simulated since she is not allowed to use hazardous laboratory equipment. She drags him over to the window to point at her favorite trees in the garden below. She bests him at the board game he taught her to play, one imitating war strategy.

Her tactics are improving. Anin is far too irritated at the loss to have forfeited for her pride.

"I must go," Anin says, brushing his palm down his chest to

straighten his uniform as he stands. "Father wants me to attend his session with his generals this afternoon."

Such an invitation is one of the many differences between her life and Anin's. She does not blame her brother. Anin lives with his parents and travels with the High King on occasion. Davia lives alone in her suite and is allowed a daily walk in the garden. The only time she sees their father is when she presents herself to his study once a month, or for a rare shared meal.

"Come back tomorrow." Davia would rather spend more time with him than anything forced upon her by her tutors. "We can play kings and pawns again and I will have the cook make those pastries you like. And then we can play—"

"Davia, I'm a prince who will someday rule Sifani Prime. I have a lot of work to do, and I can't play games with little girls when I must learn how to be a real king."

If he sounded stern, Davia might receive the chastisement better, but he is loving and compassionate. His eyes fill with pity, making it worse. "I'll always be your brother, and I'll always protect you."

She wonders as he embraces her if this, too, is a lie meant to appease her.

A week later, Davia receives a royal summons.

The High King's study is built into the tallest tower of the palace's central structure. When Davia arrives accompanied by an assigned detail of protective soldiers, High King Anahd is not alone. Several of his advisors—stern older men who stare at her with bald curiosity or feigned disregard—stand around the ostentatious room, holding tablets or drinking from glasses of dark liquor.

The High King is not a large man compared to his advisors, yet his presence fills every space of the expansive room. His bald head does not detract from his vigor—if anything, it makes him more severe and imposing—and his clean-shaven pale skin appears tanned in contrast to his pristine white garments. The green of his piercing eyes is startling by comparison.

The afternoon sun spills over the garden, and the view of

it from these chambers is unparalleled. Every flower on the entire planet is represented between the hedgerows and along the paths. Davia resists the urge to glance at them. She will be reprimanded if her father catches her not paying attention.

"I don't care how many fighters it takes," Anahd says in his imperious baritone to a lanky man with shifty eyes. "I want those supply convoys back on schedule. These delays have affected over thirty worlds this time."

"And if the terrorists attempt again to interfere?" His advisor shifts his tablet behind his back and stands erect, awaiting further instructions.

"They can only interfere if they have inside information. Identify their sources, incarcerate and penalize their families, and then broadcast their executions."

His commands strike Davia as cruel. He must have his reasons for such severity. She hopes never to have the kind of responsibility requiring her to execute people.

The advisor leaves when dismissed, and Anahd addresses the next man.

"Put an end to the miners' union before it spreads to the other colonies. They're not rising against the conglomerate. They're rising against me. If it means shutting down the mine, do it and raise the quotas in the rest of the system. Let them turn on themselves. Either way, the system is responsible for meeting the demand."

On and on, Anahd directs his advisors to execute his will across Sifani Prime until Davia and the guards are the only ones remaining in the study. Davia hasn't moved, eager to impress her father with her fortitude.

Anahd sifts through the papers and tablets on his desk. "Your instructors have informed me you exceeded Prince Anin's marks in all your subjects this term."

"Yes, Your Highness." Davia is never to address him as *Father* when they are not alone, which they rarely are.

She had not intended to best her brother's record and is thrilled to have scored well.

He makes a note on one of the pages with a stylus and then peruses the next item in the stack. "I have raised my estimation of your capabilities. You will begin the Meteus Secondary Conservatory curriculum ahead of schedule."

He has not said she will attend the Conservatory. Most likely, she will complete her studies in her rooms as she has done everything else—for her own protection, according to her governesses.

Yet the seed of an idea has taken root, and now is her only chance to see it grow.

"May I speak, Your Highness?"

He nods without looking at her.

"I wish to study where my mother did, at the Polytechnical Institute of Cenobia Duveri."

One of the few pieces of information Davia has gleaned about her mother since her death is her birth world. Duveri is part of the core systems, a place shrouded in legend and mystery except for the esteem for its secondary schools and universities.

When she was small, her mother told Davia stories of Duveri's tangled jungles and thick fragrant air. Davia wants to experience them herself.

Recognition flares in her father's eyes, as does his disapproval. They have never spoken of Jora Wallin. No one does.

Davia does not cower. She is her mother's daughter, and she is also a Sifane—she keeps her back straight and her head raised.

"Their excellence is one of the shining riches of your empire," she finishes, and awaits his judgment. Perhaps Davia has gone too far in this request. But it is made and she will face the consequences.

An aide enters the room, and Anahd beckons at the man, who approaches and whispers in his ear. The High King frowns.

"I'll be off-world for the next four months," he says, "and will expect weekly missives on your status. Achieve perfect marks for the rest of the year and your wish will be granted."

He gestures at the guards, and she is dismissed.

For the first time, Davia is angry at her father. She is expected to do as well as her half brother, yet exceeding his performance does not gain her any credit or accolades.

Davia is another detail among many—one to be managed, another flick of the High King's wrist.

She will find a way on Duveri to prove her significance.

Davia is fourteen and has never had a friend like Izabel.

They share several classes and take their meals together in the boarding dormitory hall. Izabel is from a province on the northern continent here on Duveri and knows only that Davia is from Meteus.

Anin advised during their last conversation for Davia to keep her origins to herself. "People will treat you differently once they know who you are. Now is the only chance you'll have to be judged by your merits alone and not your blood."

Izabel walks beside her in the hall after they exit their classroom. Her golden skin is unblemished by adolescence, and her dark hair is plaited in the requisite single braid down her back, like Davia's.

"Can we meet after supper tonight?" Izabel asks. "I need help with our fourth session assignment."

Three women approach them. Davia and Izabel step to the side of the hall. All three are Duveri Mins—practitioners of the obscure art of Venu Pakrim. Though their appearances differ, their attire and bearing are all the same. Each wears a dark green tunic with black trim, a dark gray shawl, and is armed with either a sword or a dagger. Each is daunting in demeanor, focused and intense. In the hallowed halls of the monastery, even the instructors step aside for them.

Once the women pass, Davia and Izabel resume their conversation.

"I thought you finished the assignment already," Davia says.

"The equations make no sense." Izabel, frustrated, hides her face in her hands.

"They are not complicated, Iza."

"You worked harder on them than anyone else, and if you had to study that much, I've no chance." Izabel's expression is petulant, but her praise is sincere.

Few of their peers share Izabel's respect for Davia's single-minded focus on her studies.

"Come," Davia says and pulls Izabel's arm. "We must not be late."

Davia insists Izabel keep her pace. She walks as quickly as she can without appearing to run from the studious halls of the third-year dormitory to the cathedral at the center of the institutional grounds.

The last of the day's sunlight spills red and orange across the foreboding turrets and towers of the riverside cathedral, brightening the stained glass as green as the water. They join the throngs of people on the causeway running parallel to the river channel. Ferries and boats of all sizes navigate toward the cathedral's docks.

Once a year, all students, staff, and dignitaries attend the ceremony of the monastery acolytes promoted to the rank of Min First Set. These are exalted practitioners of Venu Pakrim, the martial order of Duveri, ones who have completed all their trials and are here presented gray yaffa shawls denoting their new rank. Some continue their studies on Duveri, while others return to their lives off-world.

Inside the cathedral, the audience stands in the darkness, the air hazy from the wood-scented incense. All light shines on the center platform where the elders of the Jeweled Circle sit in carved stone chairs—twenty-seven men and women of elevated rank, the highest council in the monastery, revered throughout Sifani Prime.

The monastery is centuries old, and the origins of Venu Pakrim are shrouded in mystery. Many acolytes begin the journey to become Min. Few succeed. Those who pursue the path are expected to excel at their studies, with harsh punishments for failure. The trials are rumored to be grueling—over a hundred students attempt to join every year and only a handful are admitted.

Izabel grows restless after the first hour, twitching where she stands, whereas Davia has spent years practicing the art of standing still for long periods of time. The enigma the Mins present, the command they carry, the poise, grace, and feral intensity they possess despite their calm—all of it captivates Davia.

By the time the ceremony culminates and the newly promoted Mins exit the cathedral's nave, she envisions a new future, one allowing her to shine beyond the shadow of her parents.

At the beginning of the institute's next term, Davia adjusts the collar of her new uniform. She stands before the data relay station in a private chamber near the acolytes' quarters. At the appointed time, the display activates.

Her father is angry.

"You wear the colors of a Venu Pakrim acolyte."

"Yes, Father," she says, though he may not be alone. She is too excited for caution.

"You will not do this." Her father does not raise his voice, but his ire spikes through the connection like electricity. Sunlight streams into his study, emphasizing the wrinkle of his frown.

"I have already given my oaths before the Jeweled Circle."

A calculated risk, and one taken without warning her father. The ceremony had been private, in one of the monastery's wings closed to outsiders, and each moment had terrified and thrilled her. The edicts of the oaths require her to relinquish her family name within the Venu Pakrim halls, to suffer expulsion and banishment if she breaks her word.

Not a day later, Davia received a missive to contact her father. News of her participation must have reached the High King's ears, proving he has spies not yet routed by the monastery's security. Davia had not planned to tell him until their next scheduled call the following month.

He seethes, taking her measure from light-years away.

Davia is confident she will be allowed to pursue her training. If he exerts his influence and has her removed from the ranks of Venu Pakrim acolytes, the consequences could be politically damaging. Rumors might spread if she breaks her oath, which would reflect on him. So would the associated expulsion from the monastery's elite boarding school.

She endures his anger, a strange thrill in her blood.

"You will excel in this as you have done in everything else, Davia, and you will rise all the way to the Jeweled Circle."

"Yes, Father."

He terminates the connection as she speaks. A whisper of doubt is not enough to temper her relief at the lack of immediate consequences, nor to quell her excitement at his acquiescence.

For the first time, he had focused on her throughout the entire conversation, and not once had they been interrupted.

Now all she has to do is survive and conquer the next nine years.

Davia is twenty-two and fascinated by the softness of Izabel's skin against her own. They lie in Davia's bed, and she strokes her fingertips along the curve of Izabel's bare hip.

"That tickles," Izabel says. She swats Davia's hand away.

Davia mock gasps. "Such brutality, Min Izabel."

Izabel snorts. "I'm sure you can endure it, Min Davia."

They have both successfully completed their final trials for the rank of Min First Set, a year earlier than scheduled. Davia's eagerness to complete the curriculum could not be contained, and she drove Izabel to accompany her.

She did not want to rise alone.

Davia lives in private quarters in a dormitory for older students while she pursues her advanced engineering degrees. Izabel lives on a separate campus within the Cenobia Duveri, and studies to become an instructor at the monastery.

Their goals are not aligned, but they have discovered better ways to spend the time than discussing the future.

A visitor's chime echoes off the stone and wood walls. Izabel giggles as Davia scrambles for a robe before stumbling from her bedroom to the entrance on the far side of the apartment.

Davia opens the door, revealing only her face. "Yes?"

A young man with a third-year acolyte's stitching on his uniform bows past the waist and speaks without rising.

"The Jeweled Circle extends an invitation to you, Min Davia Sifane, Princess of the Exalted Kingdom. In one hour's time, please appear in the anteroom of the Grand Chambers."

The messenger rises, and only takes his leave when Davia nods in acceptance.

She cannot breathe.

Since her arrival on Duveri, she has used her mother's surname of Wallin, intent on proving herself through her marks and her dedication to Venu Pakrim instead of relying on the reach of her father's power and influence.

"Davia?" Izabel asks behind her, her eyes both awed and hurt.

Davia has always been private about her life before Duveri. Izabel has never pushed, and explaining now will take too much time.

"I must prepare. Stay here." Davia disrobes and strides toward the *en suite*. "I will be back as soon as . . . well, after."

Such a summons is unprecedented.

She arrives early, her steps measured and unhurried as befits her rank but her heart races. Two guards, both ranked Min Third Set, open the double doors to allow her inside.

Only nine of the twenty-seven members of the Jeweled Circle are present—more than enough to intimidate a lone Min First Set. They sit among three tiers of tables and chairs curved around a bare receiving area on the stone floor.

Would such attention be necessary if she were to be expelled?

"Congratulations on your recent acceptance to the Biomedical Engineering Minerals Research division," one woman says, her expression unreadable.

"I am honored to serve," Davia says.

A man in the middle tier leans forward. "You are the first member of the royal family to join the Venu Pakrim Min ranks in four hundred years. We offer you a seat in the Sifani Consortium."

Shocked, Davia cannot speak.

Duveri is its own nation-state within Sifani Prime, and the Consortium is the diplomatic body that interfaces with her father's court—with her father. More than once, High King Anahd has called on them to act in his interests. The Consortium has not always accommodated him.

If she takes this position, she would be a pawn in a greater game between intractable rulers, one where her own views might never be taken into consideration, where her own goals might never be actualized.

She pauses too long. Another Min speaks.

"This is an invitation, not a mandatory placement," this man says. "You may choose to decline and serve in other ways."

Giving her oaths to Venu Pakrim without her father's permission when she was little more than a child was one thing. Accepting this volatile political position as an adult is another.

"With deepest respect," she says, pleased her voice does not waver. "I decline to join the Sifani Consortium."

A wordless conversation occurs as the members glance at one another and back at her.

"We accept," the first woman says. "You are dismissed, Min Davia."

How she might be punished for declining—by her father or by those before her—is outside her circle for now.

Back in her apartment, she shares the nature of her summons with Izabel, who appears overcome by the day's revelations.

"You could have told me," Izabel says. "Shall I call you High One now?"

Davia is tempted to laugh despite the severity of the moment, but Izabel is serious.

"No, Iza, which is why I did not tell you." She takes Izabel's hands in her own. "I am just another acolyte here. You cannot imagine how liberating that is."

Izabel squeezes back, saying nothing.

"I swear," Davia says. "I am no different from who I was this morning."

She tugs Izabel closer, rests her forehead against Izabel's, and whispers. "I do not want anything to change between us."

"It won't." Izabel presses a kiss to Davia's lips.

It does.

Davia is twenty-five. She tosses a travel bag on her bed and activates her comm system.

"Call Iza."

Two chimes later, Izabel answers.

"You're on your way, yes?"

"No." Davia winces at Izabel's groan. "I have been called to Meteus."

She has received no clues as to the nature of the summons. Two guards are posted beyond her chambers now, and the rest of a full squadron are downstairs, outside the dormitory in an armored transport. All communications to and from Meteus are blocked, no doubt for heightened security.

Whatever is happening is more serious than she has ever seen.

"Davia, I've been waiting six months for these seats. This is the troupe's last performance."

"I know, but I have a limited launch window."

"When will you return?"

Her blatant yearning makes Davia want to evade the answer. Davia severed their romantic relationship for the second time a few weeks ago. Izabel has gently persisted in attempting to reconcile.

"I will message you when I can. Take care, Iza. Until a new day."

"Until a new day, Davia."

Davia chooses to ignore the sadness in Iza's tone.

She ends the call, fastens her bag closed, and leaves her quarters. The guards say nothing as they escort her from the university to a transport station, where an armored frigate waits to take her to Meteus.

An intergalactic news blockade has further limited transmissions, and with not much else to do while she travels from Duveri to Meteus, Davia practices a proposal to her father. He has said little about her academic achievements beyond satisfaction at her meeting his high standards. This trip might present the opportunity to speak to him in private. She has achieved the rank of Min Second Set, and is at liberty to choose her professional path, within or outside Cenobia Duveri.

If her father approves, Davia seeks an independent liaison position with one of the royal engineering divisions.

By the time the ship docks in the orbital station above Meteus, the news blackout has been lifted. From dock to transport to the planetary terminal near the palace, every banner, stream, and feed reports the same announcement.

She will not speak with her father this trip or any other.

High King Anahd is dead.

CHAPTER NINE

Ten Years Later

Davia scowls at the red mud on her polished black boots. The brush bolted to the side-entrance stairs of the two-story manor house removes most of the globs from her soles. She will have to clean the boots more thoroughly later to keep them from staining. The mineral-rich soil seeps into everything.

The overpowering scent of rich vegetation bruised by the earlier rains settles the knots in her shoulders. This planet, this continent, this city of Montalans whose distant spires spike through the jungle trees—Duveri is her true home, not Meteus. Even the humid air mingling with her skin's perspiration cannot ruin her mood.

The mud, however, is a different matter.

"Don't track sludge in here," a warm voice calls from behind the open door when Davia enters.

Candles and recessed lighting augment the early evening light on redwood walls and stone floors. This house is not Davia's, but its austere and sparsely decorated space is familiar.

As is the woman leaning against the door of the modest study.

Davia inclines her head, though as befits her rank she does not avert her eyes. "Min Izabel."

"Min Davia," Izabel answers, matching the formal tone.

Three heartbeats later, Izabel's smile can no longer be contained. Her embrace is gentle and warm, and soon becomes crushing.

"Twenty years of friendship, and I am the last person on the planet to see you." Her eyes are bright despite her rebuke. "I used to be your favorite."

"I saved the best for last, Iza."

Izabel wraps one arm around Davia's shoulder and pivots them towards another door. "Come. The wine is older than both of us. It's rude to keep it waiting."

They enjoy a light supper on a covered veranda overlooking a rocky stream. Davia recaps her latest adventures off-world on a six-month speaking tour of scientific facilities throughout the core systems. Izabel apprises her of recent events on-planet. The time passes too quickly as Davia catches up with her old—and oftentimes only—friend.

Soon, however, deeper matters arise.

Izabel takes a measured sip from her third glass of wine. "Her Exalted Highest Majesty has requested a more committed involvement from the monastery in combating terrorism."

Davia makes a rude noise. "Her Exalted Highest Majesty classifies any disagreement with her policies as terrorism. The monastery's ranks would be wasted swatting flies."

Izabel rolls her eyes. "Yes, you've made your opinion on the issue plain. We're running out of room to refuse, and we need stronger leverage."

"What would you have me do?"

"You might speak with her—"

"No." The base of the glass grates when Davia sets it on the stone table, and she winces in regret. "If I get involved, I will make it worse."

"How long do you think you can remain detached from the situation? You've been on the lecture circuit for years, Davia, and while it's excellent public relations for the monastery, you've been hiding behind it. Now you're off on yet another research assignment. Sooner or later, the Jeweled Circle will appoint you to the Sifani Consortium whether you want them to or not."

Izabel glances away, as if delivering the news is a chore. "You're the highest-ranking Min Fifth Set who hasn't accepted an appointment, and it's attracting attention. This delicate dance you've been performing may soon come to a stumbling, painful halt."

The truth of her words rings in the room's silence.

"I make no promises, Iza. I will at least speak to Anin about the throne's request." Davia hopes the offer is enough because her brother is not likely to push the issue either. "I depart tonight for Meteus."

Davia has managed to avoid the seat of Sifani Prime for over two years. Anin's summons, however, cannot be ignored.

Izabel lifts the wine bottle to refill Davia's glass. "Must you leave tonight?"

The veiled suggestion does not ignite Davia's desire the way it once might have. She loves Iza no less, and no one else holds her attention, but their romantic relationship is behind her now.

"My escort lead is particular about his schedules. I find it prudent to allow him to forget I outrank him." Davia pilots her own frigate. Royal policy dictates a defense contingent.

Izabel accepts the rejection without comment and raises her glass in toast. "To safe travels and your continued good health."

Davia taps her glass against Izabel's and pushes aside her lack of enthusiasm for the next part of her journey.

Several times during her travels, Davia is rerouted by imperial directives due to terrorist activity. She has been awake for thirty hours by the time she and her four-fighter contingent arrive at the orbital station above Meteus. Her fatigue ebbs in her excitement to see Anin.

She docks her frigate, *The Adamantine*, and relieves her escort pilots of duty for the duration of her visit, then endures multiple security checkpoints between her ship and the palace.

Anin's birthday celebration is already in progress. The orchestra continues to play as Davia enters the banquet hall unannounced. She has no attendants and is not escorted by guards despite her armaments. Weapons are illegal in the presence of the crowned royals, but no one will confiscate the sword of a Duveri Min.

Dressed in the black attire and forest green robes of her practice, she is too much of an anomaly to avoid notice, and nearby conversations pause at her arrival. She would have preferred to meet her brother in private and avoid the public politics. But for now, Anin insisted she attend his birthday ball. She has never refused his requests.

Courtiers, nobles, advisors, and aides crowd the ballroom, their appearances lacking distinguishing characteristics. Davia is accustomed to a more diverse congregation of people, since Duveri attracts students and acolytes from all over the empire. The number of faces she recognizes on Meteus has dwindled. Few if any of those in attendance are likely aware of her relation to one of the two people on the royal dais.

Though the ball honors Prince Anin, Her Exalted Highest Majesty Queen Ethelyn demands all attention as her due. The queen, whose ethereal beauty hides her propensity to solve problems with violence, sits on an elevated throne of gold-trimmed stone. Anin stands several stairs below, his head no higher than her feet.

Davia awaits recognition in his line of sight. When his eyes catch hers across the ballroom floor, he beckons to a nearby attendant and whispers in his ear.

Davia pivots toward the dining tables, hoping to eat something before she is called to pay her respects. While the other attendees gape at the decor, Davia considers the mended cracks in the architecture and the worn patina on the gold and silver ornamentation. The monarchy's ability to keep up appearances is dwindling.

A royal attendant dressed in livery too tight for his physique—another sign of the empire's shrinking wealth—appears at her elbow and bows.

"His Illuminance Prince Anin requests your presence in the royal receiving chambers at half past the hour."

So much for enjoying a meal. "I will attend."

He waits to be dismissed. When Davia says nothing more, he shuffles away.

Adjacent to the ballroom, the royal receiving chambers are more of an extravagant lounge. She enters at the appointed time, which makes her late by royal standards. Her brother will forgive her.

Davia's enthusiasm is dampened when ahe sees Anin is not alone.

Her father's wife sits in an ornamented chair near the fireplace. Every detail of her presentation—her garments, her jewelry, her hair and cosmetics—reflects the pinnacle of the monarchy's wealth and power. The decor and furnishings might hint at diminishing affluence, but High Queen Ethelyn's appearance does not.

Davia drops to one knee in deference to the queen, who does not speak at Davia's arrival. High Queen Ethelyn flicks a hand in her direction without looking at her, her habitual response to acknowledgment of the crown.

Anin pulls Davia to her feet and his embrace is as warm as Izabel's had been, if not as tight. His private grin is all the welcome Davia needs. "You've been away too long."

Despite his closely trimmed beard, her brother so resembles their father, Davia cannot speak. She comes to herself when Anin frowns, no doubt concerned by her lack of a greeting.

"We made good time from Duveri," Davia says before he speaks again to admonish her. "Not many ships waiting for wormhole access."

Anin scoffs. "Sifanes don't wait in line."

The air in the room cools though the queen says nothing. High King Anahd did not publicly recognize his younger child, and High Queen Ethelyn has never acknowledged Davia as a member of the royal line. Anin, on the other hand, has always referred to his sister as family.

Davia and Anin exchange a glance at his mistake in his mother's company.

The quagmire of royal politics is tiring and reminds Davia how long she has been away from her bed. The overstuffed and overdecorated furniture in this study would be a welcome comfort, but one does not sit in the presence of the queen of the empire.

"Central system shipping lanes should be teeming with convoys," Anin says. "Those damned pirates are insignificant insects, and their persistence is annoying."

"Terrorists nip at the heels of the empire." High Queen Ethelyn interrupts without directly participating in the conversation. "They steal valuable resources from our loyal and deserving citizens."

"How long will you stay?" Anin asks.

Davia would love to visit with her brother. Meteus, however, has its drawbacks. "My itinerary is tight. I want to travel to the outer systems before the ionic swarm."

A magnetic storm larger than most planetary systems has developed along one section of the empire's outer rim.

"Why would you want to go out there?"

Anin seems genuinely confused, which is understandable. Not many people travel beyond the extended territories. The core worlds are well established, and each has representation at court. Beyond them, the extended territories have at least some representation in Sifani Prime. The outer systems have none.

"To reassess potential resources." Such evaluation is adjacent to the truth, if incomplete. "The Rymind systems have not been inspected in decades for possible changes in status."

Many of the planets on the edge of the empire are the result of royal expansion—an informal tradition in which each king upon coming to power extends the boundaries of Sifani Prime to claim new riches for the good of the people. Most of those worlds are subsequently downgraded, offering nothing of use, and mining or colonizing the rest is too expensive.

Their great-great-great grandfather, His Royal Highness High King Rymind the Steadfast, expanded the empire by more than forty worlds in nineteen systems. Some of those planets may possess minerals essential to Davia's research.

If she and Anin were alone, she might share more with him about her work in astrometric sensor development and elemental testing. She and Anin have always shared an interest in the sciences. His mother never approved—not of the subject matter, which High Queen Ethelyn believes to be beneath his attention, and not of his relationship with Davia.

The queen shifts her weight in her chair, and the supporting pillow slips out of place. "Downgraded systems are of little value to the empire."

She lifts a finger at an attendant, who scurries closer and adjusts the pillow into position.

Davia is grateful her research takes her away from monarchic excess and political posturing.

"We've received reports of increased terrorist activity on the border," Anin says, his brow furrowing in disapproval.

"And I assure you, I will evaluate all relevant security information en route. I have a bit of time before I must leave." Not much, considering the projected ionic swarm limiting her research window, but at least a day or two to spend in his company.

"Anin," the High Queen says, "this week, we must prepare for summer court."

Anin glances at Davia in apology, and Davia performs the necessary translation. His mother will keep him too busy for time with Davia, which means any private conversation about the Consortium requests will have to wait.

"Do not keep your guests waiting." The queen rises and snaps at the guards, who open the doors to the ballroom.

Anin turns to Davia, who squeezes his hand in understanding, and embraces him.

"Stay for the rest of the party?" Anin asks.

"Of course, Anin."

Davia endures the festivities for another hour before she takes her leave, and Anin is too busy with the courtiers to notice her exit.

She will miss her brother, but will not spare his mother another thought. Davia has her own life outside this cold heart of the empire and is eager to resume it.

CHAPTER TEN

Most of the outer worlds are uninhabited. A few have smaller populations in remote outposts. Twice, the arrival of Davia's five-ship contingent prompts surrender notifications before Davia can send a greeting message.

So far, the other planets match High Queen Ethelyn's description and contain little resources of transportable value.

The data collected about the next system on her list is sparse. Several orbital bodies revolve around the solitary yellow dwarf star. Only one has ever been habitable. The history is inconsistent: some scholars claim former inhabitants destroyed the planet with nuclear war, while others posit some natural disaster drove the population off-world.

The last survey conducted via remote probe by one of the Sifani scientific guilds was more than a century ago and suggested the existence of a few trace minerals on Davia's list, ones she might use to optimize her prototypes.

The moment their ships pass through the wormhole, alarms fill the displays on the guidance console of Davia's frigate.

"Multiple contacts with no Sifani transponders." Stagg, centered and calm, is the first to speak.

"Pirates? How are there so many?" Mira asks. The youngest pilot in their squadron, she breaks protocol the most often, a transgression that has landed her this assignment. "We're too far out for any shipping convoys. No one's seen a group like this in years."

"Focus, pilot." Corvun Gale is a swaggering leader. His competence excuses his pride. "Min Davia, I advise we leave this system immediately."

Something in the data gives her pause until she finds the anomaly.

"Commander Gale, most of the ships are empty, and not one of them is less than thirty years old. They must have been stolen and abandoned."

None of the ships move to engage her squadron. In fact, many appear to be static or completely powered down, and no armaments track or target Davia's frigate or her fighters.

In any case, *The Adamantine* is the most advanced ship in the system. If she gets closer, Davia might be able to obtain more detailed information before she leaves the system.

She prioritizes her scans on the bigger ships. "Approach and determine their armament and personnel status before we leave the system."

"Acknowledged," Gale says, his displeasure plain. "Staggered formation."

"Lucky me." Dalibor's wry tenor belies the severity of the situation. "I'm on point."

"Match my vector." Davia taps in the coordinates. "Mark."

In synchrony, her frigate and escort fly forward. An opposing squadron of fighters appear to accompany a larger ship toward Rymind 17A, the planet with the minerals she has come to assess. All the other ships remain in position.

The distance between Davia's contingent and what can only be a pirate fleet shrinks. Her scans return an increasing stream of data. Rymind 17A is confirmed habitable, with breathable atmosphere. Davia must commend these terrorists on their opportunism. The imperial databases are so out of date, no one else might have ever considered that Rymind 17A could sustain human life.

The out-of-date fighters have limited armament compared to Davia's squadron.

For terrorists, they are far too passive. Before she thinks

better of it, she orders them to stand down, and receives no response.

"Corral those fighters. And do not fire unless fired upon." Bringing pirates to justice is one thing. Murder is another.

Dalibor and Mira break formation, the former moving to block two fighters approaching one of the larger vessels.

"Multiple targets advancing," Stagg says.

The other fighters, faster than Davia anticipated, have abandoned the landing transport, and closed the distance to her squadron.

Davia is not prepared for battle. Though she has trained as a pilot and has participated in her share of maneuvers, she has never been in an active engagement.

"Targets have guns and missiles only," Gale says. "No nuclear payload."

"Stand by to—" Stagg's voice is cut off when one of the pirate ships races past two of its own to engage. The pirate fires. Stagg's ship disintegrates.

Davia cannot move her hands fast enough. "Disengage!"

"Too late." Dalibor dives and weaves among the enemy ships. He and Mira attack and demolish one of them before Davia catches her breath.

An enemy missile shears one wing from Mira's fighter. Her ship explodes in stages as she screams into the comm line.

"Fall back," Davia orders.

"To where?" Dalibor asks, incredulous. "They're everywhere."

The terrorists may be outgunned, but they are relentless.

Gale engages one of the fighters. They destroy each other in seconds.

"Get to the access point coordinates," Dalibor says. "I'll hold them off."

"No," Davia says. "I will not abandon you."

Only one of the fighters has yet to engage. It limps towards the fleet vessel, escorted by another fighter.

Dalibor flies behind the escort and fires. The ship becomes a blinding white ball of energy before dissipating into nothing.

"Go," Dalibor yells.

An enemy fighter adjusts trajectory in the direction of Dalibor's ship. It never fires. Instead, it collides in open space, destroying both vessels.

Only one enemy fighter remains, and Davia is alone.

She never should have come here.

The fighter opens fire. *The Adamantine's* armored shielding will hold against guns in the short term, but not missiles. Davia finally fires back—she does not want to fight. She passes the fighter on her grazing run and alters course, intent on racing for the wormhole coordinates.

The fighter fires a missile. Davia dodges, and arms one of her own.

As she fires, one of the enemy's missiles hits her ship. *The Adamantine* is jarred from its course momentarily, though the armor holds, and her missile strikes the fleet vessel. Sections of plating erupt in a fireball, silent in the vacuum of space, the power of the explosion matched by the turmoil in her stomach.

Her hubris has cost lives. Her squadron, the pirate contingent, the people on that ship she destroyed. The pirates were guilty, yes—terrorists against the empire who deserved justice, but not murder at her hands.

She flees, and the enemy fighter follows.

"Maximum velocity forty-seven percent of specification standard," the frigate's system intelligence reports.

Escape is no longer possible. The missile impact has damaged some shipboard subroutines, and she cannot increase her speed quickly enough to lose the ship in pursuit.

If she can put some distance between her frigate and this fighter, she can assess the damage. *The Adamantine's* telemetry systems, ones she designed and configured, are technologically advanced and in impeccable condition, yet they return inconsistent data about the three moons beyond the asteroid belt. Two are gaseous balls and the other is a rock with a less toxic atmosphere, but the other data values keep changing. She concludes some magnetic or mineral interference is affecting her sensors.

She flies her frigate into the asteroid field.

Her scans of the enemy fighter must be inaccurate. No missiles. No tracking. Several data streams return null data, which means half the fighter's systems must be down. Its pursuit is like an annoying insect with little ability to bite, its persistence valorous.

In seconds, the bite makes itself known. Her entire console goes dark.

Davia frantically attempts in futility to restart the frigate's primary engines. The only weapon that could have wiped out the flight console—including the redundant systems—is an electromagnetic pulse.

Without thruster control, she cannot allay the spinning. Navigation would have been problematic at best with a damaged wing. Now she cannot steer at all. She surrenders to what she can do and engages the crash harnesses. The gyroscopic stabilizers in the pilot's station keep her from being rendered unconscious.

Pieces of the hull detach on atmospheric entry. The view through the command compartment canopy is of an all-encompassing fire swallowing the ship, the friction of her descent igniting atmospheric gases. Secure in her harnesses, unable to interact with her systems, she can no longer keep her grief, anger, or terror at bay.

Her entire contingent is gone. All their ships have been destroyed. She did not know Gale well, and Mira had barely begun her career. Davia had known Stagg for years, and Dalibor had flown with her contingent since the beginning of this series of tours and missions.

They are all dead because they had followed her orders.

Now she is alone in a broken ship in a system rife with terrorists who have proved they will not stop even when outgunned. If more arrive, she is doomed.

The frigate enters the lower atmosphere, and the gaseous flames recede, replaced by a nauseating swirl of muted browns and reds and tans of land, and the grays and blues of pale sky. Davia discerns nothing in the soup except distance, which is rapidly closing as the ground approaches.

She closes her eyes and spares a thought for the two people who will mourn her death. She sends her heart across the stars in apology, and then *The Adamantine* collides with the ground.

Davia grits her teeth as the hull scrapes the earth, wincing at every clash of excoriated plating. The frigate stops with a final strike against some external object or surface, and the sound of the resonating crash is deeper than the thundering of her heartbeat in her ears.

Metal creaks as the ship settles. All else is quiet.

The compartment is pitch black until her eyes adjust to the faint light. Orange recessed emergency lights have their own power source, separate from the primary and secondary systems and shielded from electromagnetic interference.

Gravity, heavier than imperial standard, pulls her toward the overhead instead of the deck. Consoles knocked loose by the crash lie tumbled across what is now the floor. The ones still intact are above her, within reach but inactive.

She frees herself, relieved to be unharmed, and inspects the rest of the ship. Her sleeping quarters are compressed by outside obstacles, her bedding is in disarray, and smaller items have shattered. Many of the internal access doors were open, so she does not have to manhandle them without ship power. What was not strapped down or secured is unseated or broken.

Daylight spills through several viewports, and Davia pauses to calm herself, to remember who she is.

Focus on the now. Life support, water, and food.

She sheaths her shortsword—a blade forged in the monastery's smithies, earned and claimed by her own trial—and holsters a pulse pistol in a harness strapped at her thigh, prepared to face the next challenge.

The atmospheric sensors beside each exit are analog, not digital. The one by the cargo bay door confirms a breathable atmosphere. After a brief hunt for a pry bar and several attempts that cover her in perspiration, Davia finally opens the aft bay door.

The movement shifts debris outside, and the wind blows sand and dirt into her face. She sputters, coughs, and waves a hand in front of her face to clear the air before it occurs to her to track down her yaffa shawl and wrap it over her head.

Once more, she waits for her eyes to adjust, this time to blindingly bright sunlight.

By the time the dirt settles, Davia holds her pistol ready.

The Adamantine has crashed into a crescent-shaped bluff curving around a shallow canyon. A clicking noise draws her attention to where an odd creature lies on its shelled backside with half its body pinned under the ship. Judging by the decreasing speed of its flailing, it is in its death throes. An ineffectual pincer clicks at the end of a broken, bent leg, and the creature's blood pools before soaking into the sand.

Davia does not waste a pulse blast. This thing is already dead.

She turns to assess her ship and gasps.

The sheered wing has butted against the bluff wall. The fore half of the ship is covered by sand and boulders, which explains why the flight compartment had been so dark. It is now underground. The remaining viable egress points are the side boarding door and the aft cargo bay.

Only industrial equipment could dig this ship from the ground. She spent two years on its design and customization—has spent more time on this ship than anywhere else in her adult life including her own apartments on Duveri.

She forces her despair aside.

Nothing moves in the canyon. Out of precaution or fear, she climbs the bluff, traversing the boulders until she stands on the hull of her ship to scrutinize the landscape. In every direction, only rock and sand greet her. She has crashed on a moon devoid of people, and the extent of any fauna remains to be determined.

A bright flash catches her attention. She raises one hand to shield her eyes against the sunlight. The flare does not reappear. Instead, a black plume of smoke blooms upward and dissipates as it rises. Something is on fire.

It does not appear to be a natural phenomenon, which

ignites her instincts. Yet unless she travels the distance on foot to investigate, the smoke will remain a mystery.

Perhaps her pursuer met their end. Before she can relish the indirect vengeance, she considers the possibility of survivors. Another eventuality to prepare for. She adds it to the growing list.

She has not reported regularly to anyone, an indicator of independence she regrets. The soonest anyone will notice she is missing is weeks from now when she is scheduled to present at an engineering symposium. Anin will want to search for her, assuming Queen Ethelyn allows it. Izabel, too, if she is able to overcome the Duveri-Sifani political impasse.

Both of them will be held back by the ionic swarm headed across the galaxy in this direction, one that will block any direct path for months.

Rescue may not come for a long time. In the interim, she must rely on her own resources and abilities. Survivors are a problem for another day, and fortifying her location is a higher priority.

First, though, in a flat expanse of sand in the canyon, she marks out a circle two strides in diameter and kneels in its center.

She learned many years ago when to give in, a rare occurrence, and when to persevere.

Davia is an instrument of one will—level, steady and true.

Her will is not to die here.

The contents of the cargo bay have been separated into two categories—irrevocably damaged and therefore useless, or irrevocably damaged and potentially flammable.

She piles some of the flammable items in a natural pit in the canyon and sets the stack ablaze. The movement of the flames feels like another entity has joined her in her solitude—a companion in the desolation. Though the morning is warm, Davia decides to keep the fire burning.

Back and forth, Davia moves as the mood strikes her. When the pressing dark of *The Adamantine* becomes too frustrating or unsettling, she works on the fortifications—the canyon presents opportunities for a stronger defense against an influx of the shelled creatures. When outside becomes too daunting, too foreign, she retreats to the ship and makes another attempt to fix systems beyond repair.

Several crates from her interstellar assessments were destroyed by the crash, their samples contaminated. Her self-restraint is tested when she finds the case of ale provisioned because it was Commander Gale's favorite. She makes a choking sound, quickly swallowed. An even emotional keel is the only hope she has of surviving.

The ale will not keep forever. She opens the case only to discover most of the bottles are cracked or smashed. The intact ones are suspect, for who can tend to her if she ingests broken glass?

Her anger swells. Long before the meditations at the monastery helped center her, her father taught her the importance of keeping her emotions private. Revealing them gave others too much power. Now, no one is here to judge.

She screams and throws the case against the bulkhead. The sound of shattered glass is satisfying for about as long as it takes the mess to fall to the deck, liquid splattering at her feet.

Now the bay reeks of ale.

Davia resumes her sorting.

A redundant refrigeration unit disconnected from the primary systems and undamaged in storage is somehow functional. If she rations what supplies have survived the crash, she has enough sustenance for twenty-six days. Rescue will not come that soon, which means she must determine if the shelled creatures are a viable food source. Starving to death is not an eventuality she wants to consider.

That evening in the canyon, she stokes the unnecessary fire. With the flames as company, her nerves settle somewhat, but this place is too silent for her to relax. No insects, no birds, no raindrops on vegetation—all of the familiar sounds of Duveri are missing here. The wind and the crackle of the fire are the only noise.

The wind rises and clouds roll overhead. When the rain begins, she retreats inside the ship.

Her living quarters require too much cleanup to be habitable and are too far from the nearest accessible door. She separates the mattress from the frame of her overturned bed and drags it back toward the boarding door. Near the entrance, she shoves it on the floor against the bulkhead, then retrieves some of the linens for a makeshift bunk.

The orange emergency lights are not comforting. The ship creaks, startling her as it settles into its grave.

Davia envisions a Venu Pakrim meditation form until sleep takes her.

The next day, killing one of the creatures is easy. Gutting and preparing the kill is a disgusting mess and turns her stomach more than once. Butchery is not one of her skills. She remembers enough basic anatomy from her studies to manage. Her first test of palatability is successful: the meat is edible although bitter, with an unpleasant aftertaste. She plans to cook it all and store the remainder in the refrigeration unit.

Davia abandons the task when something—someone—moves outside the ship.

The scrabble of rocks is too far above the ground to be one of the shelled creatures. The canyon bluff is an uneven crag of boulders and scree, and the creatures would have been hard-pressed to scale them.

The sound before the scrabbling had been of something else against the rock—fabric or metal, not something natural—falling out of place. She now has a more pressing concern than extending her food stores.

Only one ship had pursued her from the battle—the small

fighter, large enough for a one- or two-person crew. At most, she faces two possible threats. If they saw her, they saw the weapons she carries. The martial capabilities of pirates are a mystery to her.

She will not search at night. The ground is too uneven for dark stealth, and a light will reveal her position. They might attack at night, but she is more familiar with her ship.

At first light, she will hunt the hunters. She does not sleep. Neither does she let her mind wander in speculation.

When the sky lightens the next morning, she slips outside via the aft bay door. Leaving only the whisper of sand in her wake, she travels until the ship is hidden in its resting place, then arcs around to approach the far side of the bluff.

The threat is far less than she had feared. A coordinated attack on her ship is not in progress. She finds only one pirate, a woman with matted chin-length blond hair, her over-mended flight suit bloody and torn. The woman climbs not so stealthily along the ridge, observing the canyon and not once scanning elsewhere for threats.

She has not checked her own flank.

Davia hides behind a boulder and surveys her opposition. The woman favors one leg, the wound on her other streaming blood into her boot and onto the rock where she perches. She is an easy target, and Davia settles her drawn pistol against the rock before her, plants her fist, and lines up the shot.

She cannot, however, pull the trigger. Her own life is not in immediate danger. In space, ship against ship had been one thing. Shooting someone in the back, someone who appears to be armed with only a long metal strut, is murder.

Curiosity drives her forward to investigate further, and she closes in on the woman's position. The pirate does not react to her approach.

Davia stops outside the range of the strut, her weapons in hand, and waits to be discovered until she tires of the subterfuge.

"Drop your weapon and—"

The woman screams, whirls to face her, and drops into what

looks like a painful crouch. She winces as her eyes fill with tears, lets out a wordless screech, and then as if in afterthought, points one end of the strut at Davia.

If the situation were not so serious, Davia might laugh out loud. The woman's stance is uneven, and one strike would knock the strut from her hands.

The cold hatred and abject terror in the woman's icy blue eyes, however, reveal her true mettle and, skilled or no, keep Davia from laughing.

The woman's eyes roll into her head, and she collapses to the ground with a graceless thud.

Davia prods her with a boot and receives nothing in response. She holsters her pistol and sheathes her blade, then crouches for a closer look.

Pale skin unaccustomed to exposure is sunburnt to the point of peeling, and dehydration has shriveled and cracked the woman's lips where they are not bitten and scabbed. One hand and arm are badly burned, and the wound on her leg is a jagged, swollen, bloody mess. How the woman managed to walk is a testament to her fortitude. She may be untrained, but she is persistent.

Tear tracks streak the dirty sunburned face, and blood mingles with the soot and dirt and grit in her hair. Under the dirt and fury, the pirate is a well-favored young woman of about twenty-five.

Davia has three options, and she does not like any of them.

She can kill the woman and leave her to rot. She can turn her back and leave the pirate to take her chances against the threats this moon presents—though leaving her unarmed, with no visible supplies besides the metal strut, is another form of murder. This woman will not survive long on her own.

Or Davia can take her back to the ship and decide what to do with her.

It takes two attempts to lift the woman onto her shoulders. Davia balances herself with the woman's metal strut and works her way back to the canyon.

The Adamantine has a basic medbay. Most of the equipment was destroyed in the crash. Some of the medical provisions are intact, and Davia does nothing by half measures. Having decided to save this miserable excuse for a human being—who else would become a pirate?—she cleans the woman's wounds and bandages them as best as she can. The leg is challenging: the wound is ghastly, more like a bite than some sort of gouge. The pirate is still unconscious, and Davia administers what medication she has that might help, along with a small portion of water.

It occurs to her that she need not care for this woman at all. Yet the inhumanity of leaving anyone—even a criminal—to suffer is repellant. Davia cannot, however, allow this woman into the ship. Whenever she wakes, she might try to attack Davia, and giving ground is foolish.

Some of the larger cargo straps can serve as restraints. Staking the woman out in the open would be cruel—more sunburn will likely be the result—so Davia secures her to the purposeless gun turret under *The Adamantine's* remaining outstretched wing. It will provide some protection from the elements and limit the woman's ability to get in the way.

With no small measure of frustration, Davia reassesses her supplies since she will have to provide food and water to this woman, for even an incarcerated terrorist deserves humane treatment. The problem of the pirate has distracted Davia from the greater issue of being stranded.

Davia is no longer alone, and her extraordinary situation is infinitely more complicated.

Her frigate's beacon is irrevocably damaged. Even if it were working, this moon is on the far side of an asteroid field emitting enough interference to block such a signal. The pirate fleet stands between this moon and the only viable wormhole coordinates in this system, which means anyone who searches for her will have to fight their way through, assuming they determine where she has gone.

Her only company is a murderer who might kill her when

she turns her back. She may never be rescued—may indeed be stranded here for the rest of her life. She might never see Anin or Izabel again.

The tears surprise her, not with their existence, but with their velocity and volume.

Davia has endured trial after trial and overcome them all. This desolate isolation is more a punishment than a wild circumstance. That this should be her fate is intolerable.

She has always envisioned the core of herself as a rod of unbreakable ore, unyielding under any conditions.

The rod cracks.

CHAPTER ELEVEN

The woman eats her rations as if she is familiar with food scarcity, barely chewing before gulping down each bite. Davia ignores her practical inclination to halve the servings.

If she intends to keep this terrorist alive, she cannot leave her unprotected outside the ship. At first, a stick is sufficient to ward off any shelled creatures, but a spear is no safeguard against meteors, and neither is leaving her secured under the wing. As the days pass, binding the woman's hands or feet is overkill, even when Davia allows her inside the ship.

By the time their names are shared, Davia is convinced this criminal will not attempt to kill her in her sleep.

Kyran is still her prisoner, however much Davia concedes she is not a dangerous one.

"Clear the solar panels," Davia says. She pauses in performing the action and slows her speech when she repeats the phrase.

Kyran focuses on Davia's face—on her lips—and she shapes her own to match each enunciated word.

"Clah—" She is not embarrassed when she mispronounces a word, accepts correction without protest, and repeats the newly learned word to herself until she gets it right to her own satisfaction. "Clear the solar panels."

Kyran is curious and learns quickly. The more technical the word, the more rapidly she understands. Simple verbs, however, take repeated attempts. Kyran speaks like a child, and Davia is more patient than she might expect considering she is teaching a criminal.

Davia nods, and Kyran stands straighter. Regular meals have put some color back in Kyran's cheeks and added substance to her lean frame. She has lost the pallor of sleep deprivation.

"Clear the solar panels," Kyran mumbles to herself a few times, practicing the phrase.

"How do you say that in your language?" Davia gestures for Kyran to reciprocate.

Kyran's eyes darken and her brow furrows in anger.

Davia is not to be allowed the same courtesy.

Kyran huffs away, free to walk around the canyon as long as she stays where Davia designates. She retrieves a stick and uses it to dig a border around the firepit.

She also appears to be older than Davia's original estimation, perhaps closer to Davia's age. Despite the wound causing her to favor her leg, her gait is more certain and emphasizes her broad shoulders. She acts without waiting for Davia's acknowledgment or asking for permission, a sign she is used to working without supervision.

Kyran finishes the shallow trench around the firepit, then searches the canyon floor. At the base of the nearby bluff, flatter chunks of rockfall meet her unspoken requirements. She circles the pit with them, creating a two-tiered space where they can sit instead of lowering themselves into the sand. This intelligent solution to a simple inconvenience demonstrates a confidence in her skills that only experience can provide.

The last few stones are flat and thick, and Kyran pants from exertion. She no longer sunburns, and the tan of her skin accentuates her lighter hair. The muscles revealed by the tears in her dirty flight suit are sculpted and defined, and her sweat somehow flatters her. Kyran wipes the perspiration from her forehead with the back of one wrist, the satisfaction of a job well done sinking into her shoulders. Her competence is attractive.

Kyran stares at Davia, which means she has been staring at Kyran without realizing it.

Davia resumes her task of calculating the flow rate of her

secondary water filtration system. The rains are unpredictable. More than once a sudden deluge has driven them inside. She scratches an equation into the sand wet from a storage container's spillage. If she can determine the maximum flow, she might be able to construct a reservoir to feed into—

A shadow passes over her work and Davia flinches with the urge to reach for her pistol. She stays her hand when the shadow stills. Her distrust irritates Kyran the most. Every time Davia draws her pistol, Kyran waves her hands to imply she is no threat, when Davia's experience with her suggests otherwise. Davia does not want to irritate her today.

She also does not want to consider why her prisoner's feelings matter.

Kyran stands behind her, one hand on her hip, the other stroking her chin. She grunts, picks up a rock chip and scratches a note on one of Davia's equations. It is not a corrected error—more like an alternative approach using a different methodology and giving Davia a previously unconsidered opinion.

Davia had assumed societal misfits would be uneducated, though she nods at the input. Kyran says nothing and walks away, and the exchange alters Davia's perception of her involuntary workmate.

The sun has reached its zenith. Davia senses Kyran's eyes on her each time she draws the circle and steps inside, eager for the focus it demands and the peace it brings.

When she has finished and erases the circle with her boot, Kyran has climbed atop the ship and sits on her preferred spot on the wing. She gazes off into the wilds, looking forlorn and lost, and something in Davia's chest seizes. The urge arises to make Kyran feel better, and she has no idea how.

She works instead on optimizing the configuration of the lone self-powered refrigeration unit to preserve the bounty of her hunts. With meat in reserve, she is less concerned about them starving to death in the short term.

Her list of self-appointed tasks to ensure their survival grows daily—checking the perimeter for any trace of creature encroachment, clearing grit from the components of the water filtration system, adding sand to the waste pit, splitting wood with her pistol.

She now allows Kyran to attend to more technical tasks. They have moved into a tense tolerance phase where they exist in the same space by necessity, though they are not cordial with one another. Each of them did, after all, end up stranded because of the other's actions. Davia does not speak of it, but it is no less true. She would not be on this moon at all if it were not for the pirates, and Kyran would not be here if Davia had not tried to escape.

Davia pushes their marooning out of her head to focus on the now.

The Adamantine will never again fly—not without an impossible tow from a larger ship and a comprehensive overhaul in full space dock—so everything she designs and implements is solar-powered and intended to work indefinitely.

The fact that she is preparing for a permanent installation is another thought to be pushed from her mind, along with her grief and unproductive resentment.

When she finishes her work for the day, Kyran has already stoked the fire and stands staring into the flames in the late afternoon light. Kyran hums an unfamiliar tune, and Davia does not acknowledge it, afraid Kyran will stop.

Davia wonders how Kyran might look in a fight, the kind of hand-to-hand combat Davia is trained to perform. Would her anger manifest itself much the same way it does now, or would she exult in combat—a warrior who laughs when gaining an advantage?

Kyran turns to her, snapping Davia from her musing.

"I shoveled the waste pit," Kyran says, referring to her earlier task of burying some of the burned refuse and unusable detritus from the creature corpses—a precaution against attracting so far unseen greater predators. "You make dinner."

She points at Davia before returning her hand to her waist. Kyran never uses the words "please" or "thank you." She is polite, to an extent, but she expresses no gratitude, though Davia has saved her life more than once.

The familiarity gives Davia pause, and it takes the better part of the time she spends in food preparation to determine why.

Almost every engagement Davia has experienced with another human being for the last decade has been colored by her rank as Min, except for her conversations with Anin. Izabel never forgets Davia is a royal by birth and would never tell her what to do.

Kyran does not appear to recognize any of the Venu Pakrim designations on Davia's attire or her ship. She has no idea who Davia is and will not follow orders unless Davia backs them with a weapon. If Davia cursed at Kyran in an argument, Kyran would likely curse right back. On this moon, they are equals, an alarming and refreshing thought.

After the sunset kim venu, followed by a bitter yet filling supper, the evening comes. They sit at the fire watching the flames snap and hiss, a forced camaraderie providing respite from the endless vigilance of their harsh new life. The quiet lack of conversation is calming, affirming in its way, and aligned with Davia's tenet of gratitude for surviving another day.

When they bank the fire for the night, Davia tries again to breach one of the chasms between them.

"I am banking the fire," she says as she piles the coals, then covers the pile with ash.

"Banking the fire," Kyran repeats.

"How do you say this in your language?"

Kyran frowns in confusion, so Davia points to herself.

"I say, 'banking the fire.'" Then she points to Kyran. "How do you—"

Kyran interrupts her with a displeased grunt, her face twisting into something as captivating as it is menacing. A regal pose shapes her shoulders, her eyes flash, her jaw sets, and she appears as if she might break boulders with her bare hands.

Davia's heart pounds. She is not afraid or threatened—something else, perhaps best left undefined. She is accustomed to being around those who hide their emotions, and spending time with someone who never contains them is jarring.

Kyran is not self-conscious and shows no shame at expressing whatever she feels. When Kyran is pleased, it floods from every pore. The occasions are few—after a vexing or taxing task, or when the sunlight is warm on her skin and not hot enough to make her sweat. It lightens her gait and eases the tension from her face.

In moments like now, when Kyran is angry…

A new word, one Davia does not want to let affect her, drifts into her mental vocabulary. Kyran is beautiful. She may be young—or younger than Davia, at least—and she may be untrained, but when ignited by self-righteous anger, she is compelling.

This new discovery is unsettling.

Kyran stalks through the boarding door first. They climb into their respective bunks, Kyran facing the bulkhead while Davia stares at the deck above her.

If she has set aside her life before the crash to focus on her survival, can she do the same for Kyran despite all that has happened? Everything is changed by their plight.

By this new measure, Kyran's life before their isolation may not be within the circle either.

CHAPTER TWELVE

After Kyran rescues her from the pit, Davia's consciousness wanes, her thoughts clouded until she attempts to limp back to the canyon.

Later, she can think about the beast Kyran killed. Later, she can wonder how Kyran found her at all. Later, she can process the desperation that drove her to give Kyran the pistol, and the angry sorrow on Kyran's face when Davia requested it back.

Now, she can only focus on the physical torment that, like many things in her life, must be endured. Shifting her weight on her leg is excruciating. Lifting her weight off is worse. She hyperventilates, trying not to scream. Davia cannot remember which way or how far they must walk in the dark and hopes Kyran can guide them back to the canyon.

They move slowly forward, and yet it is too fast for Davia. Finally, their lack of progress cuts through the red fog of her mind. Her tears gather and fall.

Davia cannot go on.

For the first time in her life, she cannot overcome a challenge, work her way around it, or make it disappear. She cannot take another step.

Inside her, the rod of her will cracks again.

Kyran says something softly in her language. Davia is too stricken by pain to protest her lack of understanding. Then Kyran lifts her, settling her over one shoulder. The new position brings a different stress to Davia's leg, yet the intensity of the agony decreases now that she is not putting any weight on it.

Kyran resumes walking, this time at a faster though still careful pace. She mumbles an apology each time a rigorous step jostles Davia, who barely notices. Davia does not have to walk, think, solve any problems, or hold herself to her inviolable standards.

She closes her eyes. All she must do is breathe, manage the pain, and sink against Kyran, whose proximity is comforting in a way, a consolation against the torment. Davia cannot remember the last time she was this physically close to someone who was not Izabel.

Kyran sets her down by the firepit, and the pain brings Davia's attention back to the present. Repeated untrained attempts to reattach the torn flesh drive Davia to the edge of consciousness. When prompted to cauterize the wound, Kyran blanches and Davia wonders if she will take a turn at vomiting by the fire.

The urge to soothe Kyran briefly eclipses the torment. Then the smoking blade presses on Davia's skin. Agony turns to white hot anguish, and then the mercy of nothing at all.

When Davia was a six-year-old on Meteus, she contracted a severe illness restricting her to bed. Feverish, she thought the faces she envisioned were ghosts coming to rescue her from the cold of this wing of the palace, so different from the rooms where she had lived with her mother.

When Davia did not arrive as required for a scheduled meal with her father—a rare occasion since he preferred to dine with his wife, who would not share a table with Davia—a governess found her lying in her own sick.

For days, she lay in the four-poster bed in her solitary quarters, unable to move. During her illness, her father came to her room only once. For a time, she thought she had imagined him there beside the door. He was more foreboding than her nightmares. Though he had never said an unkind word or raised a hand to her, never said or did anything in her presence to justify her caution around him, the ways others deferred to him indicated he was a feared man, a dangerous man.

Her doctors—because her treatment somehow required more than one—bowed as they updated the High King on her condition. He nodded once while looking at her and left without offering her any reassurance of her recovery.

Davia wondered if that meant she was going to die.

An endless stream of medical personnel tended to Davia, their manner professional with requisite compassion. They offered no consolation, no comfort or affection, and displayed no joy when her health improved.

Her faint memories of her own mother suggested to Davia more loving ways to give care. She suspected her childish perceptions would not be welcome commentary.

As she grew older, Davia learned to tend to herself when she was ill, or pretend she was only mildly affected. By the time she left for secondary education on Duveri, Davia never asked for anyone's assistance with anything, trained by her time in her father's palace to reveal no weakness. The need for such succor—or the memory of its existence—faded like her recollection of her mother's face.

Here, on this desolate moon, her forced convalescence is dramatically different.

Davia is too tired to open her eyes. Someone holds and strokes her head, murmuring words she does not comprehend. Something cool and wet caresses her brow, her face, her neck, and her arms. She shivers, and someone arranges her blanket.

Someone sings in a foreign language, and Davia is conscious enough to recognize the voice. When she opens her eyes, shock makes her gasp and cough.

Davia has no strength to flinch at how closely Kyran sits beside her.

Kyran speaks in low tones in her language, lifts Davia's head to offer a few sips of water, then rearranges the blankets. The worry in her expression is astounding.

She moves past Davia's range of vision, and an agonizing pain follows. A cool sensation wraps around Davia's injured leg, offering some relief. The pain persists.

"Shh." Kyran's soft singing resumes. When the pain of the injury forces Davia to cry out, tears and sweat and mucus making it difficult to breathe, Kyran soothes her and wipes her face.

This is more care from another human than Davia has received her entire adult life. Izabel has never seen Davia this incapacitated, this dependent upon someone else's ministrations.

Not long ago, Kyran threatened to murder her several times a day. Days before Davia fell into the pit, Kyran had left the canyon and Davia had questioned her return.

Now Kyran has saved her life.

The ordeal comes rushing back on a wave of anxiety. The beast Kyran killed confirms larger predators exist on this moon. Davia had been minutes, seconds from death, and Kyran had rescued her. She had carried Davia to safety and had overcome her own trepidation to treat Davia's wound.

Davia has lain for—how many days has it been? The entire time, Kyran has cleaned and fed her and now seems genuinely concerned for her.

Kyran could have killed her, and Davia would have been defenseless.

Who are they to each other now?

They are not friends, but are they enemies anymore? If they do not raise a hand against one another, are they still at war?

While Davia heals, their days take on a new pattern. Davia sleeps more often than not, and concludes that the wound and the resulting trauma must have taken some additional toll beyond the initial injury. She is grateful the infection was not more serious since the medicines she salvaged after the crash were perishable or used in Kyran's care.

Kyran rises with the sun, guides Davia through her morning ablutions, and then goes hunting. She comes back at midday with her quarry or some tubers or firewood. Kyran stores the food, cleans up, tends to the camp, and then returns to the ship to care for Davia.

Not once does she act as if she is favoring Davia, nor does she appear resentful of the extra work. She is sometimes visibly exhausted, and never speaks of it other than to comment on the length of the day.

Davia becomes accustomed to Kyran's proximity, and because they spend so much time in close quarters, she observes Kyran unnoticed. In fact, she thinks often about what Kyran might have on her own mind.

More than once, Davia catches Kyran staring into the distance, the task in her hands forgotten. Her wistful expression spurs a tightness in Davia's chest. Of course Kyran must miss someone. Is Kyran betrothed? Is she married?

Davia wants to ask, to cross the invisible line between them.

Since she asked Davia's name, Kyran has not asked about Davia's past or about anything off this moon. When she forgets herself and speaks in her own language, she never translates the words into Sifani so Davia might understand her.

Davia has learned what is off-limits, where Kyran will not yield—not that she ever has—and for some unknown reason, Davia has respected this boundary.

Some questions, however, cannot wait.

"Why have you let me live?" Her voice is not as strong as she intended.

Kyran stills for a long moment, eyes downcast, before she shrugs. "I can't do everything."

Weeks ago, that might have been true. Kyran has revealed a deeper fortitude since then and is better able to navigate the harsh surroundings. She could survive here unassisted.

A genuine answer must not be forthcoming because Kyran returns to her task. She has repurposed a metal brace from the broken gun turret and attached a span of mesh from one of the cargo containers.

"What are you making?"

Tense shoulders ease at the simpler inquiry.

"For the sand," Kyran says, and nothing more.

Spent from the effort of speaking, Davia watches deft fingers and rough craftsmanship, dozing in and out of consciousness as the afternoon passes.

Finally, Kyran makes a sound of gratification.

She stands, brushes her palms against each other to remove dust and, after tossing Davia a proud smile, sets the contraption in the boarding doorway and lowers the door.

Kyran's handmade frame blocks it from closing. It braces the door open and allows the breeze to flow through. The mesh keeps any sand from blowing in.

It is simple and useful, and an impressive design considering their limited resources.

"Time to make meat," Kyran says, and frowns in concentration. "No, dinner. Make dinner." Having self-corrected her word choice, she turns toward the ship's aft, leaving the ship by the other door.

The puzzle of Kyran captures Davia's attention until she once again falls asleep.

Davia feels the pinnacle of the day and aches with the need to stand, to draw the circle, to kneel and offer herself in service.

She has not missed the kim venu in years, not since her trip to Meteus in the wake of her father's death. The pallor of grief colored the events of the trip, and she had fallen prey to susceptibility.

"You left Meteus a sprite of a thing," Anin had joked, the first time she had seen him in person in years. "Now you've returned a full Min. Shall I bow to you, my sister?"

He had not laughed, his mourning curtailing his characteristic mirth, but his humor had been unmistakable.

Anin had teased her about her attention to the calls of her art, and his gibes had hit her in a place of unprecedented weakness. He claimed familiarity with Venu Pakrim and assured her he respected its tenets, but he had not understood.

Distracted by her own sorrow at the time, Davia had paid the exchange little mind until later. She felt no small measure of guilt at her missed ritual—for disrespecting her art and not standing up for herself. She had dedicated herself to her studies and training and exceeded the expectations of her trials. That she would allow herself to be belittled to garner her brother's brief affection—a brother who loved her but did not defend her—was unacceptable.

The next time she performed the kim venu, Davia held her blade upraised for an hour. Venu Pakrim had given her purpose, guidance, and belonging. The only thing remaining from her old life beyond her love for her brother was a yearning for her father's approval, unresolved by his death.

Davia shifts her head in her bunk, the only indication of her restlessness.

"What's the sky look like today?" she asks, her first attempt at casual conversation.

Kyran sits nearby, her hands busy with some contraption. She seems surprised by the question and leans to tilt her head through the boarding door.

"No clouds. Bright. Clear. A deep green . . . no, blue." Kyran's command of Sifani is improving, an indication of how much they speak to one another now. Kyran has a faraway expression on her face as she gazes at the sky.

Davia traces the fingers of one hand over the neat row of scars on her other forearm. She closes her eyes, visualizes a sky the shade of Kyran's eyes, and performs the ritual in her imagination.

What would make someone choose to be a terrorist?

Kyran is intelligent, with a pragmatic and logical approach to problem-solving. She is familiar with the ship's systems, enough to converse about salvaging some of them for other purposes. She has had some education since she has a clear understanding of mathematics and the sciences if her additions to Davia's calculations are any indication.

Davia finds it difficult to believe Kyran is a lifelong criminal. She is kind as she tends to Davia, patient with Davia's incapacitation. The familiar anger from those first few weeks after they crashed has dissipated in the wake of what happened in the beast's pit.

Is she a fighter pilot or does she have some other role? Her fingers are nimble, which indicates a lot of work with her hands. She sits in the open doorway, letting the breeze clear air staled by the day's heat, sharpening long branches she has fashioned into spears.

Is she one of the farmers who protest they did not receive fair trade for their product, when they were subsidized by Sifani Prime? One of the miners who attempt to unionize when the Sifanis protect them from rival factions attempting to destroy them?

Is Kyran one of the galactic scavengers who think they are owed something from the universe, when what they are provided far exceeds their own contributions?

None of those imagined scenarios align with Kyran's recent actions. She may be reticent with her words, but she is generous with her time, her energy, and her care, and the dichotomy gives Davia much to think about, especially since Kyran has uttered the long-avoided "please" and "thank you" she had previously withheld.

If they are stranded forever, Kyran might be an unexpected equal, and a formidable ally. The more time passes, the less Davia worries about how Anin might be handling her disappearance and more about what she will do with Kyran should Sifani forces arrive.

Will she turn Kyran over to the authorities?

Despite her fatigue, the thought keeps her awake.

“I will clear the filtration catch.” Davia ventures beyond the confines of her bunk this morning. Several weeks of recovery have not completely healed her, and hobbling around on her crutch is a poor choice, but she has grown bored with staring at the bulkheads or the landscape, and is not yet recovered enough to perform her habitual physical forms.

“Already done.” Kyran sifts through the collection of spears leaning against the ship, preferring different spears depending on where she plans to hunt.

“What about the solar panels?” Sand and grit accumulate on the panels providing power to the ship’s reworked redundant systems. Every few days, they need to be cleared to remain optimal.

“Done.” Spears collected, Kyran refills a canteen to carry with her.

Davia bites back a huff of frustration. Kyran has been so diligent in tending to the chores, to the hunting, and to Davia herself that little remains to be done. The industry flatters Kyran, who appears to thrive when given a purpose.

“You have left me with little else to do besides stare at sand.”

“You could go hunting with me today.”

If she is joking, Davia cannot tell. Davia also cannot muster a response, since her accompanying Kryan would require her assistance, defeating the purpose of Kyran going on a hunt.

Kyran arches an eyebrow in assessment. “I could use you as bait.”

A dangerous joke, considering how Davia was wounded. What shocks her is not the candor of the humor, but the fact that Kyran made a joke at all.

Davia recognizes the test and keeps her response droll. “Sand can be fascinating.”

The ghost of a wry smile transforms Kyran’s face, and Davia’s heart races until Kyran takes her leave.

Boredom proves to be more intolerable than pain. Davia moves slowly, shifting her weight with each measured step. She manages to collect meat and water and chopped tubers for stew, and carries them all to the firepit to prepare their dinner.

They. She thinks in terms of both of them now, not just herself. It is not an unpleasant epiphany, and she is grateful not to be alone. She has come to . . . favor Kyran's presence, and even now wonders how long it will be before Kyran returns.

Late in the afternoon, Kyran's proud form breaks the horizon, her stride sure. When she enters the canyon, she waves in greeting.

Davia waves back before she thinks better of it.

Kyran looks tired, and chastises Davia for cooking, though after she cleans and stashes her kills, she eagerly consumes the bland stew.

They watch the sun without speaking.

Something is growing between the two of them. The silences are companionable now, the time beside the fire relaxing yet somehow charged with possibility. Kyran's proximity heats Davia's skin differently from the fire or the heat of the sun, prickling over her like a shiver and igniting an inner need.

Davia has now shared more of herself with Kyran than with anyone—not by sharing the details of her life, but by working side by side with her day after day. They have learned each other's rhythms and preferences—the way they breathe and move.

More than once, Davia has considered crossing the barrier between them into the physical—deliberate, not the touch of aid or convalescence or circumstance—despite the implausibility of anything growing between them. What she understands to be true about their origins and who they were to one another at first does not reconcile well with what she feels now when she looks at Kyran.

Kyran catches Davia observing her, and neither of them drops her gaze.

The wind rises and the moment passes, and something has

changed. Perhaps soon, on a night like this one, Davia will offer more of herself.

Perhaps Kyran will do the same.

CHAPTER THIRTEEN

Kyran sits by the fire for a long time—until the flames shrink to plasma rolling over coals—and Davia does not return.

How can so much change in so short a time?

"I am Davia Sifane," Davia had said. "The Old King was my father."

Kyran stares at the glowing embers, trying to understand how her provisional ally can be so close to her greatest enemy.

The wind rises, pulling her attention from the cacophony in her head. It's been weeks, months since Kyran has been outside at this time of night. The sky is clear, the stars are bright, and an entrancing magic covers the arid wilderness. It does not soothe her, not in the wake of the night's revelations.

Davia's family killed hers. Davia's ancestors destroyed Kyran's people. The High Queen isn't Davia's mother, but she killed Kyran's parents. Davia killed Benna.

And yet, Davia saved her life. More than once, Kyran saved Davia's.

The knots of the past and present twist and tie inside Kyran and she can't unravel them.

The fire is smoking coals by the time she stands. She's too tired to stay awake and can't sleep so close to Davia. Instead, Kyran grabs a spear and sits down near the open door. She leans against the ship and closes her eyes.

She doesn't dream.

In the morning, she wakes when Davia walks outside to

perform her kim venu. Davia pauses briefly, saying nothing, and Kyran doesn't speak a word. The silence is heavy with truth now, and it's Kyran's turn to broach the gulf between them.

She can't think here.

By midday, Kyran acts on impulse, packing some of the meat and filling two of the larger canteens. The makeshift bundle on her back is cumbersome but not difficult to carry. She is stronger than when she first arrived.

Davia says nothing as Kyran clutches a handful of spears and leaves the canyon.

No piles of stones exist to aid Kyran's navigation, and her hazy memories offer only a general trajectory. She is careful to mark her passing though she doesn't want to think about her return. None of the shelled creatures block her way or threaten her progress. Faint tracks of something larger give her pause; otherwise, only the uncertain course adds time to her voyage.

Late on the second day, she finds the otherwise nondescript location where she crash-landed months ago.

The fighter is blackened from the fire and warped, as is the explosion-scarred ground extending away from the ship. The cockpit is full of murky rainwater. Meteors have burned into parts of the hull.

The ship appears smaller than she remembers. It's not just the broken wings or the burned-out shell, and she wonders about her change in perspective since she is no larger.

Then again, she is also not who she once was.

The boulder she climbed the first miserable night is a decent spot for a protected camp assuming it doesn't rain. While she'd never have survived when she arrived, Kyran has the supplies, experience, and confidence now to fend for herself.

She sacrifices three smaller spears for a fire and sets a limited perimeter by half-burying all save one of the rest. It's not much protection from the shelled creatures, but it will provide some warning should any threats make an appearance.

The heat from the fire reflects off the stone behind her. Kyran sleeps.

The next morning, a few sips of water and some dried meat make an adequate and unsavory breakfast. With a stiff neck as her only company, Kyran's in a foul mood.

She wastes her last bite of meat by tossing it in the fire, angry at Davia for withholding information.

My father was powerful politically.

Kyran could scream. She wonders at providence—to have come all this way, to be marooned at the edge of the galaxy, and only now has she come closer to her parents' killer, closer than she might have ever done in her old life.

Fate is maddening.

Would her parents be ashamed of her for building a truce with their enemy?

Would Benna condemn the companionship that has grown between Kyran and her cousin's killer?

And worst of all, what does it matter since they're all dead?

Can she blame Davia for not bringing it up sooner? Kyran hadn't given Davia the chance to explain.

Does Davia agree with her family, with bending the galaxy to their rule and claiming the best it has to offer for themselves? Does Davia know about the atrocities committed in her name? How can they move forward if Davia is in favor of all the things Kyran is against?

Davia is not imperious or dismissive. When holding Kyran captive, she was kind—or as kind as one who keeps another prisoner can be. She does not carry herself like a member of the Sifani ruling class although all Kyran knows of higher Sifani society is based on hearsay. Much like Kyran does not conduct herself as the last of Ellod's royal line.

Kyran doesn't remember much about her parents beyond what she has been told by others. By the time they were captured by the Sifanis, they rarely spent time with her. Kyran had held so much hope for someday settling on one of the independent worlds and having the kind of family who spent time together talking of things other than the revolution.

Maybe her anger at the High Queen has more to do with the death of an unlikely future. There would never have been a day when she and her parents had lived a happy, common life on Ellod or any other planet. Life on the ground would have been spent much the same as it had been in space—improving the lives of their people. It was a duty she was raised to uphold.

While she wished for her people to be free of persecution, she did not want to be responsible for them, to lead them in a war against a corrupt regime.

Kyran is relieved the path she never asked for is now no longer an option, though it shames her to admit it if only to herself.

Always forward, never back. She cannot go back, and only two paths move forward—one with Davia, the other without.

If all other futures are now impossible, can she hold Davia accountable for a past that can't be changed?

After a long day and evening with her thoughts, Kyran resigns herself to the truth. The scored corpse of her old fighter is all that remains of her old life. Her past offers little wisdom regarding her future.

The next day, she navigates a more direct path back to the canyon, her passage quickened by the new system of stone markers to guide her journey. The day is warm, and she keeps a steady pace over more familiar territory.

Kyran does not stop along the way, choosing to eat her rationed meat as she marches onward. She's angry—it simmers in her blood—but she can't avoid Davia forever.

When darkness falls, the moonlight is bright and clear enough to continue. Kyran is restless, invigorated by the warm night and its silent calm. She feels brave and opts to finish her journey despite the danger of walking in the dark instead of camping within a few hours of the canyon.

For the first time, she wonders if Davia might be angry as well.

The fire is banked when she returns, and since Davia is nowhere to be seen, she must be inside the ship. Kyran stashes her supplies as quietly as she can and weighs sleeping outside against knocking on the door and waking Davia. If nothing else, she owes Davia an apology for leaving without saying a word.

The decision is made for her when the door slams open.

Davia has her pistol raised between them, and the shock of its appearance freezes Kyran where she stands.

"Do not think you can kill me." Davia says. "I am a Venu Pakrim Min Fifth Set, and now you will learn what that means."

With her other hand, Davia draws her blade and steps into the moonlight.

Fury pulses in Kyran's body with every heartbeat.

"You're going to kill me now?" she yells in Ellodian before she remembers and repeats herself in Sifani.

The moonlight steals the green from Davia's eyes, leaving an ethereal gray, and her features are fierce enough to have been carved from stone.

Davia steps closer to Kyran, leaving clearance for her weapons. "You left without explanation. Now you have come back in the middle of the night to kill me in my sleep—"

Kyran scoffs and raises her empty hands. "Davia, I don't want to kill you—"

"What was I supposed to think?"

Empty hands become fists, and Kyran rests them on her hips. "If I wanted you dead, I'd have killed you already."

Davia's mouth falls open in blatant disbelief. "Is that meant to make me feel better?"

"I left because I . . . I needed to be alone."

The point of Davia's pistol drops, no longer aimed at Kyran's heart. "Well, for all I knew, you were never coming back."

"I would have taken more supplies."

"I didn't know." Davia gestures wildly with her pistol-laden hand, the clearest indication of her anger Kyran has ever seen. Davia is always precise, no movements wasted.

"You said nothing when I left."

The fierceness in Davia's expression eases. "Where did you go?"

"Back to my ship, to think."

"And what conclusions did you come to?"

A hint of derision, a touch of judgment colors Davia's tone, stirring Kyran's irritation.

"That it's good yours was in better condition since mine was destroyed."

Davia sneers and arches an eyebrow. "Spoken like a true pirate."

"Pirate?" Kyran doesn't know this Sifani word.

"You take things that don't belong to you and pretend they were yours all along."

The insult ignites fire in Kyran's veins.

"The Sifani take more. They take and give nothing." She points toward the end of the ship, toward the cargo bay. "All your . . . your work. I saw the . . ."

Kyran wants to growl. Not knowing the words she needs makes this worse. "You take dirt and water and . . . and more for your science. To take more for Sifani Prime."

The proof is in the many samples stashed in the cargo bay—the vials and cases containing the bounty of a dozen worlds. Another example of Sifani appropriation without thought of impact or consequence.

"I am a scientist, an explorer. What are you? Nothing but a killer." Davia sneers. "You have given no thought and spared not one word for the people you killed that day—"

Davia speaks so quickly, Kyran fights to keep up. One thing, though, is clear.

"I didn't kill anyone," Kyran says.

She would have. If she'd had any missiles left, she'd have used them to shoot Davia's frigate to pieces.

"Well, someone did."

"Does it matter?" It's not the right thing to say because of course it does. Language keeps interfering. "We can't change it."

The past—they can't change the past. Kyran doesn't know this word in Sifani.

"Yes, it matters!"

"Why doesn't it matter when Sifani ships kill my people?"

"You broke imperial law—"

"The law? Is that what you Sifani call it when you destroyed our homes, when you—you . . ."

Sifani Prime brutalizes and murders innocent people. How can she translate this? "You hurt those who do you no harm."

"No harm!" Davia scoffs, squinting her eyes in judgment. "Don't your people kill soldiers without trial and steal their vessels?"

Flustered, Kyran can't raise a counterargument. Davia's contempt is infuriating.

"I had nothing to do with any of that." Other independents, other peoples who resist Sifani Prime use heinous tactics. Most of Kyran's people agree such methods are too expensive a price for freedom.

"Oh, I see," Davia says. "You take no responsibility for yourself."

Kyran curses in Ellodian, ignoring Davia's weapons as she steps closer. "Daughter of the Old King, are you? When you're not hiding the truth to serve yourself?"

"I hid nothing! I had no reason to tell you sooner, and it would have changed nothing if I had. I was on a scientific exploration, not some military patrol."

"What difference does it make why you were here? You took . . ." She clenches her hands in frustration. "You killed people who attacked no one."

Shock and chagrin mar the beauty of Davia's features before her anger returns. "You fired first."

That's not how Kyran remembers it. "No, you—"

"I gave specific orders not to engage unless fired upon."

Kyran doesn't want to believe it.

Davia continues, her voice pitched low. "How dare you judge me. At least I have some pride in who I am and what I have accomplished."

"What does this mean, accomplished?"

"I have done good things," Davia says, speaking slowly with veiled condescension.

Kyran leans closer. "Good things? Sifani are the pirates."

She points to the planet above them. "Your kings destroy this planet, so we moved to another one. They destroyed that planet, so we moved again. When we fight back, we die. When we don't fight back, they lock us away, take our—our small ones . . ."

Whole cities obliterated. Starships incinerated in open space. Families incarcerated, the children taken and never returned.

Davia looks mortified at the suggestion. "I have no part in any of that."

Her denial is the opening Kyran's been looking for, though the insinuation isn't anywhere near what she believes to be the truth about Davia.

Kyran twists the knife as hard as she's been stabbed.

"You want this," she says, pleased at the fire in Davia's eyes. "To be High Queen, to make everyone do what you want, to make them destroy worlds for you."

She doesn't mean the words as she says them. She only wants to singe some of the arrogance from Davia's features.

Davia raises her blade and presses it against Kyran's throat. Her eyes cool, and her face smooths into an otherworldly blankness. "You speak of things you do not understand."

Kyran freezes but doesn't yield an inch. She leans forward, raising her chin and pressing her neck against the blade. She takes a sharp breath at the pain of its stinging bite, juts her chest, and offers no surrender.

Davia shifts her weight back instead of pushing her advantage, and Kyran perceives the motion as a sign. Like her, Davia does not want to go all the way back to the beginning, nor does she want something irreparable to happen now.

Kyran speaks softly. "These things I say are true to me. Tell me your truth then."

She stands on a precipice before something dark and unknown, and she cannot turn back. She sees Davia more clearly now—the tightness around her eyes hinting at sleepless nights, the slight tremble of her chin.

A faint flush darkens Davia's cheeks. The hand holding the sword is steady. Everywhere else, she vibrates, her chest rises and falls with each rapid breath. Her gaze darts between Kyran's eyes and then she looks at Kyran's lips.

What Kyran sees is desire.

With forced slowness, she wraps her hand around Davia's wrist. Kyran pushes the blade away from her neck, from the space between them, and Davia does not resist.

She kisses Davia—firm, solid, and unmistakable. Davia's lips are cool but the rest of her emits a warmth seeping into Kyran's exposed skin. Kyran hungers for it, emboldened when Davia doesn't stop her.

Kyran pulls away after a moment, closing her eyes tightly at the possibility of rejection.

Davia kisses her back.

Pent-up aggression from their argument, the urge to dominate Davia with words now a demand to share this swelling *something* inside her—Kyran wants to have it pushed back against her by Davia's kiss. Her limbs twitch with a need she had not recognized and now she cannot quell the irrepressible compulsion to consume.

Davia's quiet moan spirals Kyran's desire higher. She clutches at Davia's shoulders, pressing against the hull of the ship.

Davia answers with her hips, and Kyran moans back. Restraint lost, she slips her hands into the collar of Davia's tunic, splits the fasteners as she widens the taut fabric.

Kyran crushes her palms against Davia's breasts, clutching and releasing, plucking and pinching. Davia has yet to drop her weapons, kisses Kyran back and cleaves herself to Kyran where she can.

In a pause to catch her breath, Kyran considers slowing down, ending the argument altogether before they tread this new ground. She claims one more kiss.

Davia bites Kyran's lip hard enough to make her grunt, and all thought of *slow* evaporates.

Kyran slides her hands down to Davia's belt and unfastens it. She pulls away to stare into Davia's eyes, to give her the chance to stop what comes next.

Davia says nothing as Kyran's hand slips lower. She gasps at Kyran's first touch.

Kyran's head swims at the swollen fullness against her fingers.

Something angry and hurt and naked swells inside her chest and she hates it. When she presses her fingers deeper inside Davia, she swallows the pleased moan on Davia's lips, and sets the feeling loose.

If Davia wanted her to stop, she'd have raised the pistol or the blade. Kyran holds back nothing, her arm burning with her exertion.

Davia spreads her legs wider and her head falls forward, her eyes closing, and Kyran can't stand it. She thrusts harder.

"Look at me," she says in Ellodian, a guttural growl Davia may not understand but nevertheless responds to. Davia raises her head with obvious effort, moaning with pleasure as Kyran grabs her by the throat and holds her in place.

Kyran pours herself into her motion—the grief and loss, the uncertainty, the need and loneliness, the anger and hope, the relief and fear. Kyran pants as she thrusts, driving past her own limits as much as she's pushing Davia.

Davia doesn't bend or break. She stares back at Kyran, unyielding as she gives everything she has, until her eyes shade quicksilver, unseeing.

For a moment, they breathe in synchrony.

Davia's surrender is complete, the glory of it shining on her face. Kyran is overcome. She bites back a sob and stops moving, her fingers aching as the tightness around them pulses and flutters. Davia sags, her pistol clanking against the hull.

Kyran withdraws, cups her hand, her fingers slickly pressed against still pulsing heat. The passion fades into something calmer and no less taut.

Davia shifts her weight so she can stand without leaning on the ship. Kyran pulls her hands away and takes a step back. Once Davia sheathes her sword and holsters her pistol, she stands before Kyran with strands of her hair wild in the wind, her tunic spread wide. She shimmers with an ignited energy, like she's been given her due and it's nowhere near what she can endure.

She is breathtaking.

Davia takes Kyran by the hand and leads her into the ship. She stashes her pistol, kicks off her boots and removes her clothes. Uncertain, Kyran turns to her own bed, another layer of grief sinking into her skin.

"Kyran."

The sound of her name in Davia's low voice makes Kyran ache so deeply, her knees tremble.

In the dark where each cry seems louder within the quiet confines of the bulkheads, Kyran attempts to make up for her earlier madness by devoting herself to Davia's pleasure, learning her in a new way.

Davia touches her like they're going to die tomorrow. It's not a constant urgency—more a reverence of the now. She pauses to cup Kyran's face while kissing her with singular focus. When the wildness takes over again, Davia is as strong in her embrace, as driven in her pursuit of Kyran's pleasure—as if this is their one chance and she is not going to waste it.

She speaks little, sometimes in whispers.

During a rest before one of them will no doubt start anew, Kyran reflects on her brief couplings on *Althea.* Nothing serious or lasting, a quick release of tension at best, and never with the power or intensity coursing through her now.

Now, fingers again slick with Davia's most recent orgasm, Kyran paints the wetness on Davia's spine. She feels as if the core of her is stripped bare, exalted, and alive.

What kind of life was she living before she got herself stranded?

She lies across Davia's hip, one arm wrapped around Davia's body and her head resting below Davia's breasts. Both sadness and elation make her cry.

She lets the tears have their way.

"If you must leave again, tell me," Davia says softly.

"I will." This is an easy promise to make. Kyran won't leave again.

Davia's breathing evens and sinks into the steady rhythm of sleep. Kyran swallows the beginning of a sob.

"I'm sorry," she whispers in Ellodian. She's sorry for everything.

Davia's breathing doesn't change. She shifts one hand to rest on the back of Kyran's head.

At dawn, Kyran is exhausted when Davia untangles her limbs from Kyran's embrace. She kisses Kyran's temple, retrieves her blade and walks outside nude. When she returns, Davia tucks her blade behind her along the bulkhead and presses her now cold skin against Kyran's.

They should rise and start the day, but nothing is as important as staying exactly where they are. Kyran caresses Davia's chilled skin with her warm hands because the privilege is now hers. In time she lulls them both back to sleep.

They spend most of the day inside the ship. At one point, Kyran is rendered speechless not by Davia's touch, but by her laugh.

Kyran shifts her weight without thought and slips onto her elbow, knocking her face against an uneven protrusion from the bulkhead. She doesn't stop alternating strokes and thrusts in a way that makes Davia arch her back.

Davia grabs Kyran's head and pulls her close to lick her cheek. When Davia pulls back, there's a small streak of blood on her tongue. She licks her lips and smiles.

Kyran thrusts faster.

Davia laughs, deep and full, until the pleasure overtakes her.

At sunset, Davia walks outside wearing her tunic and boots and carrying her blade. Kyran follows barefoot, her flight suit folded down at the waist leaving her topless.

She sits in the doorway as Davia performs the kim venu and is for the first time envious. The peace Davia exudes as part of her ritual—Kyran now wants something like that for herself.

When Davia is finished and turns toward the ship, Kyran speaks before the words solidify in her head.

"Will you teach it to me?" Kyran asks as Davia approaches.

Davia stares at her without speaking for a long time.

"No."

Kyran's heart seizes in disappointment.

"No, not yet." Davia leans over to kiss Kyran. "I will teach you other things."

When Kyran stands to start right away, Davia shakes her head.

"Tomorrow we will begin."

CHAPTER FOURTEEN

The door is open, and the evening breeze dries the new layer of perspiration on Davia's skin, adding to the lassitude in her limbs. Her heart thunders in her chest as she regains control of her panting breath, her spine twitching from a back-arching orgasm.

Davia clasps Kyran's hand, pulls it against the valley between her breasts and closes her eyes.

"I don't hate it here anymore," Kyran says, her tone a relaxed musing, apropos of nothing.

'No?" Davia opens her eyes in surprise. Kyran has given the impression their surroundings are cursed.

"Hmm." Kyran splays her hand where Davia has pinned it and strokes the skin with her thumb. "I didn't like the quiet at first. I do now."

On the tail of her revelation comes another surprise, this one more substantial.

"I've never been on a planet like this one," Kyran says. "Have you?"

Davia is silent for a long time before answering. She tests her words for accuracy—comparing them to her memories.

When Kyran kisses her jaw, Davia tilts her head to give her better access.

"I have never been on a planet with only one discernible ecosystem." She stares at the bulkhead, imagining other landscapes. "It is far more common for a planet to contain several if not countless different biomes."

"Like where?" Kyran asks with her characteristic curiosity, which has so far been directed solely at their current circumstances.

"Meteus. Duveri. Many of the central systems."

"What's the most beautiful place you've ever been? Somewhere that stole your breath."

The question is not what surprises Davia; it is the expectation of some emotional resonance associated with the answer. Davia cannot remember when last she had a similar conversation.

Kyran is so different from Izabel, from Anin.

Her body bare and uncovered, Davia stretches her legs as she thinks and sighs at a memory. "The southern continent on Duveri. In the rainy season, the air is so humid you can almost drink it. The cold is dreary and ominous . . . but the extremes lead to the richest, greenest place I have ever seen. In the forests, the trees tower into the sky, and the undergrowth is so thick, you have to walk with poles because the depth to the ground is misleading.

"And you?" Davia asks. Kyran's experience has been significantly different based on what little she has shared with Davia.

"Here," Kyran says without pause.

Davia searches Kyran's face for any hint of dishonesty and finds none.

"It's dangerous," Kyran says, "more than either of us knows. There's a truth to this place I appreciate now. "

"You never speak of your people."

Kyran's hands still. "We do not often speak of the past and the people lost. Those things are private—so they are behind me now. I speak only of what is, and what will be."

Now is not the time to ask why Kyran will not teach Davia her language. Perhaps that is another thing to be put behind by Kyran, which saddens Davia. They already avoid so much. The words from their argument still sting, and the lack of a complete common language makes true verbal communication almost impossible. This new connection between them eases the hurts they cannot otherwise resolve.

Kyran turns to lie on her back. "Now, in this place, I feel . . . true. I felt like a liar where I was."

Reminded of her first year on Duveri, Davia understands.

Kyran sits cross-legged in the sand of the area Davia uses for her various exercises and meditations. Her eyes are closed, the lids flickering with movement.

"Venu Pakrim means true heart in an ancient Duverian tongue." Davia paces the edges of the area, shifting a rock in alignment to mark a border. "Long ago, before the rise of Sifani Prime, the monastery on Duveri was a place of peace and reflection in a world torn by war and strife."

Kyran opens her eyes. "What does this mean, strife?"

Davia pauses, surprised at the disrespect of interruption. No beginning acolyte would dare to interrupt a Min on the training floor—or anywhere else, in truth.

Kyran is no typical acolyte.

"Conflict. Disagreement," Davia says, and then continues, not ungently. "To show your respect for Venu Pakrim, you will be silent when in this space unless invited to speak."

She points to the boundary of their training ground. "Here, I am your teacher, Min Davia, and you are my student, Pri Kyran. Beyond this space, we are—who we are."

Kyran frowns and her shoulders stiffen. If she cannot acknowledge the different power dynamics, the boundaries separating lover from teacher, then her training cannot continue.

Davia waits without speaking. When Kyran's shoulders relax, she continues.

"The art of Venu Pakrim was born when the monks of Duveri used what they had learned in seminary to soothe people, to settle their differences, to build a lasting peace. This is the art you will learn, by first soothing yourself, settling your own conflicts, and building a lasting peace within the heart of you, Pri Kyran."

Instructing Kyran is different from, and yet the same as, Davia's lessons with the first- and second-year Pris on Duveri.

She teaches Kyran the same vocabulary, the same basic movements, the core of the first-level rituals. Kyran asks so many questions about the nature of Venu Pakrim, Davia has to remember her own patience. She adapts to the immediacy of this new feedback loop, even when her response is to tell Kyran to question less and be more.

During the day, Davia focuses on the what, the actions of Venu Pakrim until Kyran takes the hint and asks fewer questions while addressing the task at hand—specific exercises and drills sharpening her attention and strengthening her body.

At night by the fire, Davia teaches the why, the philosophy and tenets of the art.

"The Jeweled Circle is a council of elder Mins, ones with many years of experience. Long ago, when the influence of Venu Pakrim stretched beyond Duveri, they decided no monasteries would be built off-world.

"We keep the tenets of Venu Pakrim private and within our ranks, to honor what has been given to us. We rely on each other as we rely on ourselves. You may train far from the monastery, but because you train with me the art flows through me to you. Here, you are as much a Pri as the acolytes on Duveri, and now part of the whole."

These initial lessons are designed for children, yet they are the building blocks upon which the other lessons will rise. Davia changes nothing. Venu Pakrim was demanding for Davia as an adolescent, and her life then had been nowhere near as difficult as their life on this moon. Losing sleep was a challenging trial for Davia when she was thirteen, but cannot compare to Kyran's trek without food or water—on a wounded leg, no less—to reach the canyon.

While Davia describes their lessons for the following day, Kyran's eyes are bright with firelight and more questions she does not ask.

CHAPTER FIFTEEN

Kyran huffs in frustration and opens her eyes.

"I don't feel any different." She sits cross-legged on the wing of the ship with her hands resting on her knees.

Davia sifts through collected crash debris and salvaged materials from the cargo bay.

"Sometimes you won't." She evaluates a hunk of metal from the pile, and then tosses it aside.

"So what do I do now?" Kyran would rather focus on Davia, who looks fresh and clean after their morning swim. The journey had taken some time. Davia wanted to attempt longer distances, and Kyran had suggested the lake.

Davia's hair is curly and wild today, with long waves hanging down her back. When she moves, the sunlight dances in the tendrils—much more entertaining to Kyran than closing her eyes and breathing.

"I've been doing this for hours."

"No complaints." Davia remains focused on her task. "Try again."

"If this is meditation, shouldn't I visualize something? What am I waiting for?"

She hates waiting, and this art of Davia's demands a lot of sitting still. Yet the peace Davia radiates is enticing, and the purpose she offers is compelling. Kyran wants those things for herself.

"You practice Venu Pakrim," Davia says. "Breathe in through

your nose and out your mouth. Feel the air move through you."

"For how long?"

"As long as you need to."

Kyran wonders if Davia is being deliberately unhelpful. "How do I know when I'm done?"

"You will know."

Kyran twists her body, peering in Davia's direction. "Is this some sort of torture?"

Davia offers a brief glare, then returns to her sifting.

"What are you looking for?" Kyran asks.

"Never mind me. Focus on your breathing."

Another huff bursts from Kyran. She shifts back into position and closes her eyes.

Davia adds short-range walks to her daily routine, determined to use her leg as much as she can. Kyran escorts her out of caution. What if Davia falls into another pit and Kyran isn't there to help?

She hovers so much Davia teaches her a form of wordless communication—arm motions and hand gestures providing tactical information without speech. To practice, Kyran must move beyond conversational range.

Months ago, she couldn't stand being so close to a Sifani. Now, she can't bear to be apart from her.

This morning, they walk toward the east. Half an hour later, a pod of shelled creatures crosses their path.

Kyran climbs a bluff for a better view and returns to Davia's side.

"I've got an idea. You may not like it."

Ten minutes later, Davia is crouched on her good leg in the scree of the ravine. She glances over her shoulder at Kyran.

Kyran nestles in a small space in the rock wall for cover, poised with a spear at the ready.

Seven or eight of the shellers—Kyran's estimation unless

more are hidden—make their way toward Davia. The one in the lead is the length of Kyran's arm. More motivated than the others, it scurries closer to Davia's position.

"May I remind you I have only my blade with me?" Davia's calm voice doesn't quaver.

Kyran ignores her and focuses on her quarry.

Fist-sized rocks are the only obstacle between the creatures and Davia. If they surround her, she won't be able to run fast enough to escape them.

"I just washed these clothes," Davia says.

Kyran fights down a laugh and squeezes the shaft in her hand, drawing the spear back. The creature screeches as it clears the bigger rocks and crawls faster across the rubble.

Davia doesn't move, a testament to her faith. "Any day now, Kyran."

She does, however, sound annoyed.

The creature raises one pincer to attack. For the space of half a breath, its eyes and antennae aren't covered by its shell and Kyran throws her arm forward and lets the spear fly.

The spear hits home and knocks the creature onto its shelled back, its cry of pain cut short but loud enough to scare the rest of its pod into turning back in the other direction.

Kyran leaps down as Davia stands to brush off her knees.

"Told you," Kyran says. "Taking out the lead one scares the others away." She retrieves her spear, lifts the dead creature with one arm—something she hadn't been able to do the first few months after the crash—and carries it over to a clump of rocks to gut the carcass.

"You've become quite skilled with the spear." Davia's cool tone has a measure of surprise.

Kyran plants her hands on her hips, her spear propped against her shoulder as she stands. "You weren't worried, were you?"

Davia says nothing and arches one dark eyebrow, reminding Kyran of other times she has expressed herself with a similar look.

Kyran wonders how soon they can get back to the canyon, to their now-shared bed.

Kyran entices Davia away from her usual afternoon tasks of checking the filters and clearing the solar panels. The lovemaking pauses for Davia's sunset kim venu, followed by dinner.

Afterward, they sit in a new preferred position by the fire—Kyran in her chosen spot, and Davia on the ground between her legs.

Kyran's chin rests on Davia's shoulder, the silence comfortable until Davia breaks it.

"My mother was a courtesan of the Old King."

Davia's voice brushes against Kyran's skin like the breeze blowing around them. "He pledged to marry the first courtesan who bore him a child. Five days before I was born, High Queen Ethelyn—another courtesan at the time—gave birth to my half-brother."

"Prince Anin."

Davia hums her acknowledgement. "Anin is a good man who craves his mother's approval too much to veer far from her political practices. His only rebellion appears to be his love for me."

Kyran can sense how much Davia misses her brother, and also hears the truth Davia suggested during their argument. Davia does not support the High Queen's vision for the galaxy.

Davia returns to her story. It seems more like a dark fairy tale of a distant land that should have no bearing on Kyran's life, and yet it does in so many ways.

"Anin claims she was different when he was small. Queen Ethelyn doted on him and—having secured her place on the throne by marriage to the king—was kind to those in her service. When High King Anahd's policies were too harsh, she was a temperate voice of reason."

Davia sounds doubtful.

"Though my father had married Queen Ethelyn rumor suggests he was in love with my mother. Over time, his affection for her only grew. Some at court believed he might set the queen aside and choose my mother after all."

Davia's body tenses. "I was told my mother died of a sudden illness when I was five. I overheard my governesses gossiping, certain Queen Ethelyn had had her poisoned."

Kyran gasps at this shared injustice. She squeezes her arms around Davia in apology for interrupting.

"I remember little of my mother," Davia says. "The Old King had enough of a soul that he saved me from a similar fate, plucked me from the courtesans quarters where I was raised and isolated me in a private and secure wing. I do not believe he held any affection for me, but he would not let someone murder the child of the woman he loved. Only Anin showed any fondness for me."

Davia shifts herself more snugly against Kyran's chest. "Gaining my father's approval was important to me when I was young—too young to understand how fruitless a pursuit it was. I studied harder than was required to make top marks, and soon realized the only thing that would please him would be for me to become like one of the tools in his arsenal—the men and women who dominated the galaxy in his name. I wanted no part of it, and I was too young to say anything against it."

Her regret is plain on her face.

"I left for the monastery when I was twelve, telling no one of my lineage. My years in training may be the only time in my life when I was judged on my dedication and skill instead of my blood."

Guilt twinges inside Kyran as she remembers her own response at learning of Davia's parentage.

"When I returned," Davia says, "as a Duveri Min First Set, I was more formidable than when I left, and I still had Anin's favor. The High Queen could not have me killed easily, not even with assassins as I believe she did to the Old King."

Her voice isn't melancholy or mournful, so maybe Davia

carries little love for her father now. She sounds as if she is musing to herself, and to Kyran by extension.

"You said I might share their view of the universe. I do not. I thought many of my father's policies were extreme, and I chose to separate myself from the affairs of state, to focus on my own interests and pursuits.

"When he . . . he died, I mourned him and did nothing to stop the executions offered in his honor. Perhaps I might have convinced Anin to persuade his mother toward some other course of action, but in his grief he turned more to his mother than to me, and I . . ."

Her voice falls to a whisper. "I thought myself neither strong nor powerful enough to stand against both of them."

It sounds like an apology, one Kyran has implied she wants yet no longer requires—not from Davia.

Kyran holds Davia tighter and kisses her temple. "I don't think anyone is."

The words are inadequate. She thinks of her parents and wonders how her people fare. She will never have an answer.

The fire burns to embers as they sit in silence, listening to the wind.

CHAPTER SIXTEEN

Kyran is wrong.

That night, their lovemaking is as passionate as it was in the afternoon. After Kyran drives Davia to new heights, after every cell of Davia's body is spent, Kyran slumbers as Davia lies awake unable to sleep.

Davia misses the soothing cacophony of the jungles of Duveri. Here, the night is quiet save for the distant whisper of wind—not enough to distract Davia from her thoughts.

It is not true no one is powerful enough to stop the High Queen.

The Jeweled Circle of the Venu Pakrim is an institution older than the throne of Sifani Prime. Though they publicly defer to the throne, they are clandestinely an independent neutral party—one occasionally called in to mediate between lesser factions. They have privately suggested changes in policy to the royal court.

On five separate occasions, they have offered Davia a role as royal liaison to the Sifani Consortium. Davia recognizes their gestures for the political ploys they are. If Davia became a member and was successful in furthering their agenda with the crown, the Jeweled Circle would have exerted their influence in secret. Should she fail, the Jeweled Circle could blame it on her personal shortcomings, and no one would know any attempt on their part had been made.

The field of land mines is more treacherous from the other

side. If Davia were to act on the empire's behalf and succeed in implementing the demands of the throne, the High Queen would claim credit. If Davia were unsuccessful . . .

She does not entertain such a scenario often.

Davia has avoided all requests or suggestions to choose one position over the other. Neither offers her any advantage, any path that would keep her dignity intact, or preserve her independence and sense of self. In fact, they cast her as a pawn.

A third option exists, a frightening one she has always pushed from her mind.

Davia is a Venu Pakrim Min Fifth Set. With such a distinction, paired with her father's blood, she could claim the throne of Sifani Prime. The Jeweled Circle would have no choice but to support her in overthrowing the High Queen. The unprecedented opportunity to influence galactic rule would be difficult for them to ignore.

Her only challenge would be in eliminating the one true obstacle between her and the throne. She would need to remove her brother from his birthright. Anin would never stand aside of his own volition—forceful removal would be required.

Davia cannot kill her brother.

In the deepest parts of herself, she also fears she might become like her father—or far, far worse, like Queen Ethelyn. Cold, vindictive, devious, absolute.

Queen Ethelyn was born into a noble family on Meteus, with parents who machinated for a closer connection to the throne. With their numerous off-world holdings in mining and ore refinery, they were prominent enough at court to position their daughter as a courtesan for young Prince Anahd.

After Anin's birth, Queen Ethelyn was cool with anyone who was not her husband or her son, but affectionate and warm with family. High King Anahd, on the other hand, was less satisfied with his marriage, a situation ripe for court intrigue. Perhaps jealousy, or the scathing dismissal of her due respect, drove Queen Ethelyn to her own machinations.

When crossed, the queen retaliated out of proportion to the

affront, thereby ensuring it was never repeated. If the obstacle couldn't be outmaneuvered, the queen eliminated it altogether. Members of the court learned to stay out of her way whenever possible and to curry her favor when avoidance wasn't an option. Whispers of disappearances, of suspicious deaths, of outright murder in the form of execution on suspicion of treason—all of it served to keep everyone except Prince Anin and High King Anahd under her control.

Rumors in the darkest corners of the palace suggested the Old King had been an obstacle Queen Ethelyn decided to remove.

Davia wonders what she might use to justify her own heinous actions should she ever commit them. She listens to the wind for a long time before sleep takes her.

The next day, when the dawn comes and Davia begins teaching Kyran another series of lessons in Venu Pakrim, a niggling doubt has taken root in her brain. Her devout focus on only what she can immediately affect shifts to what she might control given different opportunities and circumstances.

Anin is persistent and will have his people search for her until he finds a body or his path to answers is blocked by celestial phenomena comparable to a black hole. Sooner or later—tomorrow or years from now—Anin will find her.

What will become of Kyran then? She is a terrorist, a traitor to Sifani Prime who will be summarily executed.

She and Kyran have saved each other's lives, and now have crossed into new territory changing everything. Davia will not let Anin or his mother hurt Kyran, but what will happen to Kyran's people? The weights on the scale change every moment. Would Kyran accept Davia's protection if she could not secure freedom for her people?

If she and Kyran are rescued and separated, will Davia ever see her again?

Speculation is a habit she thought long broken. The rod within herself—restored somewhat from recent cracks—and twenty years of training remind her nothing can be achieved by positing various outcomes to circumstances that haven't yet arisen.

When Kyran smiles at her with a soft glance meant to ease the tension in Davia's shoulders, Davia feels like she is hiding from the truth.

Kyran is wrong, and should their predicament end, Davia may have more influence than she cares to admit.

CHAPTER SEVENTEEN

"No, pivot this leg here." Davia shifts Kyran's foot with her own boot as she lifts Kyran's arm into position. "When you raise this arm, you center your weight and are harder to push off balance."

Kyran has known pain in her life. She's known agony. She's been near death, and she's been so mentally, emotionally, and physically exhausted the thought of dying in her sleep sounded like a comfort. She's never experienced this tingling, bone-deep ache.

Davia's instruction sinks through her skin into a part of her wanting to stretch past its limit, to do something she's never done, to be someone she never thought she could be.

The light of early afternoon through patchy clouds casts short shadows on the canyon. Davia parallels the position beside Kyran to demonstrate in tandem the series of movements yet again, her patience endless.

"Again. Slower this time."

It takes hours of practice for Kyran to complete the form without Davia's aid.

When they curl up together in the bunk that used to be Davia's alone, Kyran groans when she wraps her arms around Davia.

Davia laughs.

Kyran is even sorer the next morning when Davia stirs.

"Wake up." Davia shakes Kyran's shoulders, and the touch hurts.

"I can't move. I'll take a massage when you get back, even if your hands are cold."

Davia smacks her on the naked flank of her backside. "No more sleeping late. Now you join me."

Kyran perks up when the words sink past her mental fog.

Outside, the chilled dawn breeze makes Kyran shiver and worsens the ache. A few clandestine stretches on the way to Davia's ritual space keep her from groaning aloud.

Kyran stands nearby while Davia marks her circle. Today, Davia adds a line behind it.

"Kneel here."

Kyran considers resisting out of pride then remembers it doesn't serve her. She asked for this, and Davia delivered. The proper respect is due.

She lowers herself stiffly into place with only minor correction from Davia, who takes her usual position within the circle.

"Repeat only the first two lines after me," Davia says.

Kyran takes a deep, centering breath without prompting, ingrained by her training so far.

"I have no mother, no father, and no house to call my own. I have no shelter but the stars and no home but where I kneel."

A potent ache rises in Kyran's chest as she repeats the words, their truth resonating through her entire body and filling her eyes with tears.

The shallow valley is the fourth one Kyran has checked today, and the results are the same. She stashes her worry into a mental compartment to be revisited later.

Kyran pushes her luck by staying on the hunt as long as she can as the day fades. For the last several days, she has seen no movement anywhere. Her only catch is a few tubers from the small scrub forest nearby.

She relents and returns to the ship. At least she won't return empty-handed.

They have plenty of cured stores thanks to Davia's precaution, but they're running out of fresh meat. When she gets back to the canyon, the fire is stacked for dinner and unlit. The sound of heavy breathing and clanking components draws Kyran to where Davia is hard at work on the far side of the ship.

"Need help?"

Davia has tucked the sleeves of her tunic into themselves at her shoulders, and the taut muscles of her forearms and biceps are on display as she wrestles with unyielding bolts.

"No." Davia pauses when the bolt gives way. "I've realigned the solar circuits so they feed power to one of the filter flows."

"You mean—"

"Hot water. Well, tepid water."

Kyran raises her eyebrows, impressed. "Well, that's one success for the day."

Concern furrows Davia's brow. "Nothing?"

"No trace of them. No tracks, no scat. Perhaps they've all gone underground."

She's considered the possibility her hunting has driven her prey from the area, but she isn't the biggest predator—not if the creature she killed in the pit was any indication.

"We could dry more of the fresh meat that's left," Davia says.

Kyran hums in agreement, but the ropy dried strands upset her stomach and are far from appealing. "How about I make stew tonight? We can assess the rationing in the morning."

Davia secures her tools and brushes dirt and grime from her hands. "Spar while we wait."

Kyran smiles despite the bleakness of the situation. Maybe this time, she'll gain the advantage.

She doesn't.

Davia knocks Kyran flat on her backside so many times Kyran is certain her bones are bruised. Each time, Davia extends a hand to help her up and gives Kyran a moment to recover and set herself anew.

"You are improving," Davia says.

Kyran wonders if it's said only to ease her pride. Then again, Davia doesn't slow her punches anymore. At first, Davia only parried Kyran's blows. As Kyran grew more familiar with the strikes, Davia would connect with little force behind them.

Now, her strikes are focused and powerful. She weighs less than Kyran yet hits harder. Kyran has the bruises to prove it.

The next time Kyran lands on her back, she considers sleeping in the dirt for the night.

Davia prods her leg with a boot. "Up. Try to land one solid hit before dinner."

Kyran grasps Davia's outstretched hand and rises to her feet.

That night, when Kyran lays herself on Davia's bunk, she swears her joints creak and bites back any complaint. It occurs to her Davia has never complained about anything—not the weather, not their limited resources, not their circumstances, not the fact Kyran is to blame for her being stranded.

Kyran's admiration of Davia grows.

Davia doesn't lie beside her. Instead, she kneels naked next to Kyran's legs, rubbing her hands together briskly, palms flat against each other before she presses them to one of Kyran's thighs.

Kyran gasps. Davia's palms are hot as she massages into Kyran's muscles. It hurts at first, and then the pain eases to a pleasurable ache.

Davia repeats the action over much of Kyran's body. The relief spreads, a languorous hum singing in her blood.

When Davia stops, Kyran draws a breath to speak, to thank her. Davia kisses the skin above her navel and the words never cross Kyran's lips.

The attention begins anew as Davia paints her in kisses. Arousal sweeps through her, and then desire. She waits for Davia to finish, to have her way.

Davia is nothing if not diligent and attentive to detail.

When she lies alongside Kyran, Kyran rolls on top of her, wet and eager and straining against impatience. Davia is insistent, pulling Kyran's thighs outside her own, spreading Kyran's legs into a straddling position. Davia slides a hand between them, then purrs at what she finds.

Kyran can barely hold herself up, so deep is her fatigue, and she pulls from her waning energy reserves to raise her hips over Davia's hand, pushes onto Davia's fingers, and draws them inside.

Her nerves are over-sensitized, her skin hot where they touch. Sweat breaks out on her spine, and she can't breathe between kisses to Davia's perfect lips.

Kyran speeds the rise and fall of her hips; Davia matches her and as one they strive for the same goal. When Kyran peaks, Davia doesn't stop, and Kyran's euphoria expands, seeking a new height, fatigue forgotten.

Davia flips them over, sinks down Kyran's body, and adds her tongue in counterpoint as Kyran arches her back. Kyran slips her hands into Davia's hair, pulling her head closer, and offers everything she has because now it's not only her pleasure. Davia is asking something of her, Davia wants more, Davia demands her due with mouth and hands, and Kyran is helpless and must obey.

This time when the orgasm swells, when she cries out, it's a keening for the person she used to be, someone she doesn't recognize anymore. She is not the same.

Davia's thrusts slow, her brazen and wild kisses a benediction. She stills her fingers and doesn't draw them out, rests her cheek on wiry hair, hums without making a sound and settles herself as if she has no intention of moving ever again.

The dark behind Kyran's eyes is welcome, the warmth of Davia's skin against her a reward.

Kyran is sanctified, reborn.

CHAPTER EIGHTEEN

Multiple sandstorms have led to poor performance from the solar cells. Training is suspended as Kyran clears the panels between storms.

Davia considers herself resourceful, and Kyran's endless tinkering with scavenged materials has further inspired her. Together, they have devised solutions to many of their logistical problems, including the creation of an aft-bay sand-lock—a repurposed airlock to keep sand from accumulating inside the ship.

"Aft panels are clear, but the wind has shifted." Kyran stomps on the deck of the sand-lock. Sand and dust cloud around her legs. She tugs a strip of worn fabric from over her nose and mouth, and hangs it on a hook before she closes the door. "I'll have to do it again before dark."

The other current challenge will require more than ingenuity. Davia does not draw out the bad news.

"The meat is spoiled." She wipes perspiration from her forehead.

Kyran stares as she sits on a waist-high cargo container, her eyes communicating her understanding of the real issue: the stores of fresh meat are empty. "I've harvested all the tubers within half a day's walk. There's a clear path to the northeast where I can push farther since I can navigate back in the dark. Extending hunting range in that direction might yield more results, too."

Both are dangerous yet calculated risks.

"We have enough full rations of the dried meat for eleven days," Davia says.

"I don't think my stomach can handle so much rope." Kyran offers a wry smile. "Half rations at most."

"We would not want to cause you any distress." Davia does not comment on the worry darkening Kyran's eyes.

"As long as we don't have to resort to the worms," Kyran mutters.

Davia crosses the cargo bay to stand between her legs and brush the hair from her face. Kyran's hair has grown past her shoulders, and the wind has blown it into knotted disarray.

"Today, we have what we need," Davia whispers.

Kyran seals the discussion with a kiss.

At dinner, Davia attempts to give Kyran the larger portion. With a disapproving glance, Kyran spoons the extra food into Davia's bowl until the contents are equal.

The rigor of their daily existence has increased. Their limited diet leaves them deficient in necessary vitamins and minerals, and considering their reduced rations, it would be smarter to reduce their caloric expenditure, but inactivity is dangerous for both of them. Kyran busies herself with sharpening her spears, constructing a lean-to by the firepit, assembling a sled to carry water containers from the lake, and using stones to build stairs to the best vantage points on the bluffs.

Now, too, her hunting expeditions have grown longer.

"I'll camp along the route tonight." Kyran does not look at Davia as she collects her spears for the hunt.

Davia freezes mid-motion. Under the wing at the worktable, she has sliced a few of the shriveled tubers from Kyran's recent foray. They may not dry well. Davia will make the attempt anyway.

Kyran meets Davia's gaze, her face carefully blank. "I'll

return late tomorrow."

Davia sees through her to the grave concern beneath. She sets down her knife and bids Kyran to wait while she retrieves her pistol and holster. She remembers the first time she did this—handed her weapon to Kyran—and spares a thought for how far they have come, how important Kyran's safety is to her.

With weapons secured and a canteen strapped to her back, Kyran kisses Davia's temple before she leaves, a new gesture whenever they part company. The tenderness of it warms Davia from the inside.

Kyran is hours gone when Davia notices the rations left on her seat at the firepit.

Kyran has come far in her training. Her movement flows, her attacks are crisp and precise, her defenses graceful and effective. She executes the beautiful dance of Venu Pakrim, its signature trait. Deadly grace, centered power, fluid presence.

Davia must fashion the weapon Kyran will soon earn.

What took Davia years to accomplish as an adolescent, Kyran will most likely achieve in a handful of months. Davia practiced Venu Pakrim alongside other children where the most demanding training was conducted only a few hours a day. Since they were also pursuing their studies, strenuous instruction paralleled school classes and projects and other demands of their young development.

Kyran has no need for such temperance and has the benefit of a master's singular attention. When she is not hunting or foraging, she fills the remaining time with constant practice and focus, receiving instant correction when she makes a mistake, and she is a quick learner.

She is impetuous yet resilient, impatient yet resourceful, prone to emotional outbursts yet persistent. What she has already endured on this moon is far beyond what Venu Pakrim training demands of younger students.

And she is not a child. She is a mature woman who has experienced loss, death, and more than one kind of pain. Though Kyran shares little of her origins, she did mention she had never studied an art like Venu Pakrim before, so she has no martial training she must unlearn.

Davia doubts Kyran will have the same difficulties she did with her own first dagger—forgetting it was under her pillow, knocking it off surfaces or holding it awkwardly when her sheaths broke. If Kyran were an acolyte on Duveri, she would be in her fifth year of training, approaching the most feared and anticipated challenge of her development. With only one weapon and a supply of food and water, acolytes are sent into the wilderness full of swamps and jungles and, most frightening to adolescents, the unknown. The journey is called the halem venu, and its completion is one of the final tests for Pris.

Yet here on this moon, such a challenge is more like an afterthought. Kyran performs such trials every few days. Her time on this moon has been an endless halem venu.

Davia considers making the challenge more difficult somehow, and ultimately leaves the directives unchanged. Kyran's training has been easier in some ways than it might have been on Duveri. She is older than most acolytes and better able to temper her emotions and responses. If Kyran were to set foot inside the monastery—an impossibility, of course, considering their circumstances—she would not need to justify her presence. A simple list of her experiences since the crash would exceed many of the requirements.

An acolyte's first blade is a gift bestowed by a master. Every blade after is chosen by the acolyte. Swords, sabers, rapiers, daggers—all are tools, no more and no less, and not items to be anthropomorphized or named. At first, many students choose ornate, provocative weapons. By the time they advance to Min, they have tempered such frivolity in favor of versatility of function.

Davia has designed and begun construction of a dagger to be presented to Kyran when her Pri trials are complete. The blade will be a simple one since the materials at her disposal are limited. The thought of creating it reminds Davia of something she hasn't thought of in years: the other ways blades are given from one to another.

When a Venu Pakrim Min marries, they offer their blades to their beloved. The offering is symbolic and permanent—in the rare instance of separation or split, the blade is not returned.

Davia has known love in her life. She loved her mother. She loves her brother and knows it is reciprocated. She loves Izabel, though she does not return the depth of love Izabel has felt for her.

She has never been in love. The challenges her identity presents make true connection difficult. Her brother's warnings and her father's missteps live long in her memory, and romantic relationships require an unfamiliar vulnerability.

Her feelings for Kyran are too immense for her body. They overflow every night in Kyran's arms—an ache to hold and keep Kyran close.

Kyran knows who Davia is and does not seem to care. Perhaps it is Kyran's origins—someone who rejects the crown would most likely not pay the proper respects to any royal. She never refers to Davia by any title, never extends any obsequious courtesy. She is simply Kyran, who is now always kind to Davia, who asks Davia for nothing save the instruction in her art.

She touches Davia as if she is precious. Not fragile, but—and the irony does not escape Davia—exalted. When they argue—more heated disagreement than violent confrontation—Kyran is careful with her words and no longer attacks with them, not like the night that led to their first union.

Whenever Kyran returns exhausted to the canyon after a hunting and foraging trip, her eyes brighten upon seeing Davia. She pulls Davia close when they lie together, even if she's deeply asleep. A kind of gratitude fills her eyes when they perform the kim venu, and at night when they're together by the firepit, Kyran's affection spills into every gesture.

It is the most egalitarian relationship Davia has ever

experienced. Neither of them is too self-important to butcher the meat, or to muck the waste unit when it clogs. There is never talk of what is deserved and what is owed. They merely exist, taking turns with the difficult challenges, ebbing and flowing based on who is more capable of completing the task at hand.

It is liberating. Davia is stranded, starving, and alone with someone she thought was her enemy, and she feels freer in Kyran's arms than she has ever felt anywhere else.

And so, for the first time in her life, Davia wonders what it would be like to love someone deeply enough to perform such a gesture—to separate herself from the blade that has been the heart of her for so long.

Whenever Kyran looks at her, eyes bright with something she cannot wait to share, Davia begins to understand.

In any of these moments, Davia is grateful she does not have to choose between the empire and her lover's well-being. She is grateful that being stranded on this moon, even with dwindling resources, has led her to this vibrant, powerful woman. If she dies here, if their circumstances never improve and she and Kyran waste away to nothing, Davia will die knowing what she has found with Kyran has been worth the price.

A breeze rises in the canyon, cooling the sweat on Davia's skin as she lies in her bunk. Her thoughts dance between memories of her young years on Meteus, her formative adolescence on Duveri, and her decade as an adult full Min. All these experiences have helped her to adapt to the challenges on this moon.

Davia rarely wonders who she might have been had she not become a Min. Tonight, alone in the dark, she tries until sleep overtakes her to imagine another life—and whether that life would have crossed paths with Kyran's.

One afternoon, Kyran kneels behind the line for instruction. Davia's leg aches worse than usual and has failed her twice today, so she paces the sand with a limp.

"The diameter of the circle is no wider than your reach." Davia holds Kyran's gaze with her own. This point is important, the basis of all Venu Pakrim. "Working within this circle teaches you never to overextend past your limit. Within your reach, however, is your responsibility to control."

In rapt attention, Kyran sits in silence. Her fingers no longer twitch, her feet do not wriggle in the sand, her body does not shift from position even after extended periods of time. Kyran has learned stillness and is no longer tentative when holding her own space.

Such is the nature of Venu Pakrim.

"There is no shame in failure, but do not make it a habit. What is ours to manage must be mastered. What is within this circle is mine to protect, mine to mold, mine to center, mine to master."

She beckons Kyran to rise, and squares her shoulders.

Kyran has progressed to weapons training. Davia had one staff in her personal belongings and has crafted a second from a wind-compressed water-starved branch from one of the squat trees. It might not sustain extended high intensity use, but will be enough for Kyran to begin the practice.

Davia tosses the new staff to Kyran, who catches it and holds it gingerly. Davia fights the urge to flourish hers with the skill acquired by the many bouts in her experience, and instead levels it before her.

"Your staff is the same length as the circle's diameter, as the width of your own arms outstretched. This will teach you the ebb and flow of your space, the limits and opportunities within it."

Davia does not mention that Kyran is lucky to learn on sand and not stone, and she has no intention of going easy on her.

The practice goes on for weeks until Kyran reaches a plateau in her training and the frustration bleeds into her movements. A series of parry-and-strike combinations ending in a leg sweep is difficult to instill in her muscle memory, and every time she makes the attempt, Davia knocks her to the ground.

New acolytes spar with one another as they learn the forms and strikes. Kyran is no child, and this far into her training, she is strong enough for full contact with no one else to spar with besides Davia. When Davia hits Kyran, she hits hard, and this time, she breaks Kyran's skin.

Sitting on the ground, her elbows on her knees while she catches her breath, Kyran wipes a streak of blood from one cheek like an afterthought.

"I'm never going to learn this," Kyran says, exasperated at her lack of progress.

"Speak not of the future, Pri."

Kyran grunts at the correction and the appellation. Such a response is a hair short of insolence and another sign of her frustration.

"No complaints and no castigations. Listen to your body, to the signals it sends you. You must teach it new paths for those signals. Visualize the movement and your body will follow."

Disbelief joins the consternation on Kyran's face. She appears tired enough to be done for the day. Davia cannot let her stop here.

Though it hurts her leg to do so, Davia lowers herself to one knee.

"I will not say quitting is the easy way out." Those are words for a child learning perseverance, not an adult who has fought and defeated despair with intelligence and skill. "The consequences for giving up can be expensive."

Nothing is gained, nothing is learned. Kyran says nothing, her posture suggesting she is listening to every word.

Davia softens her voice.

"There are many lessons here, and the one I want you to focus on is this. Do the next task in front of you, limit your vision to it, and the entire endeavor simplifies. If it is a journey overland or up a mountain, focus on the next step. If a creature attacks, focus on the next blow. If it is a bout such as this, rise to your feet. You learn nothing from the dirt—"

And with a snap of her teeth, Davia stops speaking in shock.

She nearly called Kyran "beloved."

Unaware of Davia's epiphany, Kyran rises, brushes the sand and dust from her tattered clothes, and takes first position of the fighting stance she has learned.

Davia recovers and stands, filing away this new revelation for later study.

Kyran begins again.

CHAPTER NINETEEN

For the first time in months, Kyran wakes before Davia.

It's dark outside, but not for much longer. She doesn't move—she wants to let Davia sleep, wants to lie in the abject hopelessness for a moment before they get up and pretend they can do anything about their fate.

The last of the fresh meat spoiled seventeen days ago. They halved their dried rations and halved them again. Now, they add only a few of the remaining shriveled morsels to the evening soup.

Soon, they'll be down to water and tubers. Kyran travels farther and farther from the canyon to find any of the roots at all.

After everything they've been through, she can't believe they're going to starve to death.

Davia's features are serious even in slumber. Her sleep is heavier today, her body eking as much rest as it can. As if sleep alone can refuel a body desperate for nutrients.

Kyran doesn't let herself cry at the injustice of it, that someone as strong as Davia can be broken by something so insidious as a lack of food.

When Davia stirs, Kyran forces the sentiment down deep. They rise, dress, and begin the day. Outside, Davia's limp is more pronounced. Her cheekbones show the hollows of her cheeks in stark relief, yet her strength has not waned and neither has her drive.

Kyran has seen her wince more than once. Davia's poorly healed injury is bothering her again.

They spar less, and Davia tutors more in the philosophy of Venu Pakrim.

"Focus on this movement, the one your opponent makes now, and take action. Do not consider what they might do in the future. You control only what happens in the moment, and hold your head up as you face its consequences."

Kyran wonders if Davia is teaching a lesson or convincing herself.

"Those consequences may not be positive. Take solace in doing your best at what needs to be done. This is all you can do, and it is enough."

While their prospects dim, Davia does not succumb to depression or inactivity. Even now, Davia sits away from the fire, hunched over some task that sounds like scraping metal.

"What are you doing?" Kyran asks from her seat by the firepit.

Davia passes the metal over the stone a few more times before she pauses to respond, breath short at such minimal effort. "Making something we will need soon."

Kyran doesn't bother asking for clarification. Davia uses the fewest words possible to express herself, and if she'd wanted Kyran to know more, she'd have said so.

Kyran has little imagination or curiosity left to puzzle it out.

Though it's a futile pursuit—she hasn't seen prey in weeks, and the last two trips she didn't return with tubers either—Kyran collects her hunting gear and a canteen full of water and leaves the canyon.

The scraping sound stops. Kyran senses Davia's gaze boring into her back.

Kyran is forced to take more breaks. She tries to ration the water. It keeps the hunger pangs from twisting her guts and tempers the headaches. Her searching yields no more prey and fatigue drags at her heavy limbs.

In the distance is the outline of trees. Where there are trees, there may be scrub brush. Where there is scrub brush, there may be edible roots.

Returning to Davia empty-handed is unacceptable.

Kyran adjusts her load and walks toward the possibility of food.

"How, Davia?" Kyran fights her own despair that night. Her muscles ache, her stomach hurts, her head is tight from holding back tears. "How can you just . . . keep going?"

They choose the comfort of skin and the warmth of clinging to one another at night over the insulation of layers between them. Davia is pressed against Kyran's side, her head tucked into Kyran's shoulder and her arm across Kyran's belly.

"Today, we had enough to survive," Davia murmurs in the dark. "We are alive. Tomorrow, we will rise and begin anew."

It sounds simple the way she says it, and yet it's so immense it astounds Kyran.

"Once I thought my mother was the strongest woman I'd ever known." Kyran speaks now in a rasp not much louder than a whisper. It takes less effort than normal speech. "When no one else did, she believed in a future of possibility and promise for our people."

Kyran shifts her legs, searching for a position that doesn't strain her back. "Later, Benna—"

She pauses, waiting for the mourning ache, but it doesn't come. Maybe her grief has eased, or maybe she's too tired and weak to give in to it.

"Benna was the epitome of that same strength."

"Benna?"

It's the one thing Kyran can't resolve—her anger at Benna's death despite her feelings for Davia. She has spent months pushing it down, like her shame at failing her parents and her people.

"Commander Benna Dobri. Our grandmothers were sisters."

Kyran swallows against the lump in her throat. These things are too recent to feel like another lifetime.

"She led the fleet across the outer rim from Ragan to Ellod. Backbone of metal and stubborn as hell. Never let me get away with anything."

Saying this warms Kyran, this first thought of Benna that doesn't hurt deeply enough to bite.

"What happened to her?"

Kyran doesn't want to say, doesn't want to bring one more painful thing between them that she cannot change. As the days pass, as Davia becomes more a part of her, withholding anything—even the things she doesn't want to talk about—is much harder.

"She was on the bridge of *Althea* when—when the missile from your ship destroyed it."

A gasp in the dark, a clenching of the hand at her waist. Davia starts to pull away.

Kyran holds her in place, refusing to let her go, and kisses Davia's temple. "You would not have been allies, but you are similar in so many ways."

The silence stretches until Davia speaks in a pained whisper. "How can you not hate me for this? For what I have taken from you, for what has become of you?"

Minimizing her response or muttering platitudes would not be honest, and Davia would sense it. Forgiveness isn't possible for either of them. If it weren't for Kyran's attack, Davia might not have fired that shot. If it weren't for Davia's attack, Benna might still be alive.

She weighs her words, stroking her hand down Davia's back to ask for patience while she untangles her thoughts and feelings.

The truth surprises her with its power. "I'm not sure I'd trade where I am now for my old life. Of course I'd want Benna back but I—I am . . ."

She doesn't want to say she's happy because she's not. She's terrified and empty, and all that is left is a newfound core unwilling to concede. Some cold, dark part of her is secretly grateful she doesn't have to choose. This time and place with Davia have more value to her than anything she's ever held before.

She is too hungry and tired and despondent to think about how that betrays Benna's memory. And what does it matter when it's all impossible? Her anger and grief change nothing, but also . . .

"I belong here," she says. It's nowhere near enough and will have to suffice. "With you."

When Davia turns her head to bring them face to face, tears glint in Davia's eyes. Kyran closes her eyes at the sensation of Davia's lips against her own and tastes the salt she herself can't spare.

Two days later, a half day's walk from the ship, Kyran comes across tracks so large, she doesn't recognize what they are at first. The pattern resolves—the winding marks through the sand are similar to the shelled creatures she hunts, and several times larger.

Bigger than the one that almost killed Davia.

She doesn't see the creature and cannot judge how long ago it passed, and continues on her way, more wary in its wake.

Movement in the rocks near the valley's floor captures her attention—a pod of the animals she's been searching for.

The threat of famine makes her run when she should be silent. She doesn't want her prey to escape. She's not quick enough, and by the time she catches up to them, they've crawled into a crevice where she cannot reach.

She hears scratching and skittering behind boulders too large for her to move. She'll have to draw them back out and has nothing to use as bait.

When the idea occurs to her, she's certain it's insanity born of desperation.

She crouches near the hole and bares one arm. She's

watched Davia do this countless times, and Kyran hesitates with the point of a spear over her arm. It's not easy and takes several painful tries, made somehow more difficult by the thinness of her skin. She finally cuts well enough for the blood to bead.

She hisses at the pain of tearing her own skin to make the cut deeper.

Kyran leans her bleeding arm over the ground in front of the hole, squeezing a fist to encourage more blood to flow down her arm and into the sand.

The scratching gets louder. Forced to decide to commit or give up, she stretches herself across the ground. Any creature will have to reveal itself if it wants what it senses.

Finally, one appears. Kyran fights against her urge to move. She must wait for the creature to clear the opening entirely before she attacks, or it will skitter back inside.

She lies still until one pincer grabs at her arm. Before it clamps, she raises her spear and stabs at its unprotected face, blinking at the blood and whatever else squirting out when she pulls the spear back and stabs again.

Her weakness makes for a messy kill. She jabs at it until it's too wounded to retreat, then shoves herself to her knees. She drags the thing further away from its hiding place, flipping it over and stabbing it again.

She stops when she's spent, hoping it's close enough to death that she doesn't have to stab it anymore. When it stills, she guts it where it lies, letting the blood pool while she gathers her strength.

By the time she's prepared the kill for travel, the sun is setting. She hangs her head, exhausted, and begins walking toward the distant pile of stones marking the path home.

She pays more attention to the shadows on the way.

They force themselves to ration their bounty. The soup they make in the middle of the night is almost too much. Kyran sits, clutching her belly, willing herself to keep the food down.

Davia is so unsteady once she eats, she doesn't leave their bunk for most of the next day. Neither of them is able to eat solid meat at first, and not much beyond the kim venu gets done around the canyon.

Kyran is diligent about preserving and making sure none of it goes to waste. If her hunting yields no results for a few more weeks, they'll survive until then. The looming threat of starvation has been averted for now, and they slowly recover.

Many days later, when they've regained their strength well enough to spar again, Kyran resumes her suffering at Davia's more skilled hands. The time it takes Davia to get the best of her, however, grows. Kyran still finds herself in the dirt more than once, but with increasing frequency they break away from each other and regroup, Davia unable to press her advantage.

One afternoon, the bout is more evenly matched than usual.

Drenched in sweat and focused on Davia's movements, Kyran no longer thinks. She parries one of Davia's combination attacks, spins as she lowers to the ground and sweeps Davia's legs out from under her. Davia stops her fall from doing any damage to the back of her head, and her surprise is audible.

Kyran stands and steps back, breathing heavily, blows a few strands of her hair from her eyes and grins. Davia arches an eyebrow in acknowledgment and begins to rise. Kyran stretches out a hand to help her up.

They both take their positions for the next engagement, and Davia nods her head at the achievement.

"Do it again," she says, "and I'll cook dinner."

CHAPTER TWENTY

After dinner, Davia says words Kyran doesn't understand.

"Your halem venu begins at noon tomorrow."

Kyran waits for an explanation. Waiting is still painful. She endures it as required.

"You will travel into the wilderness alone, for three nights, and return to this fire at sunset on the last day."

When Davia says nothing more, Kyran bursts.

"Do I need to bring something back?"

"No." Davia checks the boiling pot of sinew from Kyran's latest kill.

"Do I need to go somewhere in particular?"

"The goal is to be unassisted. I doubt the terrain will make it any easier for you."

"What can I take with me?"

"Rations, water, and your spears. Or the pistol, if you wish."

Kyran waits for some added challenge or complication. Judging by the way Davia is acting, there isn't one.

On her knees in the sand a day's walk from the canyon, Kyran performs the kim venu alone for the first time. She faces the sunset, her eyes on the first stars twinkling beyond the cloudless purple sky.

For the first time, too, Kyran gazes upon Ellod without

grief or anger. Despite everything, maybe she is still in Ellod's embrace.

She finds a near-perfect location for the night, one with a nook where she can rest beside a clearing for a small fire. Falling asleep takes awhile, mostly because of boredom. No solar panels to clean, no filtration catches to inspect. She misses books, not that her days in the fleet provided much time to read for pleasure.

She stares at the stars as she lies warmed by the fire and eventually closes her eyes.

Late in the morning on the second day, she finds another set of larger tracks. These are headed in a direction away from the canyon, which is good. The creature who made them is nowhere in sight, and following something so big alone is too much of a risk. She must remember to talk to Davia about their fortifications in case this thing returns.

That night, she chooses to sleep in a crevice of a bluff. The night is cold, and she shivers as she visualizes her forms until her breathing settles. Eventually, she sleeps.

As the hours pass on her journey, Kyran chooses to focus on only the present moment and now understands its value. The path through the rocks, the sand shifting in the wind, the passing of clouds overhead. She looks forward to seeing Davia, enjoying the anticipation, and it doesn't change the fact that all she can affect right now is the pace of her stride.

The last day, she travels to the lake. Wading in the shallow water feels like a cleansing of more than her body. She fears predators—especially the larger one somewhere in the region—but none are attacking her now. Vigilance is within her circle, and that is all that's required.

When Kyran returns to the canyon's fire at sunset after three nights in the wild, Davia waits in the ritual space and has not yet drawn her circle. Kyran starts to kneel in what is now her usual space behind Davia.

"Stand here." Davia points to a spot a few steps to the side and one step behind where she stands.

Kyran does as she's told. Though she's curious about this change, she keeps her questions to herself.

Davia comes to stand before Kyran and looks into her eyes for a long time. Kyran is not discomfited and meets the gaze steadily.

Davia draws a dagger from her waist. The hilt is a finely sanded warp of shell, the ties binding it to the blade made of boiled sinew and strips of leather from Davia's own scabbard. The blade itself is a honed bracket from the landing strut Kyran brought to the canyon, its form edged and sharpened.

Rough and primitive, the dagger is nowhere near as fine as Davia's blade. Instead, it is a forthright reminder of what they have experienced on this moon, and no less deadly in its functionality.

Davia holds it across her palms and raises it between them.

"This blade is an extension of you. Your blade is the heart of you, and your heart is this blade. Carry it with you everywhere you are without exception. If you are naked, it is close at hand."

So, all these months of Davia sleeping with hers close by have been more from training than vigilance.

Davia places the blade in Kyran's hands.

"I thought my trials difficult at the time, and they were. What you have accomplished here . . . you must never question what you have done to earn this blade or what it represents."

Kyran understands Davia's true meaning. She holds this blade with an esteem similar to the way she carries her own.

Davia begins to mark her circle.

"The circle embodies the locus of what you can affect. Within it are all the things in your control, including your own mindset. Beyond it are things your action cannot change. Be vigilant and stay aware of them, for your ability to affect them may become possible over time and under different circumstances. Focus your action on the things within the circle."

Davia is answering questions Kyran has had for months, not

only about this ritual, but also about the kind of woman Davia is—one who has never complained about their predicament and instead has focused on how to endure it, how to improve it, how to survive within terrible constraints.

She points at Kyran to mark her own circle and Kyran mirrors her actions.

Davia lowers herself to her knees. "We kneel for the kim venu because regardless of birthright or status, we are not all-powerful."

Kyran doesn't need this explained. She's lived it most of her life.

"Repeat after me, every word I say."

Davia speaks the words of the ritual. Kyran memorized them months before. As she says them now, they somehow strengthen her resolve to live on, to face another day, to walk forward whether she knows where those steps will lead or not.

"I have no mother, no father, and no house to call my own. I have no shelter but the stars and no home but where I kneel. My heart is this blade, offered true and without shame despite its flaws."

When Davia draws her blade across her arm, Kyran does the same and no longer finds anything barbaric or foreign about the gesture. She's bled more than once to serve something greater than herself and this is no different. In fact, this is something worth far more.

"I serve to live and live to serve, with faith and hope this day I will be worthy."

Kyran raises her dagger before her eyes, her arm stinging from the new cut. Her hands do not tremble.

She hopes she is worthy.

She lowers her arm when Davia does, wipes her blood on her leg and secures her new blade at her waist. She'll have to build a sheath for it.

Davia smiles at her, her eyes shining.

Kyran breathes in something sweet she cannot name.

The pride Kyran feels is not arrogant, not the expansive

better-than-someone-else pride of winning a competition, not the birthright her parents claimed on her behalf, not the destiny Benna insisted belonged to her.

This is the pride of well-executed hard work, earned with her own sweat, her tears, and her blood. When she stands, her weight is centered over a solid stance, strong, unyielding.

Kyran is who she is, and she is enough.

CHAPTER TWENTY-ONE

The night is hot—the air thick with humidity only a storm will dispel. Inside the ship, condensation beads on the bulkheads. Ventilation would work if only there were a breeze, which there isn't. Nothing in the night moves, nothing eases the immense pressure of the heat.

Kyran could not care less.

She can't hold up her head, and she raises an arm to brace against the wall. She feels like her cells are about to divide as Davia thrusts hard and deep and fast, breath hot on the back of Kyran's neck. When Kyran thinks she can't go on, Davia goads her with one more pinch, another undulating thrust of her body along Kyran's back as she spreads Kyran's legs apart with her own.

Davia is a giving lover. Tonight, however, she is demanding with her touch, relentless, and Kyran is just as insistent. It's far past the middle of the night, and their loving is feral in its intensity, like the first time they were together. Neither of them speaks and neither stops—each peak is a chance to begin anew. It's as if they're proving their ability to survive with this one act. Davia will not give in and Kyran will never concede.

When Davia thrusts deeper and bites Kyran's shoulder, Kyran cries out her release, savage. She reveals herself to Davia, holding back none of her need, and Davia not only accepts her, but pushes Kyran to new heights, and Kyran would bleed for more.

With a groan, Davia shifts Kyran in her arms and covers Kyran's body with her own, seeking her own pleasure. Kyran wraps her legs around Davia's hips, drowns in the messy kisses attempting to devour her, slips her hand between them to stroke where Davia is so distended by arousal, it takes only seconds for Davia to join her.

Davia collapses, and her moans sound disappointed at peaking so quickly.

The aching joy in Kyran is overwhelming. She fights back tears, clenches her hands in Davia's hair, pulls Davia into her tightly with her legs and holds on, clinging to Davia's existence like a lifeline, as if holding Davia, spent, in her arms is her only requirement for survival.

Their ardor cools. Her need does not.

Kyran caresses Davia's skin, follows the lines of scars and blemishes with her fingertips, kisses her favorite places because they make Davia gasp or moan. She pauses between each touch, watching its effect with a hyper-vigilant awareness as Davia arches or tenses or sighs. She pushes herself down Davia's body until she rests between Davia's legs, splays her hands against firm muscular thighs and lowers her mouth with an eager groan.

Kyran feasts, communicating with her lips and tongue through sensation everything she has no words for. She takes her time, unsatisfied until Davia sinks her hands into Kyran's hair and pulls none too gently. Davia's thighs tremble and her hips arch. She calls Kyran's name as she comes again.

When Davia's breathing evens out, and the pulse in Davia's body no longer races, Kyran rises over her. The warm air briefly cools the sweat on her skin. She wipes her chin in blatant carnal satisfaction and smears the wet across her breasts, smiling down as she holds herself over her prey, her hair falling like a curtain around their faces.

The wonder in Davia's eyes is out of sync with her earlier passion, and it stills Kyran where she hovers. Her question must be written on her face because Davia speaks.

"I wish you could see what I see. The woman you are now."

Kyran lowers herself to kiss Davia's neck. The scent at Davia's pulse point makes Kyran want to start all over again. "Am I truly so different?"

She's physically stronger and emotionally calmer than she was before Davia's training. What other changes has Davia noticed in her?

Davia wraps her arms around Kyran, slides her palms down Kyran's back and molds them to Kyran's hips. "The first time I saw you, you were . . ."

It's rare Davia fights for words. Kyran is nothing now if not patient. She kisses the join of Davia's neck and shoulder while she waits.

"Fury."

Surprise pulls Kyran away so she can see Davia's face.

Davia winds tendrils of Kyran's hair around her fingers, appraising and comparing this version of Kyran with her past self. "You were this manifestation of pure fury I thought might destroy me from its force alone. You were wounded, hungry, your lips and skin broken from wind and dehydration. Your weapon was no threat against mine, you had no skill at all, and you were terrified, but . . . had you tried to kill me then, I suspect we might have been evenly matched, will for will."

Kyran remembers it differently. She'd been angry, yes, and so weak she doubts she'd have been able to raise a hand for anything past a first blow. And Davia had been the epitome of an undefeatable foe—fierce yet placid, deadly yet serene. Untouchable.

Kyran doesn't think about those days much, those eons ago when she hated Davia with everything she had, when she thought only of vengeance, when she was more driven by fear and desperation than she might have wanted to admit.

Now, this sweeping, visceral need for Davia cannot be encapsulated by a term as simple as love. She has fought for Davia, killed for Davia, and would die by Davia's side.

A pensive frown furrows Davia's brow. "Now, that molten fury has been forged into . . ."

Davia reaches for Kyran's face, clasps her chin with a firm gentleness stealing Kyran's breath. "This strength—your strength. Your power, Kyran."

She shakes her head in disbelief. "You shine with it. It pulses through you, and sometimes it burns me."

She sighs as if her words have failed, and Kyran thinks she understands. Kyran traces the elegant line of Davia's jaw with one finger, brushes her thumb along Davia's lips, barely feeling their warmth. She keeps her touch light, trying to memorize the precise curve of their bow until she can't resist them.

The kiss is as measuring and deep as every one prior, a slow call and response their hips soon match.

Davia flips them over, clenches their hands together and pushes Kyran's arms overhead until they lie flat behind her head, and then Davia takes her turn. Kyran can't keep her eyes open against the onslaught.

When she opens them again much later, a new expression radiates from Davia's face. It's like the earlier wonder with something else—something like admiration, something not demanding, but pleading and raw—and whatever it is, it renders an invisible blow wide in Kyran's chest, every part of her exposed, fraught yet jubilant and wild.

Her breath comes faster. The sensations grow, drawing through the muscles in her thighs, a screaming intense wave crashing into her and rushing deep inside her. She arches her back, wants to close her eyes before the tears fall.

Davia grabs her hair with her other hand, clenching against her scalp.

"Stay with me."

Holding Kyran's head in place, and Kyran forces her eyes open as she cries out, as the pleasure fails to crest and expands until all of her is aflame and weightless, pulsing in time with the contractions pounding inside her. The moment it begins to wane, Davia kisses her, tongue and teeth claiming what little Kyran has left to give.

—~— —~— —~—

Pale light bends through the holes in the ship when Kyran wakes the next morning. Beside her, Davia is dressed against the chill and pulling on boots.

Kyran grunts as she stretches and starts to lift herself from where she lies on her stomach. Davia stops her with a touch to her shoulder.

"Rest. After the halem venu, you are allowed three days of rest without ritual observation."

She kisses Kyran, a slow deep exploration stirring Kyran's desire.

"That's not restful," Kyran says when they part, and settles back into the blankets.

Davia fetches her blade and holsters her pistol before she opens the door.

Kyran closes her eyes and burrows into the remaining warmth from Davia's body heat, relaxed despite the mild unsettled feeling of missing the morning ritual. How quickly it has become a habit for her.

Her mind is clear, her worries gone. The lassitude from a long night full of Davia's affection warms her insides as she sinks into a delicious half-sleep.

A loud rushing sound like a violent wind pulls her from her dozing. When it stops, she thinks it's a dream.

Moments later, she hears voices. A lot of voices, of men who speak in authoritarian Sifani.

She sits up, alert, confused and alarmed. Adrenaline freezes her when she hears Davia's footsteps—a gait she has memorized—near the door. Davia appears, looking back the way she's come.

"One moment," she says, emotionless and cold.

Davia isn't speaking to her.

"Yes, High One," a man says, and it sounds like he's right

outside the door. "Stand down!"

Another voice, farther away, acknowledges him. Kyran reaches for her dagger, the shock staving off all other thought as she prepares to leap into the unknown.

Davia steps inside, makes a fast movement with one hand using the signals she taught Kyran for combat and hunting.

Be silent and still.

Davia unfastens her holster and sets it and the pistol on the nearby shelf. For a moment, she rests her hand on her blade's hilt at her hip, then grabs her shawl and turns without another word or a single glance in Kyran's direction before walking out the door.

Kyran waits, arms straining against action, trusting Davia's warning as she listens to her footsteps fade. She counts her heartbeats, forcing herself not to follow.

The rushing sound repeats—an engine, a ship's engine—roaring and fading away. She hears no more voices.

Kyran dresses, clutches her blade, and leaps barefoot for the door.

When she steps outside, nothing is amiss. Nothing is different—not the firepit or the work area under the wing or the boundary wall at the edge of the canyon. A shocking number of boot prints mark the dirt and sand. The men who made them and their ship are nowhere in sight.

A circle in the sand lies undisturbed and empty.

Davia is gone.

PART THREE

CHAPTER TWENTY-TWO

One thought blazes across Davia's mind when the ship appears, looming black against the pale blue sky.

Protect Kyran.

The circle before her is drawn, and she stands within its boundary as the space she imagines inside it swells far beyond her physical reach. The heavily armed cruiser—a larger class of vessel eight times the size of her crashed frigate—hovers in midair not far from the canyon, low enough to drop several dark figures to the ground.

Dust clouds stir as they hit the ground. In seconds, they advance to the wall and Davia has not moved.

Protect Kyran.

Warning Kyran would reveal the presence of another person inside her ship.

Behind the approaching figures, the cruiser lands. Boarding bays open and another group of soldiers disembarks. They rush in formation across the sand, preceded by the squad now scaling the rock wall, and the dam of shock in her mind breaks and thoughts flood.

Rescue has come, and all Davia can think of is keeping those soldiers away from Kyran.

The first one—a tall, rugged man with ruddy brown skin, broad shoulders, and bulging muscles—glances between her face and a handheld device before he bows his head on the debatable side of respectful. He assesses her from head to foot, his expression communicating she has been judged lacking.

He is mistaken.

"High One," he says without inflection, tucking his device in a pocket. "His Illuminance Prince Anin has sent us to retrieve you and return you safely to Sifani forces for transport to Meteus."

So much information. His eyes say he had expected a fight and will follow orders even if it means forcing her to obey. Anin has sent them, not the Jeweled Circle or the High Queen, which is no real surprise.

Most importantly, he has not called her Min Davia, instead referring to her by the generic title of a courtier. He does not know who she is, which means she has little leverage with him.

If they see Kyran, they might shoot her before her presence can be explained. Worse, they might execute Kyran, and assume Davia is compromised.

The only plan she can set in motion in the next thirty seconds is to steer these men off this moon, thereby assuring Kyran's safety.

The first step is the hardest.

She holds her hand up in a waiting gesture and turns to the ship. The soldier is close behind her, the other five closing in.

"One moment," she says, and steps inside the still-open boarding door.

"Yes, High One." He tells the others to stand down while he lingers. If he leans forward and tips his head inside, he will see Kyran.

Davia will be out of his line of sight only for seconds. Her quick hand motion warns Kyran not to move, and Davia prays Kyran will obey without asking questions.

To her relief, one she endeavors not to show, Kyran stays frozen in their bed.

How soon Davia might return for Kyran—and she will return for her—is unknown. Kyran will be forced to carry on alone. She will need the pistol, which Davia removes and shelves in seconds.

Davia touches her blade and for a long moment—time she does not have—she considers leaving it with Kyran where she herself belongs. Reason drowns her heart. Removing it now might raise questions—hopefully ones she can avoid despite leaving the pistol. Instead, she reclaims her shawl, a potential excuse for returning to the ship.

She wants to look at Kyran one more time before they are parted but must not. The soldier will notice.

Walking out without a word is like a slice across the chest. Davia gestures for the men to follow her and prays not one of them stays behind.

"Move faster," she says in feigned disgust as she crosses the canyon floor to climb over the wall. "I want us off this barren rock in five minutes."

She quickens her steps toward the ship, resisting the pull back to the canyon.

These men are not Sifani soldiers. Not one of them bears a sigil or a marking of rank or affiliation, and they all defer to the first man who addressed Davia. They speak only to one another, not her—she is a parcel to be fetched and delivered.

They are mercenaries, which means they will likely only take orders from whoever hired them. She does not sense any true danger to her, but she will not be able to influence them.

Years of training and discipline straighten her back as she strides toward the cruiser's boarding ramp.

The leader beckons to another man. "Our mission is complete."

The second man nods and uses a handheld device to capture Davia's image. "As soon as we clear the asteroid field, I'll send proof for payment."

They trade rough jokes with the other mercenaries as they all board and take their seats in an open transport area. The leader guides Davia to a seat by a small window providing a limited view of the outside. The tightness in her shoulders eases—though not much—as the ship launches.

The cruiser gains altitude quickly, too high for a final glance at the canyon. The farther they progress from the moon's surface, the safer Kyran will be, and Davia resists the urge to clench her fist as she wills the cruiser to move faster.

Twenty minutes ago, she was warm in Kyran's arms. Davia bites her cheek, draws blood until she tastes it, so deep is the pain of leaving Kyran. She should be elated to leave, but she has left too much of herself behind.

Protect Kyran.

The ship weaves through the asteroid field, deft and versatile despite its size. Rymind 17A—Ellod, as Kyran had called it—fills the viewing window.

Before it sits the stationary pirate fleet, and a Sifani battlecruiser.

Davia's mind races. First, she needs to get away from these mercenaries trading gibes and stories of previous missions, and then the Sifani forces, which means she needs her own ship.

"Where are we going?"

Conversation stops and the men glance at each other.

The leader answers. "Our original directive was to locate you. Thanks to that damned ion storm, it took us months to get here. Our revised orders are to deliver you to the official transport above Rymind 17A."

"And if I request to be . . . delivered . . . elsewhere?"

His expression does not change, and his body shifts as if he anticipates a confrontation. "That would be against our orders."

Davia will not fight this battle. It is useless in the short term, and she lacks information.

"If you require anything prior to docking—food, water, a shower—"

One of the other men snickers.

"Data node access," Davia interrupts. The rest can wait. She must get a sense of how much has changed in her absence.

His eyes darken at the interruption and the request, and then he looks thoughtful, as if he expected a different answer. He points in the direction of an access portal.

Moments later, the pilot announces the ship has cleared the

asteroid belt and the ship's flight stabilizes. Her legs tremble and wobble from the shipboard gravity while Davia uses mounted handholds along the bulkhead to make her way to a small nook with a bolted-down chair and a basic interface module. The portal activates as she claims the seat.

The data station is limited but does patch into the greater imperial networks. She does not attempt to connect to any of her own systems, which are most likely still active, for fear of leaving a path for unsolicited access.

By the time they dock with the other ship, Davia has determined how uphill the battle ahead will be, and how long it might take to acquire a ship of her own. She has been presumed dead. Her personal funds are inaccessible, and many of her accounts are locked.

The mercenary leader is the first to rise from his seat.

"Set a course for the wormhole generation coordinates. We'll launch when I return." He approaches Davia's compartment. "Shall we?"

A small contingent awaits them in the docking platform's receiving area. The battlecruiser's commander stands before six other men, all of them in black and gray Sifani Armed Forces uniforms. The mercenary extends a palm-sized tablet as soon as he is close enough to present it.

"Please confirm the personnel transfer," the mercenary says without introducing himself.

Davia's arrival is nothing more than a transaction. The commander's demeanor is cool with the mercenary, implying the man's existence offends him. He makes his note and hands back the tablet.

"We'll detach immediately," the mercenary says in parting to the commander, nods at Davia, and returns to the boarding doors.

Once the platform doors close behind him, the commander nods at his staff and all but one of them leave through two other doors.

"High One," the commander says. "I am Commander Bruse."

He bows his head in respect. "I can only imagine what you have endured. Please allow me to offer you every accommodation I am able to provide this far into the outer systems. Rest assured we'll be leaving for Meteus shortly."

The thought of returning to Meteus so soon after all she has been through is . . . too much, and requires preparation.

He continues. "Our best private quarters await you, and His Illuminance requests your immediate contact."

He extends an arm towards one door. "This way please."

They navigate the decks and corridors through the ship, Davia wordlessly accompanying the commander. Ship's officers and soldiers stare at her as if she is a malnourished refugee, not a formidable Min—an odd circumstance Davia cannot yet process—and salute the commander as they pass. Bruse returns each one in a manner reflecting his assurance in his position, a man used to being in charge.

A long viewing window in one of the corridors reveals the iridescent greens, blues, and browns of the planet below, the immense cloud formations and what can only be oceans. A shuttle launches from the battlecruiser's bay and tilts toward Ellod.

"What is the current situation on . . . Rymind 17A?"

Bruse frowns. "You're in no danger aboard this vessel. The insurgent vermin are being tended to."

He misunderstands.

"And what does this tending involve?"

"That's beyond my purview. I will obtain a summary for your review while we travel to Meteus."

Davia stops walking. "I will not leave this system until these details have been communicated to my satisfaction."

The corners of his eyes crease as he assesses her, perhaps judging her seriousness and what it might cost him to deny her request.

"I'm sure the internment director would be happy to apprise you."

Internment implies incarceration. Unease twists Davia's

already unsettled stomach.

They arrive in a quiet corridor and stop before a nondescript door. Bruse keys an access code into an entry panel.

"Your quarters." He extends one arm through the door, and after she passes through, he stands beside the communication station near the door. "And the means to contact His Illuminance the Prince."

With another bow—deeper this time—the commander strides through the door as if his attention is better served elsewhere.

Lights blink on the comm station, awaiting instructions. What can she say to Anin? How can she tell him what has happened to her, how and with whom she has spent these lost months?

Fatigue wears at her limbs, though little time has passed. She cannot speak to Anin looking as she does and visits the *en suite* to clean herself.

By the time she has dressed in the only clean nonmilitary clothes available, her sense of time is distorted. Distracted by concern for Kyran, she strains to focus on the present moment.

An access inquiry chime announces a steward who delivers a tray of freshly prepared food—more than Davia has seen in what feels like forever. Her mouth waters but after the steward departs, Davia settles for some weak tea.

Another chime announces a new visitor. When she opens the door, a man of average height and build with forgettable features bows low. She forgets his name as soon as he introduces himself.

"It is an honor to meet you," he says.

Davia has never met an internment director—a softer title than prison warden—and is not sure what to make of this one. His eyes light up at the prospect of interacting with her—he does not yet know he has no hope of making a good impression.

"I was told you could provide the most information about the activity on . . . the planet."

"Ah, yes, of course you'll want to update the Imperial

Council upon your return." His bearing is confident without being haughty. "I was transferred at their behest to the director position here four months ago."

The Imperial Council is the political arm of the High Queen. The prickle of unease down Davia's spine intensifies.

"And the parameters and scope of this . . . installation?"

Davia does not suppress the disapproval in her tone, not that he appears to notice. His back straightens with professional pride and he smiles at her.

What she learns is alarming.

"The Sifani Forces impounded the enemy ships on arrival. My understanding is the subversives wouldn't talk until extreme measures were taken, and I'm not privy to those details. I'm sure Commander Bruse can provide them if you wish. That's more his area of expertise."

Torture. Bruse, or perhaps the mercenaries, had tortured the Ellodians for information.

The director continues, oblivious to her horror. "Once they'd captured and incarcerated the planet-side terrorists, my presence was requested based on the standard protocol."

All this in the name of the empire, and common enough for established procedures to exist.

He gestures toward a larger display on the far side of her temporary quarters, little more than a viewing lounge outside her sleeping room. When she nods, he bends over the keyboard and enters a string of commands.

"All of the stolen ships have been confiscated. The remaining pirates on board were taken into custody and incarcerated planet-side in internment centers for reconditioning. With your permission?"

Davia steps to one side—not to give way, but to keep herself away from him, apart from him, as if the work he has done for Sifani Prime is a disease, a virus that might spread to her via contact.

The display changes from a hemispheric map to a series of regional feeds, sequential images of various locations.

The pictures of the people nearly undo her.

The men have all been shorn, all hair shaved to the scalp. Their attire is mismatched, and they cluster together in small groups in outdoor fenced yards with minimal cover. Figures huddled on the ground in the background demonstrate the lack of separate sleeping quarters.

Another image reveals a similar compound for women.

"With limited personnel at my disposal, I've been forced to relegate all my staff to guard duty, and we've enough of the riffraff to tend to basic tasks."

He laughs to himself. "I'll say this for these vermin—they scouted fertile terrain. Before we arrived, they'd begun farming. The early crops are coming in now, and we'll be able to harvest the bounty at the end of the season for shipment back to the core systems."

She does not want to ask, she does not want to know, but she must have all the information available to her.

She will not hide from the truth.

"And the children?"

He straightens and frowns, linking his hands behind his back. "I must apologize—the limited staffing and resources here have led to delays in reconditioning. We will soon begin to process adoptions for the younger children, as required, and the older ones will progress into the existing infrastructure as they come of age."

Davia clenches a fist until her nails bite into her skin. She had thought Kyran's mention of abducted children to be the hyperbole of an isolated case, or an exaggeration twisted by limited language skills.

In the name of Sifani Prime, families have been divided and children systematically stripped from their parents.

The director misunderstands her irritation and attempts to placate her. "Please understand this installation is not as well-entrenched as some of the others. A population of this magnitude usually merits a staff six times the one I was assigned, and I was given this project on short notice."

His spine returns. "I assure you, I have extensive experience. I directed the installation on Nerrus Cardinal and the three installations across the Apori Alpha system. We will take longer than usual, I'll admit, but we will meet our targets."

Even if she were to shut down this instance of horrid barbarism, countless more of these abominations exist across Sifani Prime.

Even if she rescues Kyran, how can she justify what has been done to Kyran's people?

"What are the specific charges against the . . . subversives?" The word feels wrong on her tongue.

"The ships were all stolen from reclamation depots along the outer rim, and we have no details of who stole what. As for the subversives themselves, if they're evading imperial forces, they're guilty of something."

Guilty of returning to a place once theirs before the Sifani Empire claimed it as a prize, and now they are treated as dangerous criminals as a result. Is it a crime to be affected by circumstances outside one's control?

He grows nervous at her lengthy silence. "Are there any other questions I can answer?"

Davia cannot speak. She shakes her head, and the man bows his head in confusion and exits.

Saving Kyran is not enough. The misfortune that has befallen Kyran's people is undeserved, and their piracy is at least understandable, if not to be condoned. Their fate demonstrates the treatment awaiting those who dare disagree with the High Queen and her policies.

These are the expressions of Queen Ethelyn's directives. Those who stand against her must be subjugated even to the point of penalizing their children.

It is too immense for Davia to console herself with tears.

She contemplates her next actions and the order of operations gives her some pause. She has already neglected to respond to Anin's messages. Some instinct tells her she will get only one chance to convince him of the horrors committed in the imperial name.

When Davia summons the battlecruiser's commander to her chambers, he bears the weary impatience of a man who believes himself the ultimate authority within his tiny corner of the universe yet forced to play nice with a royal courtier.

Davia omits the pleasantries. "Recall all Sifani forces and make haste to depart this system. Set course for Apori Alpha and proceed at best possible speed." Her plan must be executed in the proper order.

His glare is condescending, exasperated. "High One, His Illuminance Prince Anin has requested my orders are to return you to Meteus."

Davia is exhausted, unsettled, emotionally spent, and mourning the loss of the presence most precious to her, and she is also something more.

"Commander," she says, calm and without emotion. "Do you outrank a Duveri Min Fifth Set?"

His expression changes from tired irritation to self-preserving concern. He pauses long enough to make her point. She waits for him to say the words.

"No, Min . . ." She watches him realize he has never asked her for her name or the proper way to address her.

She holds his gaze until perspiration beads over his lips, and then tilts her head to communicate how much this man is testing her patience.

"Min Davia," she provides.

"Yes, Min Davia. I shall prepare to leave the system, but . . ."

He swallows, too nervous to continue speaking until she arches an eyebrow.

"We don't have enough pilots to fly all the confiscated ships."

"Leave them."

Davia turns to gaze out the viewing window. "They are substandard and most likely require complete refits, and we have other places to be. Withdraw all—and I mean all—Sifani personnel from those ships, and from the planet. Ensure we leave this system in no more than six hours."

Her tone dismisses him, and the hurried click of his boots on the deck confirms his exit.

Ellod is beautiful from this vantage point, and the stars are as majestic as always. Davia stares instead in the direction of the asteroid field and one of the moons beyond it.

Kyran is strong enough to hold on a little longer.

CHAPTER TWENTY-THREE

All day, Kyran is too stunned to do much of anything except wait.

Thoughts churn and fade, and nothing takes hold as she sits at the firepit and stares into the sky waiting for a ship that doesn't appear. By the time she comes back to herself, it's late afternoon and the fire is smoke and charred embers.

The circle from Davia's kim venu that morning is still etched in the sand. Although Kyran's completion of the halem venu granted her a holiday, she draws her own circle beside and behind Davia's, kneels, and speaks the ritual words in little more than a whisper. Her eyes fill with tears when she cuts her arm—but not from the physical pain. She lets the breeze dry her face as she holds her outstretched dagger in front of her.

She wonders what the measure of her worthiness might be, if the ease of her halem venu will now be paid for in this new isolation. That night, she sits by the fire far later than is her habit. More than once, Kyran turns expecting to see Davia only to be brutally reminded anew that she is alone.

Davia will come for her.

The next morning, Kyran awakens with a start when she doesn't feel Davia beside her. Her heartbeat slows as she considers the events of the day before.

Davia would only have told her to stay back if she thought Kyran was in danger. Maybe Davia didn't think the Sifani soldiers would listen to any explanations. Maybe she was afraid they'd arrest Kyran or, worse, kill her on sight. Maybe they thought Davia was compromised, and had taken Davia into custody—

And then Kyran remembers who Davia is.

A royal. A royal whose brother will be High King when Queen Ethelyn dies.

Davia's rescue had been inevitable. Kyran is an idiot for not having considered this before. She fears the impossibility of a Sifani princess lowering herself to come back for an Ellodian rebel, and then she remembers who they are to each other and severs that line of thought.

Davia will come for her.

Kyran performs the kim venu, then eats a quarter ration of meat. She clears the filtration catch, cleans the sand-lock, and brushes the boarding door mesh. She carries ash from the fire ring to the waste pit, then practices her forms in the training area until the midday kim venu. After another quarter ration, she decides to wash in preparation for rescue.

By the time she returns to the canyon, it's time for the evening kim venu. She allows herself a full serving for dinner since she won't need to go hunting again, and stares at the fire until long after the moon rises.

Davia will come for her tomorrow.

Kyran cannot bring herself to clear Davia's circle. By the fourth day, some of the outline has been erased by the wind, and she doesn't want to mark it herself because Davia made it.

She is disgusted at having become pathetic.

Davia will not leave her here. Kyran is not doomed to spend the rest of her life alone on this rock. She trusts Davia. Pretending to ward off the fear Davia will not come, however, is easier than the deeper terror.

As a Sifani royal, Davia may ensure that Kyran is rescued, but is most likely bound for the core systems of Sifani Prime.

What Kyran buries deeper than anything that's ever hurt her before—including being marooned, Benna's death, the death of her own parents—deeper than all those marrow-deep pains is the terrifying thought she may never see Davia again.

Kyran bites her lip hard enough to cut skin, hoping the pain will keep her tears from falling. If she starts crying, she'll never be able to stop, and resisting hurts. Trying to do anything at all hurts.

She surrenders to the sobs. If it's weakness, so be it. No one is here to see.

At sundown, she marks what remains of Davia's circle with stones.

Each night, she practices Venu Pakrim forms by firelight until she can't raise her arms and her legs tremble from the exertion. It doesn't make her fall asleep any faster, but the exhaustion keeps her from tossing and turning as she lies in the dark, and the wind lulls her into a daze.

Something thumps the overhead hull of the ship. Something big, and not a meteor, because the next sounds are heavy sliding and scratching noises followed by another thump.

Kyran clenches her fingers against the pistol she doesn't remember drawing.

Whatever it is moves over the top of the ship from the direction of the aft bay doors. Barefoot and half-dressed, Kyran skulks toward the boarding door, held open by the makeshift screen, and sinks to the deck to peer through the mesh.

A shadow blocks the moonlight. Kyran holds her breath as it passes over the canyon while another thump reverberates through the ship. The shadow resolves itself into a familiar shape.

It's a sheller—far bigger than the one in the pit. Its pincers are as long as Kyran is tall, and the length of its body stretches longer than the overturned wing, its size slowing its gait.

Kyran stays in her uncomfortable crouch, watching its every movement. The ship is too well buried to be moved by the sheller's side-to-side winding crawl, and Kyran is likely safe inside the ship. Her heart races. This beast is far too big for her to handle alone, and the pulse pistol isn't enough firepower to stop it unless Kyran gets not one but several clean shots to its head.

The creature continues its path after crossing the canyon, and Kyran listens at the door until she can no longer hear its motion across the sand and rock.

She retreats to her bunk, curls in the blankets with her back against the bulkhead, one hand on her dagger and the other on the pistol as the wind whistles through the holes in the hull. Sometimes she counts her breaths. Sometimes she mentally recites the kim venu.

Sometimes, she mentally recites the kim venu in Davia's voice.

Midmorning the next day, Kyran builds a perimeter beyond the canyon with stripped wire and anything in the debris piles that makes a clanking noise.

What has she done to incur such disfavor? One catastrophe after another her whole life—has she been cursed?

Is this new punishment because she's learned the martial path of her enemy? She doesn't think of Davia that way anymore, but Davia is still Sifani. Maybe some god she doesn't know about sees it that way, too.

Kyran has endured more difficult times than even heroes in stories have survived. Has she done something to merit this endless suffering after years of countless trials? Something about her warranting the absence of joy?

If so, how can she repent and redeem herself if she doesn't know how she has sinned?

When Kyran is more rational, she's aware none of those things is true. Her emotions get the better of her the more time passes.

It does not stop her from kneeling three times a day and raising her blade, asking the stars to judge her worthy.

The silence is maddening. Kyran went hours without speaking in Davia's company, but this solitary quiet unsettles her. She's alarmed into alertness every time a pebble shifts.

By the third week, her dwindling food supplies force a hunting excursion. She doesn't venture far from the canyon. Since she's the only one eating, she dries most of the meat. Her appetite has waned, and she can only eat half of what she usually consumes.

Once the food stores are addressed, she explores the territory within half a day's walk, confirming nothing has changed and no new tracks have appeared. After she trips and falls flat on her face from moving too quickly in one direction without checking first for obstacles, she slows down. She's uninjured, and remembering no one can help her if something more serious happens dampens her mood further.

She returns to the canyon and takes her old position on the wing of the ship with a plan to sit and attempt to meditate until it's time for the kim venu. The sadness creeps in again, the ache for the sound of Davia working at the table below, and she pushes the pain down deep. Nothing can be done. She must focus on something else.

Instead of closing her eyes, Kyran watches the clouds form and dissipate in the midafternoon sky, and contemplates the puzzle of fetching more firewood from the nearby forest considering she must complete the task with extra caution.

A fast-moving hazy cloud turns into a slow-moving rock before sunlight glints off it and reveals it to be a ship.

Kyran leaps to her feet, and stares at it long enough to

convince herself it's not her imagination. The ship adjusts trajectory and veers towards her position. She knows who it is, who it has to be, and blinks away tears as her hope swells.

Davia has come for her.

Right after that thought comes another. Davia may not be alone.

Kyran takes precautions. She checks the charge on the pulse pistol, cinches the loose straps and connectors on her flight suit, and makes sure her dagger is cocked for easy draw. She fetches her spears though they likely won't do her much good. It feels better to have them close by.

By the time the craft lands in a clearing not far from the canyon, Kyran has identified the markings classifying it as a Sifani transit shuttle with only enough capacity for a small squad.

Kyran crouches behind a boulder in a defensible position.

The ship-width door at the stern disengages with a loud clang and a hiss. As it lowers, a single female figure is revealed, dressed not in the dark Sifani garb Davia wears, but in a spotless white version of Kyran's own filthy flight suit.

Kyran forgets about her cover and stands, dropping her spears in shock as the woman removes her helmet.

Benna stares back, eyes wide.

CHAPTER TWENTY-FOUR

By the time Kyran convinces herself this isn't some kind of fever dream, Benna has crossed the distance between them, her eyes shiny with tears.

"It's true. You're alive." Benna drops her helmet and crashes into Kyran. She wraps her arms around Kyran so tightly, Kyran can't do the same.

Benna pulls away and clutches her shoulders. "We couldn't find any wreckage after the battle, and we searched but your trail was lost and . . ."

The words speed up and Kyran doesn't catch them all. Benna is alive and breathing right in front of her and must be real because she looks so different.

Her hair is shorter, roughly cut and more red than brown. Her skin is darker than the pale Kyran remembers, with freckles across her nose and cheeks. She is leaner and so far from dead, Kyran can't speak until she can.

"I thought the command deck was destroyed. All this time I thought . . . wait, how are you here?" Rationality returns, splashing through her like water. "How did you find me?"

Confusion and hesitancy slow Benna's speech. "An odd story I can tell you on the way back."

"Back?"

Kyran sways when it hits her. She's leaving this place. Benna is here to rescue her from this rock, never to return.

The sudden pang for Davia slams into her guts, and some

small voice of caution keeps Kyran from mentioning her name at all.

"Look at you, Kyran." Benna's horror and pity add to the unease growing in Kyran's belly. "I can't imagine what you've been through."

With Benna's pristine appearance as comparison, Kyran scrutinizes her clothes with new perspective. Davia had offered her spares more than once, but their different dimensions made wearing them more of a hindrance than a help. Though Kyran has done her best to keep the tattered flight suit clean, the many bloodstains are permanent as are some of the deeper stains of dirt. Punctures and tears, both accidental and deliberate, have torn away sections of the arms and legs.

Kyran appears as if she's been through a war, and she has. She is also stronger and more capable than she's ever been. Each scar demonstrates her will to survive. How does Benna compare her to the memory she has of Kyran from all those months ago?

"Well, let's go. I want to show you our new home." Benna pulls Kyran by the hand toward the shuttle.

"Wait." Kyran can't leave. Not yet. "I need to . . ."

What word can possibly describe what she has to do? "I need to prepare."

Benna's expression is indecipherable as she releases Kyran's hand. Kyran retrieves her spears and turns back toward the canyon. Benna's foreign presence is like an itch in the small of her back.

They're side by side when Benna stops at the boundary wall and gawks.

"This is where you've been living all this time?"

"Not at first, but . . . yes." Discomfited, Kyran waits for the obvious question: what happened to the pilot of the crashed ship?

Benna doesn't ask.

The first thing Kyran does is cover the firepit's coals with sand. They would burn out on their own, so the gesture is symbolic.

And then her steps slow as she evaluates everything—all the collected shells, the carefully crafted tools and the makeshift inventions she and Davia have constructed over the last several months that have saved or improved their lives and won't be needed elsewhere. Either all of it is valuable enough to come with her or all of it should be left behind.

"Is that a Sifani frigate?"

"Yes. My fighter crashed a few days' walk from here and there was no salvage. I—I followed the smoke to this ship."

The disquiet inside her worsens. She wants to be happier about Benna's arrival, about the fact she is alive, but her cousin is a stranger.

Maybe later Kyran will fill in the details she's omitting. Her emotions are too close to the surface, with the potential to shake her apart.

She rests her spears by the ship's door and climbs inside, eyes adjusting to the lack of light.

"What is all this?" Benna's disdain gives Kyran pause. She leans out the door to see Benna peering at the meat drying rack, at the rudimentary tools on the workbench, and the broken components awaiting repair.

Benna turns her head, wrinkling her nose at whatever she smells. "It's a wonder you survived like this at all."

"Considering the many ways I could have died, this place has been a haven."

Benna is chagrined. "I am grateful you're alive, Princess."

Yet another jolt hits Kyran and for a long moment, she considers the life she left behind and what it will mean to return to it. She has to focus on what she can control now, not what might occur later.

Back inside the ship, Kyran reassesses its familiar contents, searching for some token or memento of her time in Davia's arms—something she can take with her. She contemplates the threadbare blankets of a bed she'll never share with Davia again. Nothing here will suffice.

That's not true. She has Davia's pulse pistol in a holster

strapped to her thigh, and she has the knife Davia made for her.

She draws the blade and holds it in her hands.

"Do you really need that thing anymore?" Disapproval drips from Benna's lips where she stands at the door.

Anger surges through Kyran though she doesn't speak or move. Benna takes a full step back, one arm raised in defense.

"Sorry, I just . . . I mean it looks like . . . well, where you're going doesn't require that kind of weapon."

Her tone is more polite, but the damage is done. Kyran slides her knife back into place and rests her hand on the hilt for a moment before letting her hand fall.

"Yes," she says, because explaining will take hours. The more she thinks about it, the more she wants to keep her life with Davia to herself.

Benna nods, her brow furrowed.

When Kyran shuts the door of the ship, the finality of it shatters something inside her. Kyran gazes around one more time, delaying the inevitable.

She can't leave without stopping at the ritual space one more time.

What she did on this span of dirt built her into who she is now. Davia healed her, helped Kyran become someone new. Someone who can face the uncertainty of returning to her old life.

Benna is probably wondering why she's staring at the ground.

Kyran drops down to one knee, touches the stones as she searches for any faint marks remaining from the circle Davia drew. She needs to go, she wants to go, to not be here anymore, but she doesn't want to leave. Leaving means putting everything she shared here with Davia behind her, and she doesn't think she'll ever be ready.

"What are you doing?" Benna asks, hesitant and not unkind.

Kyran closes her eyes. She tries to imagine how she appears, down on one knee staring at a circle of rocks in the sand. Benna wouldn't understand.

Kyran pictures Davia drawing her blade across her arm and raising her blade to the sky.

Before the ache in her chest can manifest into the tears burning behind her eyes, Kyran stands and turns toward the shuttle.

"Saying goodbye."

With each step out of and beyond the canyon, she pledges to remember what she has learned, and who taught her.

As she approaches the shuttle, she wonders how she ever thought Davia would appear in such a ship. It's a basic unarmed transport, the kind Ellodians often use to move personnel and goods. It occurs to Kyran as they're boarding Benna never answered her question.

"How did you find me?"

Benna claims the command seat and engages the engines. The shuttle hums and Kyran flinches at the vibration. Nothing is wrong; it's been forever since she experienced the normal start-up sequence of a ship. Benna begins the preflight check and dances her fingers with familiarity over the various buttons and switches.

"Four days ago, we received an anonymous relay from the core systems containing only your name and these coordinates."

Davia.

Kyran swallows and her heart feels like it's pounding a path out of her chest. "Four days?"

"I thought it was a trap. The Sifani occupation ended three weeks ago, and we argued about it until I decided to take the risk myself."

"Occupation?" Kyran is aware she's repeating words back to Benna.

"Let me get us in the black and I'll tell you from the beginning." The ground pulls away as Benna flies from the canyon. Kyran clenches a fist in her lap and the tears come. She wipes them away.

How much of herself is she leaving behind?

Then again, getting off this moon is the first step in a path leading back to Davia.

Once they've ascended above the lower atmosphere, the weightlessness that used to be so common is foreign.

Benna settles in behind the controls. "After the battle where—where I thought I lost you—"

"How did you survive, Benna?" Kyran can't help interrupting. "I saw the explosions on the bridge."

"When the attack came, I was so worried about you being exposed in open space, I'd gone down to the flight deck to meet you. Afterward, we scanned for remnants of your ship. We didn't find anything."

Kyran relives her side of the events Benna describes.

"When no additional Sifani troops appeared after the first squadron, we thought it was a random patrol. We hoped we'd covered our tracks well enough, so we proceeded with the colonization."

Benna wipes a hand over her face, the gesture revealing her weariness. "Things were going well until some Sifani soldiers arrived four months ago. They interrogated some of us for information about the previous squadron. It was like they were looking for something important, and we couldn't figure out what it was."

Not what. Who. The whole time, the Sifanis had been looking for Davia, so close and yet so very far.

"And then things got worse. More of the Sifanis came and corralled us on the planet's surface. They imprisoned the men and women in separate sections and isolated all the children." Her eyes are shadowed by the horrors she must have seen.

"Then three weeks ago every single Sifani loaded up and left."

"The planet?" Kyran asks.

"The entire system." Benna doesn't sound happy about it. "They even abandoned the ships they'd reclaimed."

Kyran can't form the puzzle in her mind—there are too many pieces. She knows without question Davia is the solution.

"When we received the message about you, we couldn't trust

it, since no one else has been in the system with us besides the Sifanis, but I . . . I had to know."

The shuttle clears the asteroid belt, and Benna pivots toward the planet enveloping the view.

Kyran is captivated by its brilliance. This is the world her parents used to say would someday be her home.

I have no shelter but the stars and no home but where I kneel.

The words pass through her mind and the feelings are overwhelming.

"Strap in," Benna says as she prepares for atmospheric entry.

The silent vacuum of space gives way to the roar of thermosphere, followed by the placid calm of stratosphere.

Kyran hasn't been on a world like this in what feels like half a lifetime. Before being marooned, it had been years since she'd stood planet-side, and that distant world had been nothing like this one.

Glorious colors stun Kyran the most. The greens and blues are different from the browns and reds she's been staring at for months. The mountains are purple and white, the lakes the shuttle flies over are as blue as the sky, the high-stretching trees are plentiful and have too many shades of green to count.

A clump of white resolves into a small settlement as they approach. Colonization tents surround more permanent structures under construction. Nearby, a field of churned-up mud reveals the former landing spot of a large spaceship.

People move between the tents and buildings with purpose, carrying supplies and operating machinery. It's all so much, Kyran finds it hard to breathe. These are her people, but . . .

"Benna, I can't—"

She's not sure what to say, and Benna nods.

"Why don't you clean up first before you return to the masses?"

"Yes," Kyran says, because that's part of what she wants and nowhere near what she needs.

On the far edge of the settlement, another field is a designated landing area, with more personnel darting between several grounded transports. Though Kyran is unprepared, the shuttle is once again on the ground and powering down.

Benna stands at the stern while the boarding door opens. Bright sunlight and temperate warmth await.

Kyran takes her first breath of the clear and crisp air, and it stings in her nostrils with the scent of growing things.

"You first," Benna says, eyes full of questions. "Welcome home, Princess."

No home but where I kneel.

With one hand on the hilt of her dagger to center herself, Kyran steps onto the green grass of Ellod.

Hot water sluices down Kyran's body. Dirty water swirls at her feet and disappears into the drain. She rinses everywhere before she reaches for the soap, and then the dirt removal starts anew.

She fights the sobs for fear of the sound carrying past her stall, though Benna made sure the communal washroom was empty. She's back with her people and Benna is alive, and still Kyran cries. It doesn't feel like relief. It feels like mourning.

Two full wash and rinse cycles later, she steps into the dressing area to dry herself and freezes at her reflection in the full-length mirror.

Her naked body is all angles and strength as if chiseled from stone, nothing but muscle and bone. Her hair—longer than it's ever been and so blond it's white—falls halfway down her back.

Her skin is tan in contrast and riddled with scars and scratches. The largest scars—the rough blemish of the burn on her arm from the crash of her fighter, the healed gash on her leg from the first shelled creature's bite, a few more bites on her other leg and her lower back—are darker than the rest and remind her how far she's come.

Kyran is weary of crying. She wipes her face with the towel and eases into a clean ill-fitting flight suit. She adjusts a few straps, pulls the pistol holster, her dagger, and the dirty threadbare belt from her old suit, and ties them in place.

Her last act before leaving the washroom is to toss her old flight suit into the waste bin. It feels disrespectful, but she cannot look back.

Benna is waiting outside, and Kyran can't let herself look forward either.

"You ready?" Benna asks with a nervous smile.

Kyran isn't. She nods anyway.

The flight from the moon to Ellod and the tilt of the planet itself have added hours to Kyran's already taxing day. Everyone in the settlement gathers for the evening meal, and the path from the landing area to the largest colonization tent is blocked by several groups of people.

The colonization supervisor, Fillip Jonas, is first. He greets her with a warm smile and keeps his distance as if sensing her reticence. The dam is burst by their interaction and a small crowd forms, all familiar faces.

Benna guides her through another group, and the next. Kyran has to have been greeted by everyone in the fleet by now. When she follows Benna through one of the side entrances, more people await inside the tent.

A cheer in welcome swells, complete with stomps and whistles. It's all for her and she's grateful, and it's too much, and too loud, with too many people.

Once again, Benna runs interference.

"We're all glad to have Princess Kyran Loyal back with us." Her voice is distorted and tinny through the aged public address system. "Let's give her a chance to settle in before we put her back to work."

Everyone laughs and applauds the well-delivered joke, and Kyran's shoulders tense further. The role she played as the fleet fixer will be in high demand as the colony grows. Benna may not mean for her to resume her duties immediately, but Kyran will be expected to contribute sooner rather than later.

Everything presses in as Kyran joins Benna at a table near the front of the room. Kyran ignores the seat she's bidden and moves to one along the wall so no one can approach her without her seeing them first. Benna frowns and offers to bring her dinner.

No matter what direction Kyran turns her head, someone is looking at her. Some wave, some offer reserved smiles, some stare. The names don't come to her quickly, and she wonders what they think of how she appears.

A closer look at some of the settlers reveals hollow eyes and faces hungry for something other than food. Some hide flinches when another gets too close. The children are silent when they should be vibrant and energetic. They have all been through something as harrowing as her own experience, and when they meet her eyes, she senses their need for something she can't define and has no idea how to provide.

By the time Benna returns to the table, Kyran is staring at her hands and trying to regulate her own breathing.

Benna sets a plate heaped high with food in front of Kyran. Back on *Althea*, the rations hadn't been this plentiful. Steamed, grilled or mashed root vegetables—some varieties Kyran doesn't recognize—along with meat and bread spill over the sides of the plate.

"I wasn't sure what you'd want or how hungry you might be."

The uncertainty in Benna's voice stirs Kyran's guilt.

Conversation rolls around her. She doesn't speak. Instead she tries to listen, to learn more about the life being built here. Outside, the sun has set and she twitches with the need to perform the ritual that has given her respite these last few weeks since Davia left.

At the thought of Davia, a wave of nausea upsets her overfull stomach. She winces.

"More food than you're used to?" Benna appears to regret her words once they've crossed her lips. She doesn't seem to know what to do with Kyran.

"It's good." Kyran sets aside her discomfort. She struggles to remember how to pretend to be social. "Isn't this where I ask for the tour?"

Relieved, Benna nods and stands. Kyran rises as well, holding her mostly full plate.

"Leave it for the kitchen crew."

Kyran shakes her head. "No need to make more work for anyone."

She carries her plate over to one of the people standing by the serving tables. A young woman as tall as Kyran, with ebony skin, chin-length black hair and rich brown eyes, bounces on her toes at Kyran's approach.

Kyran doesn't recognize her. She gestures with her plate. "This is delicious, and I don't want to waste it. Can I store it somewhere for later?"

Surprise joins the eagerness on the woman's face. "I can take care of it for you, Princess."

"Call me Kyran."

The woman takes the plate. "Don't worry about this, Kyran. When you want it, ask for me."

Kyran stares. The woman stares back until Kyran can't resist a wry half grin. "It might help to know your name."

"Oh. Lora. I'm from *Ellod's Light.*"

A moment passes while Kyran pulls the name from her memory—a passenger vessel transporting many families with small children.

Kyran stretches out her hand. "Pleased to meet you."

When she clasps Lora's hand in her own, the fingers are gnarled, as if they have been broken and reset poorly more than once. Lora squeezes back and her eyes crinkle and disappear as she smiles.

Exhaustion weighs her limbs, but Kyran can't sleep.

She lies atop the bedcovers fully dressed including her boots, which has attracted more than a few curious glances. The bunk rooms aren't as crowded as they'd been on *Althea*, where dozens of people slept in the same hot racks around the clock. Here each of the smaller temporary buildings contains a handful of double-stacked bunks, some of them permanently assigned and decorated with flowers or vines.

The day has been far longer than normal, and every cell of her body is spent from the ups and downs of adrenaline and its aftermath. Kyran is unable to relax. The unfamiliar sounds of other people breathing in sleep, the foreign ticks and whines of equipment settling into the ground or shifting in the wind outside—all of it combines to deny her true rest.

Benna sleeps nearby. After she got Kyran settled with a bunk along one wall—intuiting Kyran wouldn't want to be exposed by the open bunks in the middle of the room—she disappeared to take care of other duties. When Benna returned, Kyran closed her eyes and pretended to be asleep, avoiding any more questions about how she was settling in.

Neither does she want to talk about her life while she was marooned. Her time with Davia might not be easily explained. That she was stranded with a Sifani and made peace to save her own life would be difficult to share, yes. Although Benna might understand.

Her relationship with a Sifani royal, however . . . Kyran can't find the words to begin that conversation and chooses not to have it at all. Nor can she explain how she feared Benna dead and never managed to avenge her.

She gives up pretending she can sleep. More importantly, she's left something vital undone.

With stealth she's honed over months in the wild, Kyran rises and tugs the blanket from the bed. She tosses it over one shoulder and slips out the door.

Outside, the stars are familiar, a constant detail bringing a small measure of peace. In a nearby glade between the bunkhouse and the landing area, the leaves on a dozen trees whisper in the breeze. Kyran finds one tree with more dirt and grass at its base than scrub brush. She throws the blanket over the thick roots and walks a few paces away from the tree.

She etches a circle with her boots and kneels in its center.

Three weeks of separation haven't eased the wrongness of Davia's absence beside her when she performs the kim venu.

The ritual words wash away the remnants of the day's stress, though not the longing for Davia. When Kyran draws her dagger across her arm, her heartbeat settles into a rhythm that eases her mind. She raises the blade to the sky and asks the stars for worthiness, and the tears do not come as she feared they might.

After, Kyran curls into her improvised nest at the base of the tree, covers herself with the blanket and lays her head on the root at her shoulder.

Here, the only sound is the wind. She's asleep minutes after she closes her eyes.

CHAPTER TWENTY-FIVE

From Ellod to Apori Alpha, from Nerrus Cardinal to Ragan and now on Forge III, Davia demands the battlecruiser's commander escort her through several Council-mandated installations in the realm. In transit, she relearns what she thought she understood about the governance of the empire, and what she discovers changes everything.

Across Sifani Prime, one hundred thousand prisoners are incarcerated in these "reconditioning" or "internment" stations. Thousands of children have been separated from their parents.

In addition, millions of people in the outer regions have lost livelihoods and resources in tithes to the empire, and their worlds suffer the consequences of the core systems' opulence.

Anin has sent several messages requesting real-time communication, and the more she learns, the more Davia is certain she must collect as much evidence as possible before they speak. Otherwise, she will be eliminated as a treasonous threat to the crown, and nothing will change.

Time passes quickly and slowly at the same time. Kyran is always on her mind and in her heart. She cannot give in to her yearning. Protecting Kyran means more now than keeping her free. She trusts someone received her message and rescued Kyran from her isolation.

"Min Davia."

The battlecruiser commander trails after her. He sounds out of breath, not that Davia cares much about his well-being. Davia has grown weary of his blatant self-interest and the sound of his voice, which lately borders on whining.

The wind whips through her cloak, cutting through her clothes to her skin. The sunlight on Forge III is weak and watery, the atmosphere almost too thin to breathe. Davia is undeterred as she marches across the open loading platform between shipping bays.

"I have a tight schedule, Commander Bruse." Several shipping convoys converge on this production base, and Davia has been informally inspecting manifests. Acting in an unofficial capacity means no formal requests need to be filed, and the only way to obtain what she needs is to personally interject herself in the transport of freight from one connection to another.

Face to face, no one will refuse a Min Fifth Set.

The exchange of goods from the outer sectors to the core systems is all one-way. Few services or materials are distributed back to the outer rim, and Davia has discovered many reports of the constant delay of promised medical or financial aid.

The empire takes much and returns little.

"Yes, I understand . . ." Bruse's next words are stolen by the wind.

Davia steps into the shadow of a hangar bay door. The structure blocks the elements, but the cold persists. This is the third such spontaneous inspection Davia has performed this week. Her plan needs time to coalesce, and sooner or later word will reach one of Ethelyn's many spies and Davia's movement will be anticipated and restricted.

"Min Davia, please—"

The pleading attracts her attention. Bruse has been increasingly deferential, but he has never resorted to begging.

Davia stops. "Five minutes."

He passes a hand over his thinning hair in nervous discomfort. Bruse is a lifetime military man, and not one to break protocol even in posture. Davia is not looking forward to what he has to say.

"His Illuminance Prince Anin—"

She fights the urge to roll her eyes. Her brother's messages have become more insistent.

"I will review the missives later—"

"Please forgive the interruption, Min Davia," he says to Davia's surprise. "A channel is open right now and the prince insists he will not disconnect until he speaks with you, and—and—"

Blatant fear fills his eyes, suggesting he has been threatened. Davia can no longer avoid the inevitable and requests the call be routed to her private quarters back on the docked battlecruiser.

The connection completes, and for the first time in nearly a year Davia sets eyes on her brother. The tears come so quickly, they stun her. She wipes them without shame and offers a wan smile.

"Hello, Anin."

His shoulders rise and fall with the rigor of his breathing, and his brow is furrowed in anger, but his eyes are wet.

She wants to tell him about all that has happened, how her entire being has changed, and this open communication is no place for such vulnerability. She had forgotten this, the commonplace tension to all their distant conversation conducted as if someone is surveilling them.

"I had begun to doubt they had actually found you." He has aged in her absence, with a new tightness around his eyes.

"And yet here I am."

"Not where you should be. I expect that obsequious pimple of a man to deliver you so I can welcome you properly back to the living."

"Not on Meteus."

He frowns. "Why not? Must you bow to the Jeweled Circle before you can return to your family?"

She cannot tell him yet. Not like this. "Proving I still live is taking longer than I anticipated. I am nearly finished."

"I thought you were dead for months, Davia. Even when Mother tried to convince me otherwise, I persisted and paid for the search from my personal treasury—"

"Once I have access to my funds, I can reimburse you the cost of—"

Anin explodes. "I do not care about the damned coin, Davia."

He has not raised his voice to her in decades, and never in anger. She is not afraid of him but it silences her, because she has never seen her brother lose control like this. If anything, she worries about him, and what her disappearance exacted from him.

His face clears of his outburst, an apology in expression if not words.

"I cannot come to Meteus yet, Anin." She will not speak a word anywhere on that planet of the treason she plans. Neither of her father's children are fools. "Perhaps this is an opportunity for a long overdue personal tour of those wineries you are so fond of. Your favorite one."

Davia deliberately omits the name of the place she proposes, and in the next instant, recognition and wariness flash in her brother's eyes, conveying his understanding.

"So, all this . . ." he says with a gesture of decadent humor, matched in his voice and not his eyes. He may not like it, but the confrontation at least is resolved. "All this is merely your attempt to make sure we reunite over my finest vintage."

"It has been a long while since I have enjoyed decent wine, and I want the best."

He stares at her for a full minute and then nods. "Agreed."

Davia's relief is palpable.

He reaches forward as if to sever the connection and stops. "I am pleased to see your face, Davia."

"And I yours, brother."

In her ever-expanding game of kings and pawns, Davia has claimed a crucial piece.

Anin rescinds his directive to Commander Bruse, who stops pestering Davia to travel to Meteus. Her final instruction to him is to deliver her to Duveri, which he does at best possible speed.

The battlecruiser docks at a looming space station in orbit. When she takes her leave of the ship, she limits her gratitude to a nod at Commander Bruse, who accepts it with a bow. Once she disembarks, she is on familiar territory with no need of escort or assistance.

The last time she was here, Gale and the others were with her. She mourns them anew, but does not allow her grief to pause her forward motion, and secures a shuttle from the station to Duveri's surface.

Davia's heart soars when they approach the planet. Outside the planet-side transport station, Davia visits an ancillary meditative garden abundant with hedges and rich vegetation, muting the sound of nearby transports. She closes her eyes and breathes in thick, humid air—some part of her returning to its center.

For the longest time, Duveri was home, the place she felt most herself, free and complete. Whenever she left, her return was marked by rituals such as these: a solitary moment in a garden like this, where the fountain and the insects calmed her thoughts, where she centered her being after a visit off-world.

Now, Davia finds that home is a person, one who is far away. Every familiar sight is one she is eager to share with Kyran, and much work remains before such a dream might become an achievable reality.

The frenetic pace she has kept since her rescue comes to an end. The scent of Duveri soil reminds her to adjust the universe to her pace, not the other way around.

Although she is tired and craves rest, one more reunion is in order.

A hired ground transport takes her from the city's center to its outskirts. The manor house door is open before Davia sets both feet on the ground.

Izabel looks the same—her hair is the same length as it was on Davia's last visit. At the sight of Davia, Izabel's composure breaks, her eyes fill with tears, and she leaps from the porch.

She meets Davia halfway up the flagstone walk. Izabel says nothing as she wraps Davia in a bone-crushing embrace. She does not let go until Davia pulls away.

Izabel clasps Davia's arms, looking her up and down.

"The reports we received said all ships were lost. I would have come myself if I'd thought . . ."

She blinks more tears away.

"I doubt you could have done anything, Iza." The thought of Izabel somehow embroiled in all the internment installation horror . . . Izabel is capable, without question. Davia would want no one she cares about involved in the debacle.

Izabel's searching gaze bores into Davia's. Not for the first time, Davia feels as if the analysis is intensified by Izabel's will. All her life, Davia has kept secrets, and most of the ones she's successfully kept from Izabel are because Izabel did not dig any further out of respect.

"Something's changed," Izabel says.

Davia hides nothing. She had hoped to reveal everything in her own time. Izabel is too observant.

Izabel's eyes widen as her lips part with a gasp. Sadness sparks in her eyes before she schools her face to something less revealing.

The smile she offers is bittersweet and soft. "Tell me about her."

The afternoon hours pass to evening as Davia tells her tale. A pummeling rain falls as they sit at Izabel's dining table much as they always have, with delectable food and delicious wine filling the space between them. Davia consumes far less of each than was her habit on previous visits.

She recounts the battle, the lives lost and the crash, the months on the moon, and the relationship that developed between her and Kyran. The memories sweep through her as she conveys the highlights. She keeps many of the details to herself—of Kyran with her untrained stance and meager weapons yet formidable presence, of Kyran on her knees in her own circle, of Kyran in her arms covered in sweat, spent yet hungry for more of Davia's touch—and she aches at the thought of them.

Davia shakes off her musings and tells Izabel about the internment installations.

Izabel leans back in her seat, a measuring look in her eyes. "You believe the Jeweled Circle knows something about the situation?"

"Yes, and I must determine how much before Ethelyn shuts down any further investigation."

Izabel arches an eyebrow at Davia's treasonous disrespect of the High Queen's title. "How long do you think you can hide from the High Queen?" Izabel asks.

Her implication is accurate, but it does not keep Davia from making a rude noise. "I am merely being cautious, not hiding."

Izabel rolls her eyes. "Fine. How long do you think you can . . . evade the High Queen's attention? Does that soothe your ego?"

Some chagrin settles Davia as she sips from her glass of wine. "As long as I have to."

She is reluctant to disclose much more. She still trusts Izabel. That hasn't changed.

The lights framing the garden spill into the dining room where they sit in the dark.

"What's next?" Izabel asks. "It's not in your nature to let this go on as it has, and you're here, which means you already have a plan to stop it."

Davia allows herself the luxury of a deep and audible sigh. "First, I must prove I am still alive. If possible, I sway the Jeweled Circle to my cause and then—"

"After all this time of refusing their invitations to join the Consortium, you're going to attempt to garner their favor? You don't ask for much, do you?"

Perhaps it seems outlandish from Izabel's perspective. Davia knows the political weight of the Jeweled Circle is contingent upon the belief their position is intractable, infallible, and just. The atrocities committed under the express sanction of the throne will shatter that perception. Either the Jeweled Circle knew of the internment installations and did nothing, or were unaware and therefore less omnipotent than the image they project.

"The Jeweled Circle's next formal session isn't for another two months," Izabel says. "I suspect you don't have that long to wait."

"Min Estebin has already agreed to see me, to provide witness to my continued existence." One of Davia's old instructors is now a member of the Jeweled Circle. "I will apprise him of what I have learned."

Davia will approach him alone and offer a way out of the potential political quandary. The Jeweled Circle has far more to lose than she does.

"With his guidance, I am counting on the Jeweled Circle to . . . consider the bigger picture."

Davia slides her glass away, finished for the night. Even in this moment of relaxation, she cannot afford to let down her guard. "Then I will meet with my brother."

He is the linchpin. If she can convince Anin of her cause, Ethelyn cannot stop them. If not . . . Davia does not want to think about what she might have to do to fight both her brother and his mother.

Izabel arches her elegant eyebrows in shock. "You're going to Meteus with this."

"Absolutely not. I will meet him elsewhere." Davia shares no more about that, for Izabel's safety.

Izabel turns uncharacteristically timid. "Are you doing all this for her, Davia?"

Over the hours since Davia's arrival and revelation, Izabel has kept her sorrow to herself, and now her characteristic confidence leaches from her voice.

"Not for her, Iza." Davia's plan is not some kind of romantic gesture. Some of the faces Davia has seen in the last few weeks haunt her, and the impact of what she must do is immense. "I admit were it not for her, I would not have paid attention. I've spent far too many years turning my back on the monarchy and the empire, and so it is because of her I must face the truth."

Davia strokes the stem of her glass. "I can no longer deny what is within my circle, and doing so now goes against everything I am, everything we are."

When the night comes to an end, Izabel offers Davia a guest room, and their parting is less tense than Davia might have imagined considering who they used to be to each other. In the morning, their goodbyes are brief and heartfelt.

Davia climbs into the back of another ground transport. By the time the manor house has receded from her view, she is already focused on the next challenge.

CHAPTER TWENTY-SIX

Kyran no longer has nightmares about shelled creatures finding her in the woods, though she often dreams of Davia. No messages have come from Sifani Prime, and Kyran can't initiate communication of her own without attracting attention or questions for which she has no answers.

The idea that she and Davia are lost to each other forever is too terrible to contemplate, so she waits and adapts somewhat to a busy life on Ellod.

On the tree-lined bank of a stream not far from the main settlement, Kyran has erected a simple, functional, single-occupancy structure with its own *en suite* and kitchen area. Her new home has more room than the overturned corridor on Davia's ship where she lived for most of a year.

After her sunrise kim venu, Kyran explores the nearby wilds until duty calls her to her people. She assists with the colonization efforts, an endless endeavor with an ever-growing list of projects. Sometimes Benna expects her to participate in sessions with the Ellodian council—former captains of the larger fleet vessels, elders, and leaders of various settlement task groups, all led by Benna.

Kyran adds little to those sessions, and her time would be better served elsewhere. Benna, however, is insistent.

When Kyran returns to her tent after a long morning of fishing, Benna is pacing in agitation.

"You're late. Again." Benna follows her inside. "The council has a full docket today, not to mention Farr's trial."

Farr was an old compatriot of Kyran's father, and after the Loyals were executed, he became one of the more militant members of their community. His ilk believe independence is worth any cost, no matter how bloody.

Kyran puts her fishing gear away and washes her hands. "The council doesn't need me. They're smarter and more capable than you give them credit for."

"Are you listening? Farr's trial is today."

During the Sifani occupation, Farr and his minions devised a plan to destroy the docked ship serving as their enemy's command post. Four Ellodian children had been in the ship's medical bay receiving treatment for some plant contagion, which hadn't stopped Farr from attempting to execute his plan.

Two of the children were injured in the explosion. One lost an arm, and the other lies in a coma.

The Sifanis captured Farr and his people. When the occupation ended, the council decided the militants would stand trial for their actions.

Farr had few supporters to begin with, and the handful of people who followed him have already been tried and penalized. Only his trial remains.

Kyran sits on her pallet and swaps her hunting boots for a less rugged pair she wears when in the colony proper. "How could I not hear you? You're practically screaming."

Benna crosses her arms over her chest, and Kyran readies herself for another lecture. She holds up a hand to try to stop it before Benna starts.

"I understand you think I should be at the council meeting. But why should I be on the judgment panel for events that happened when I wasn't even here?"

"After all everyone endured during the occupation, your presence will bolster morale. You need to be seen as part of the leadership."

"Benna—"

"What is wrong with you?" Benna's frustration bleeds into

anger. "It's like you don't care what everyone else has experienced around here. Every single person on this planet has been through some kind of trauma, and they still care for one another, support one another, contribute to this world we're trying to build together. You act like you're the only one who's been through something terrible. No—"

Benna wards off any interruption. "No, I don't know what it was like there, and no, I don't know what you've been through. You won't tell me. You never talk about it and bite my head off when I ask, and not once—not a single time—have you asked what I went through while you were lost, not the torture I endured or the grief I felt when you—"

Shame flares inside Kyran. Benna has always been strong, and the pain in her eyes demonstrates that sometimes strength isn't enough against the unfathomable.

"Losing you felt like a knife in the guts," Benna says. "I—I try to remember you've always closed yourself off when you're in pain. I don't like it, but I understand.

"What I don't understand is why you're not trying to fit in. This is our home now, Kyran. These are our people, and you hold yourself off from them like they're beneath you somehow."

"That's not true."

"You won't stay in the bunkhouses. You take most of your meals alone. You disappear for hours at a time, and no one has any idea where you are."

"I can take care of myself." Being alone helps Kyran with the loneliness, the ache of missing Davia.

"That's not the point. You're supposed to be preparing to lead these people, and instead you're like a ghost. You practice some ritual no one has ever seen, you carry a Sifani pistol and that ugly knife with you everywhere. Are you even Ellodian anym—"

Kyran is on her feet before Benna can finish her sentence. Benna stops talking in shock.

The words have burned like acid. Kyran seethes, forcefully slowing her breaths until she can speak without raising her voice.

"Benna, you are the only family I have left. I can never thank you enough for all you've done for me, for us, and for Ellod, and I am grateful."

She tilts her head forward, undeterred by the fear in Benna's eyes. "You speak of things you don't understand."

Memories flicker through Kyran's mind of Davia speaking those same words, and where that moment has led them. The images squeeze her chest as always.

She straps her boots and leaves without another word. Benna follows silently behind her.

Will they ever again feel at ease around each other, or has another thing been lost?

A long folding table acts as the council's panel. Twelve others, one of them Benna, fill out the rest of the table, while Kyran sits at the end. The afternoon is warm, and the air in the mess tent is close with too many bodies and not enough ventilation.

Farr stands defiant several steps away from the table, hands bound before him. He is a tall and slender man, with an unyielding temperament diminishing his good looks. Behind him and around the sides of the tent, most of the settlement's residents sit or stand in attendance.

"Were you aware children were on board?" Benna asks.

"Yes, and I was saddened by that." Farr doesn't look regretful at all. "But it would have been foolish to waste the opportunity we had to rid Ellod of those tyrants."

So, he was willing to pay the price with the blood of children. Kyran wants to strike him where he stands.

His meager defense is presented, much of it the usual diatribe against Sifani rule and little about his actual crime.

Kyran isn't bored, but she peers out a nearby window at the bright day outside because she isn't contributing either. Her vote is only necessary when the council's total results in a tie. This man is a threat to their future, and as the council deliberates, she hopes they will not be lenient.

Benna clears her throat. "Farr, you have been found guilty of reckless endangerment, conspiracy, and acting against the authority of the council. We will now discuss your punishment."

"I choose the old law," Farr says. "Princess, I ask for your judgment."

Kyran turns in surprise as he glares in challenge. Classic Ellodian law states a citizen can ask the reigning monarch to deliver punishment, circumventing the traditional judgment by council or jury. What is implied is a request for clemency.

Benna sputters. "This is outrageous. No one has cited that law in decades and she hasn't been crowned yet."

"Are we or are we not Ellodian?" Farr's tone is scathing, taunting Kyran as their staring match continues. "We came to this planet to rebuild what we had lost, including the old ways." He addresses Kyran. "You are the heir to the throne, and whether you accept the crown or not, you must abide by its traditions."

He sneers at her. Her whole life, he's indirectly accused her of being an ineffective puppet for her parents' thwarted idealism, which he claimed was too lenient.

She stares back without blinking while Benna speaks again.

"Princess Kyran is the rightful heir, yes, but—"

Benna stops when Kyran raises her hand.

"Today, this one time," Kyran says, and her voice sounds weary to her own ears, "I will stand by the old law and offer judgment."

Farr holds his head higher, a twist to his lips as if he knows what she will do.

Kyran is not the young woman he remembers. When she was younger, she found him intimidating. Now she is not as timid or uncertain or lenient as he must believe her to be.

The council makes their recommendations for his punishment. One suggests death, and the others quickly suppress the idea. They've all come too far to start killing each other now, Benna says, and in some ways Kyran agrees, but a domineering coward like Farr will never change.

The councilors fall silent. Farr is smug in his certainty of what comes next.

"Exile." Kyran offers her judgment without moving, without looking away from him.

He dares to smile. "Ellod is a big planet. Our paths will never cross again."

Kyran shakes her head. "You misunderstand. Ellod has no place for you."

Farr's eyes widen, the only indication of his surprise.

The silence in the room is heavy. Kyran can bear it. "You will be given an unarmed transport shuttle, flight rations and water, and you will leave this system. If you ever return, you will be shot down."

Incredulous, he protests. "You can't expect me to survive with one ship and limited supplies."

"I did." Kyran neglects to mention she wasn't alone. The restrictions were the same, and she owes him no justification for her decision.

"The law states—"

"You cite the old laws, but you do not understand them."

His true face, one of conceited self-righteousness, reveals itself. "You presume to tell me—"

"Protect Ellod's future." Kyran interrupts without raising her voice. "One of our greatest tenets so our children, our hope and light who shine as brightly as the stars, are protected and given every opportunity. Safety is the minimum requirement of that obligation. Which you have apparently forgotten."

He glares, persisting in what he must think is a battle of wills, except she isn't fighting. He has no leverage here and has asked for her absolute judgment.

Kyran will give it to him.

She leans forward and keeps her voice as calm as before. "This betrayal of who we are will not be tolerated, from you or anyone else. Your name will be stricken from the records, and we will not speak it. All who remain will understand this can never happen again."

Confusion and a small measure of fear finally appear in his expression.

Kyran eases her shoulders and settles back in her chair. "You asked for and have been given consideration by the old laws. My judgment is final."

"You can't do this," he says though he's already lost. "Rudd Loyal would not have gone this far. You call this mercy? Even Althea—"

The dam bursts, and she is on her feet.

"Do not invoke my mother's name."

No one makes a sound. Kyran has never raised her voice like this to anyone in present company.

"You justify your blatant disregard for the well-being of our children, and you want my mercy?"

She clenches her fists at her sides to keep from coming around the table. "Fine. Death on Ellod today or take your chances elsewhere. If you dare to set foot on Ellod again, I will shoot you myself. Choose, and choose now. Either way, I'm glad this is the last time I'll see your face."

She waves at the guards and refuses to look at Farr anymore. "Take him away. Whatever he decides, resolve it within the hour."

He'll choose the ship. As far as she's concerned, the matter is complete.

Benna stares at her like she's a stranger.

Kyran wants out of this room, but more work remains to be done. Something always needs doing. She doesn't wait for the guards to remove their stammering charge before she reclaims her seat and speaks again.

"What's next on the council's docket?"

CHAPTER TWENTY-SEVEN

Before her presumed death, Davia had acquired enough personal wealth in addition to her minuscule share of the family's expansive treasury—a provision of her father's—to fund four lifetimes. She has poured a quarter of her substantial gains into a vessel equipped to escape official detection if necessary.

She christens the ship *Fidelity*.

Davia could live the rest of her life on board. The amenities are standard, and the functionality includes advanced concealment technology, making her difficult to track, and extensive redundancy of shipboard systems. *Fidelity* is fast for its cruiser-class size, and the trip to Barria is brief.

Barria is a technologically reserved world, with more rustic cities and infrastructures. Anin has many pet projects, and his holdings on this planet have received his favored patronage for over a decade.

His private estates recognize her identification, and she docks without ceremony. By the time she reaches the adjoining bay, Anin is there to greet her.

Davia cannot help her tears when she sees him in person. She had thought she might never see him again.

"Hello, little sister," he says, an old joke since they were born less than a week apart.

His eyes sparkle with his own tears, and he looks like he has aged several years in the past one.

It is undignified for a Min to run when it is not necessary.

She does not care.

He wraps his arms around her, and another piece of Davia's self falls back into place.

Autumn has come to the vineyards on Barria's northern continent. The rows are free of staff since all the grapes have been harvested. Dappled sunlight filters through trees stretching four or five stories tall, framing sections of the vineyard. Some are evergreen, and a few others have lost all their leaves. The rest are red and golden in the afternoon light.

If Davia were not so focused on Anin, she might be captivated by it all.

There's a weariness to his comportment that makes her feel guilty as the news she brings will not lighten his load. If all goes according to her plan, his shoulders will soon bear the weight of the empire.

Between the mansion and the rows of dying vines lies a garden full of late-blooming flowers. Knee-high hedge mazes weave around multilayered water structures—the perfect place for an uninterrupted conversation, particularly one that should not be overheard.

Anin has dismissed his personal guards, and none of them are within earshot. Steadfast and dedicated, they refuse to let him out of their sight.

Davia trusts Anin, and if he disappoints her and betrays that trust, she has no hope for anything else anyway.

Anin looks more like a successful vintner on holiday than a prince, dressed as he is in layered casual linens in deference to the cooler air. He never lets Davia walk more than an arm's length away.

She shares his need to be close. She has missed him, is grateful and glad to be with him.

"Before you share your secrets," Anin begins, as insightful as ever. "Tell me the truth."

He rests a hand on her shoulder and squeezes with affection. "Are you well, Davia? This isn't about some malady related to your ordeal?"

Her appearance must be as jarring for him as his is for her.

"I am fine." And she is. Her body has settled somewhat into its more balanced diet after months of malnourishment. While her meditations and forms have not returned to their pre-crash strength and power, her overall condition has improved in recent weeks.

At least physically. Her longing for Kyran has only intensified.

Once he is convinced of her well-being, Davia begins her story—her arrival in the system he knows as Rymind 17, the battle, the crash, and how she was marooned and managed to survive. He interrupts her so many times, she finds it difficult to sway the conversation in the direction she wants—no, needs for it to go.

By the time she is explaining her delay in coming to him—the numerous visits to secret military installations on outer rim planets—he barely lets her finish her sentences.

"These are all confirmed Sifani colonies, Davia. And have been for decades—some for centuries. I fail to see how—"

"Anin." Her interruption is not an admonition, more like a reminder to allow her to finish her tale.

He visibly reins himself in. "Why is all this secrecy necessary when you are telling me what I already know?"

Davia gestures to a nearby stone bench, and with an impatient sigh, Anin joins her. When he does, she gazes at him with intensity.

"Listen to me carefully, brother. What I am about to tell you I have corroborated from multiple sources with supporting data, so it is all the complete truth without my own interpretation. Do you understand?"

A shadow flickers in his eyes, but he matches her intensity when he nods.

Davia tells him of all the evidence she has collected, her

sources' positions if not their specific names, and the steps taken to verify what she has discovered.

"Thirty-eight different installations, Anin. All on the periphery of the empire, deliberately stationed in the territories beyond core systems to evade more stringent penal law. All under military supervision, with no other sanctioned oversight. Independent governance that goes right to her personal security advisors, with all associated proceeds siphoned into personal accounts."

His incredulity is obvious.

"Do you believe her capable of such subterfuge?" His mother's calculating nature is well-known. This, however, is a conspiracy of epic proportions.

"Children, Anin. Children taken from their parents without trial—and before you say it, not all those people were guilty of treason."

By the time she details the manifests, the limited and high-reaching chain of command, the illicit funding, the hidden adoptions and the torturous reconditioning, Anin has risen from the bench and paces a path before her.

"Stop."

It is more of a request than an order, and Davia understands. The sheer amount of damning intelligence is overwhelming. He sits beside her again, and takes her hand, and retreats into himself. They sit in silence as the sun sinks toward the far-off hills.

"I hear you, Davia, but I . . ." He shakes his head.

He needs time. Davia cannot give him much.

"Break bread with me," Anin says finally, an indirect appeal for a recess. "It's been a long time since we had a meal together. Perhaps a game after supper."

"Dinner and Barrian wine sound sublime, brother, but the charm of playing kings and pawns has worn off."

—~— —~— —~—

They steer away from the difficult topics over dinner. Instead, Anin shares his perspective of their time apart and, with a blush unbecoming a prince, mentions he is engaged to be married. He endures Davia's teasing at having found a suitable match. Anin is besotted with the woman—a noble, to be sure, and also an accomplished scientist in her own right.

"I hope to meet her before the wedding," Davia says. "I must warn her about you."

He snickers in a manner unbefitting a royal. "Believe me, Gwynn knows what she's getting into. Mother has seen to that."

The mention of Ethelyn dampens his joy for a moment, though he recovers. "I had not planned on love. I never thought I'd believe someone who'd marry me would be interested in the man and not the crown."

Davia understands. "It is alarming, is it not?"

She has forgotten herself, and his focused squint at her mistake means she has yet another tale to tell.

"I thought Min Izabel could never see past your bloodline."

"No, not Iza." She takes a deep breath, prepares for another long conversation, and tells him about Kyran.

In the mansion's study, with a wall of windows overlooking the bare vineyards, Anin watches Davia pace from his ornate chair near the veranda, a glass of wine in his hand.

"She saved my life, Anin. I cannot stress this enough, and you must understand this is not exaggeration or hyperbole. I would be dead if not for her."

"And you feel you owe her some sort of recompense?" He does not appear angry, only confused.

"No." Davia pauses in her pacing and turns to face him. "She was the catalyst, but this is not about her, or her people."

"The terrorists."

Her brother does not share her points of reference. "No, the Ellodians. And many others."

She pivots her approach in an attempt to drive him to focus on the deeper truths as opposed to the surface details.

"The queen . . ." Davia has not addressed Ethelyn by her title in weeks and it is sour on her tongue. ". . .executed her parents in the series of events preceding the Old King's sepulture."

Anin's only response is to raise his eyebrows.

She continues. "The world they have reclaimed—"

"You mean marauded."

Davia sighs. "The planet's inhabited areas were destroyed by nuclear war during High King Rymind's conquest of the sector."

"They probably did it themselves to ruin the ground for us," Anin mumbles into his wine and Davia ignores him.

"We annexed the world and deemed it uninhabitable but flagged it for imperial expansion at some point in the distant future since we could not afford to develop the sector. They are colonizing a previously uninhabited region of one of the southern continents."

"On a planet that is not theirs. You see what I mean? Thieves."

"Anin . . ." Davia is exasperated. "Yes, some terrorists are pirates. Yes, some have done untold damage. Yes, many raised arms against the throne. If I concede all these things—in fact, agree with you about their verity—will you let me finish?"

He leans back in his chair, irritated, and waves a hand for her to continue.

Davia conducted substantial research to determine the origins of Kyran's people. She discovered some of their older records and began studying their language to help her translate them.

"In the aftermath of their planet's destruction, they emigrated to a new world on the outer rim, which had not yet been conquered by Sifani expansion. When High King Landin's forces came, they fought again and lost, and took to the stars once more to escape. What they had called New Ellod, we renamed Landin Four, and later, Luca Piloh."

Anin stills, his eyes registering the name and the timeline.

Named for one of their countless ancestors, Luca Piloh had been home to one of the bloodiest and most contentious colonizations in recent history. The people on-world refused to surrender, the commanders went too far, and several brutal massacres resulted. The remaining residents retreated and subsequently escaped.

The implication is clear. The Ellodians have cause to rebel against the throne.

Anin does not concede the point.

"Is this . . . some kind of vengeance, Davia?" he asks sadly, with kindness, and is without question suggesting her motives are less than altruistic. "For all the ways you were mistreated?"

This doubt coming from him pains her.

"It might seem that way, but no. I . . ."

She will not apologize for telling him the truth, even though she knows it upsets him. The time has come to say what must be said, regardless of the potential damage to their relationship.

"This . . . situation is unsustainable. The extended territories are crumbling under the weight of her demands. The regional governors know she will not acknowledge any malfeasance, the courtiers profit, and her own council labels anyone who protests too loudly as a terrorist.

"She is no longer fit to be queen."

Even the night goes quiet at her words, the earlier breeze through the windows gone.

His face hardens. "And you think you would be better."

Shocked, Davia stiffens in response. "No matter what you may have been told, brother, I have no interest in your birthright."

She softens her voice. "I love you, Anin, so I will let pass how much your suspicion wounds me. I will also be clear. I do not want, and I have never wanted the crown, but the empire will fall if this continues."

"Davia." Anin washes a hand over his face, and though his

eyes do not water, they are red with the depth of his frustration and sorrow. "Please tell me you aren't . . . asking for my permission to kill my mother."

His breath hitches, and Davia is not sure if he laments the suggestion for his mother's sake or Davia's.

She kneels beside him, a hand on the arm of his chair. "No. No, Anin," she whispers, though there is no one to hear them.

She stretches her hand to his arm, wary of pushing him too far, and pushing nonetheless. "Sifani Prime will not survive under her rule."

"Speak plainly, Davia. I am weary of shadows."

The backbone in his request, the expectation that a royal will not endure dissembling, is exactly what she wants to see.

"Anin, the time has come for you to take your place as High King."

CHAPTER TWENTY-EIGHT

Service for the midday meal is almost finished when Kyran waves at Lora and fetches herself a plate. Her usual table—near the kitchen and by an exit—is empty, which means it's been designated as hers. She appreciates the gesture yet resents the fact that her birthright grants her preferential treatment.

Halfway through her meal, Benna joins her. A tension exists between them that wasn't there previously. Kyran is grateful for familiar company because Benna doesn't ask endless questions about her time on the moon, but she's also annoyed that Benna's presence hints at things Kyran is not yet ready to do.

"I heard you visited the eastern fields today," Benna says by way of greeting.

The growing season is nearing its end, an abundant yield thanks to the fertile soil. Some members of the community have built permanent homes closer to the fields. Kyran has worked with the logistics team on an effective transport layout encouraging growth while also optimizing travel from point to point. She's spent most of the morning supervising the construction of a gravel and dirt road between the eastern farm and the central settlement. Someday far in the future, a city might stand here.

Now, though, she feels like Benna is keeping tabs on her.

"You know, I'm not going to suddenly disappear." Kyran aims for the heart of the issue.

Benna lets her fork fall against her plate. "I'm just making conversation, Kyran."

"You're keeping an eye on me under the guise of assuring my safety, and it's as unnecessary as it is insulting."

"Why are you so angry at me?"

Kyran pauses, utensil frozen in midair between her plate and her mouth. Is she angry at Benna?

"I'm not." It feels like a lie. Her appetite is lost, and the words won't come.

Benna eats in silence, and when she's finished, Kyran hasn't resumed her meal. The exchange is typical of them now. Benna is either irritated or hesitant, as if Kyran is a bomb about to explode.

Benna stands, holding her empty plate. "Will you be joining the afternoon council meeting, or do you have other plans?" Her tone is tentative, for once asking what Kyran prefers.

Kyran fights against the sigh swelling in her chest. "I'm right behind you."

The walk from the mess to the command tent is short. Summer temperatures make for warm air inside, even with the window flaps open. A light breeze does nothing to alleviate the closeness of too many people in limited space.

"What do you think, Princess?"

Since Farr's trial, Kyran has been pulled into every discussion. She has communicated to Benna that the council deferring to her input sets a poor precedent, since the others have more experience than she does. Benna perceives it as Kyran's perpetual resistance to claiming her birthright.

So far, Kyran continues to refuse coronation. The people of Ellod are in a perfect position to build a more egalitarian government. The council disagrees, and the cycle goes on. She cannot convince them to dissolve the monarchy unless she takes the throne and orders it, which defeats the purpose of her request.

The sun crawls inexorably towards sunset. Kyran longs for the clearing near the stream, for the silence and peace, and the comfort drawing the circle offers.

She clears her throat and speaks. "Jivko, you're more familiar with the capabilities of the communication grid. How do you think we can improve its range?"

The technician in question nods in acknowledgment, and Kyran's encouragement makes her sit taller in her chair.

Kyran peeks at the window, estimating how much time remains before the sun goes down. The session continues, and Kyran tries not to tune it out. She visualizes a Venu Pakrim form until the gathering ends.

Practicing the motions of what Davia taught her is difficult without Davia here to correct her imperfections. Kyran does her best. The gravity on Ellod is less than on the moon, and she feels much stronger when she does her forms. A few fighters in the settlement have experience in various martial arts. None of them have the kind of training Davia passed on to her. Kyran spars with them, sometimes getting the better of her opponent, a few times not, all of it keeping her fit. She worries about her form slipping.

She's cleared an area outside her dwelling, and she draws the circle within its borders at morning, midday, and sunset. It helps ease the aches in her heart and in the deepest part of her, where she knows who she is but does not know her place. Though she gives to the community as best as she can—more so all the time if fewer arguments with Benna are any indication—it doesn't feel like home.

That evening, a flat-topped boulder offers a comfortable perch beside the stream, and Kyran sits as she does most nights when the weather allows. Her need for Davia is more potent at night when she's alone with the stars, and she gazes at the constellations in the direction of the core worlds.

Every aching question of why she has not heard from Davia is answered by her own inability to send a message herself. What can she say? How does an Ellodian rebel contact a member of the royal family to pledge her affection?

Over four months have passed since her rescue, five since she last saw Davia's face. Kyran does not cry herself to sleep anymore when the nights are rough and the ache most poignant, yet her feelings have only deepened.

She never shared them with Davia, and Davia never spoke of her own heart. Yet Kyran wants to believe Davia felt the same way about her—still feels the same way about her.

She wants to believe that somewhere, out in the stars, Davia aches for her in return.

Ellod should be home, but it's not—not when she yearns so much for one thing more.

Kyran adds another item to her "firsts" list. For the first time, she's taken someone with her on one of her fishing expeditions.

Lora is a gentle companion and a force for positivity. Kyran soaks in Lora's exuberance whenever they're near one another. Her temperament surprises Kyran, considering the torture Lora endured at the hands of Sifani soldiers.

Kyran has begun to think of her as a friend, a space only Benna has filled before now. When Lora asked about the fish Kyran brought to the kitchens one day, Kyran invited Lora along on her next trip.

Kyran often fishes with hook and line, a method she demonstrated to Lora today, and when she's restless, she switches to spear fishing. She doesn't catch as much and ends up drenched from the stream. It's enjoyable on a hot day and keeps her spear skills sharp. Today her competence yielded six fish, three of them as long as her leg.

"Where did you learn to do that?" Lora asks as they're walking back to the settlement.

"A skill I picked up along the way," Kyran says.

"Was it on the damned rock?"

Kyran laughs, a rare thing. Lora makes her forget to be so serious. "On what?"

Skipping down the path, Lora manages to touch half the flowers as they pass. "You don't talk much about the time you were lost, and when you do, you call that place 'the damned rock.' Maybe that should be its name. 'Beware the perils of

The Damned Rock.'"

Kyran throws her head back and laughs so hard she almost trips. With the sun on her face, a full catch hanging from one shoulder, and this new friend beside her, the constant ache in her chest eases. The last time she felt this good . . . she had been holding Davia in her arms by the firepit in the canyon.

The memory tempers her joy. That was another lifetime, even if it wasn't long ago. This is her new world, and her life here is a good one, however incomplete.

Small groups of people talk in urgent voices when they return. No one is bustling with action, so it's not an invasion, but it must be something equally important. Kyran hands her catch to Lora with a promise to visit the kitchens for the yield from the river's bounty and goes in search of Benna.

The command tent is full. Benna leans over the communications console with Fillip and a few members of the council. Kyran catches her eye, and Benna disengages from the discussion. With a nod she calls Kyran over to one corner of the tent, the only privacy they can manage in the crowded space.

"Are we safe?" It's the most pressing question Kyran has.

"For the time being. I'm not sure how long it will stay that way. High Queen Ethelyn has been overthrown and taken into custody."

Worry for Davia eclipses Kyran's other concerns. Davia had no love for the queen, which doesn't mean she escaped a shift in power unscathed.

Kyran focuses on the potential effect of the coup on Ellod. They are far from the core systems, but still within reach of Sifani Prime.

Benna steps closer, though warily. She is careful with her movements around Kyran. "Her son, Anin, has taken the throne, and here is the crux of it all. We've received word from several of the outer rim planets. They think this is the perfect time to push for formal independence."

Across the room, Fillip mentions his connections on one of the systems near the border of the outer territories. "I can travel there in about ten days to determine what they're planning that they might not share over comms."

Jivko turns from the console.

"We've still got contacts in the Beglan Syndicate," she says to Benna. "They're dealing in ranged ground weapons now, which is exactly what we need to protect the settlement. I'd have to take one of the larger transports, though, to bring anything back."

Other members of the council add to the discussion, each with an idea of how they might reach out to the other independents, travel to other systems, offer their new foodstuffs in trade.

Kyran listens and disapproves. Every suggestion splits and diverts their resources from strengthening Ellod. They're trying to address things outside of their control and weakening what they can affect, which means they'll fail. After all they've endured and accomplished so far, she is certain this moment will define their future.

"No."

Conversation stops as Kyran crosses her arms over her chest.

"No, we keep everyone and everything here. Leave the lines of communication open with the independent worlds, and if a fight breaks out, we'll talk about how to respond. For now, we strengthen our position on Ellod."

Benna looks uneasy. "The council will vote on it."

The council might vote in favor of doing these things that would erode or destroy what they've built. Kyran knows what she must do and it doesn't frighten or upset her the way it used to.

They might not be convinced to see reason. They can be commanded to act on it.

She uncrosses her arms and centers her weight with her hands at her sides. "Vote if you must. No matter what the council decides, I claim my birthright as the last daughter of House Loyal, and I won't yield on this."

Kyran stands as if the circle is drawn around her, and her voice does not waver. "I alone speak for Ellod."

CHAPTER TWENTY-NINE

Davia has not spent this much time in the royal wing in her entire life.

These are the rooms her father kept from her when she was a child. They are not as warm or ornate as she had imagined. Old tapestries hang on the stone walls and worn carpets line the lengths of the halls, all opulent beyond belief, aged, and outdated.

The child she had been had hoped for a future that never came to pass. Her life is rich in other ways, for which she is grateful—her relationship with Anin, her friendship with Izabel, her duty and life as a Min.

More wondrous still, she knows what it means to feel an overpowering love for someone else. She has received no messages from Kyran and has sent none either. Whenever she comes close, a voice within her whispers the time is not yet and much remains to be resolved.

Their story is not over, Davia is certain.

In the meantime, the circle is full of work she must do.

Once the scandal hit the media outlets, complete with data to corroborate the revelations, the court scrambled to protect itself from the fallout. Ethelyn's tower of support crumbled.

The former High Queen is in custody, incarcerated in her own royal rooms. The current political climate means few of the wealthy courtiers want to be seen supporting her when opinion of the less fortunate public is so blatantly against her.

Given enough time, however, the furor—the protests, the demands for explanation and immediate resolution—will pivot to some other injustice, and Ethelyn's previous allies might be swayed to her cause. Davia must suggest Anin transfer Ethelyn to a more removed estate away from court. Ethelyn cannot easily align support if she is in guarded isolation.

Davia follows the corridor to the royal study, ignoring the guards who acknowledge her passing. She enters the room only moments before her brother walks through a different door.

He marches to the serving station along one wall without greeting her, pours himself an ample portion of spirits, downs it, and then pours another.

"Twenty-two worlds," he says as he pours another glass alongside his. "Twenty-two worlds have been swayed to join an 'independent coalition.' Our spies have sent word these pirates are now retreating and pulling out of every confrontation. They've blockaded wormhole generation locations so goods can't travel through."

He delivers the glass to Davia, a most un-kingly thing to do. Neither of them relies much on formality in private. "It's not enough for them to steal our ships. Now they're interrupting the shipping channels."

"They have good reason."

His anger is palpable, thickening the air in the room. "How can you say that?"

"Because it is true, Anin. Their worlds were conquered, the beauty and bounty of their lands stolen without recompense, and when they protested, they were labeled traitors."

"For the good of the empire, Davia. The Sifane legacy is the story of the galaxy."

"Yet the history so proudly taught throughout Sifani Prime omits the civilizations squashed by expansion. While many worlds were eager to be colonized by Sifani advancement, some were not. That some would prefer independent governance is no surprise."

"But this . . . this piratical response—the mentality that they are owed something and if not given freely, it will be taken by force—is so similar as to be identical to the absolute rule it professes to resist."

Davia shakes her head in sorrow. "I do not condone violent protest. I am a Sifane. I love many things about the empire, and the great advancements we have achieved. This, Anin . . . this is not one of them. These people were promised a brighter future in the empire, which was never delivered. They are owed much from us in exchange for what they have given."

His anger fades into a pensive frown. He sips his drink, head bowed in thought.

"Have you sent anyone to talk to them?" Davia asks.

Anin freezes, incredulous, before he remembers himself and speaks. "Talk to them? If I had forces in the sector, I would obliterate them into the void."

If the pirates—and she thinks of them less as pirates of late and more as colonies who have rejected their overlords—have banded together in some fashion, it will take more than the occasional Sifani contingent to stop them.

It will take war, which will damage Sifani Prime severely.

"Have you considered diplomacy instead of catastrophic destruction?"

Anin paces and drinks until his glass is once again empty. He is a rational man. He will come to the same conclusion Davia has about the cost of a war.

"Do you believe I can convince pirates—terrorists, Davia, who have spent decades in arms against the crown—to have an intelligent, productive conversation?"

By the time the words have formed in her head, a nervousness has risen within her at the implied possibilities. "I know one, and I will speak with her on your behalf."

He tilts his head in consideration. "Have you spoken to her since your return?"

Davia's silence answers for her.

His glass clinks on the glass of a side table when he sets it down. "Then how can you be sure she will listen?"

Davia is not sure . . . but she has hope.

—~— —~— —~—

Anin insists on a full battalion to Ellod. Davia negotiates him down to a single battleship. He also demands a promise that she not maroon herself again.

To her surprise, the Jeweled Circle also offers an escort—six Min-commanded cruisers.

In preparation for the potential of a hostile engagement, one she hopes will not come to battle, Davia resumes her studies of the Ellodian language. Since her rescue, such education has been part of her research of Kyran's people, from old primary school instruction and dated recordings of New Ellod holiday celebrations to intercepted communications, surveillance registers, and prisoners' interviews.

She discovered a reference to the Loyal family, one as royal to the Ellodians as her own to the empire. The shock takes some time to wear off.

Alone on *Fidelity,* docked inside the larger battleship, she practices until confident an incorrect word or phrase will not accidentally incite the war she works to avoid.

It distracts her from the queasy anticipation. She is here to negotiate to the best of her ability on behalf of the new High King, but she is also here for Kyran.

They have not seen or spoken to each other since the morning of her rescue, and Davia trembles with the need to see Kyran's face.

A proximity alarm signals arrival at the last stop before entry into Ellod's star system.

Davia checks the logs and telemetric data, a precaution fed by her nerves. After a short meditation, she gives the order to advance.

CHAPTER THIRTY

"How many?" Kyran strides into the command center flanked by her council advisors.

Two months after assuming her role as the newly crowned head of Ellod, with a symbolic coronation held during yet another council meeting, Kyran leaps into the first true test of her leadership. Sifani ships have arrived—the first contact of the new regime.

Jivko updates Kyran without looking away from the consoles she's monitoring. "Two dozen fighters static before six cruisers and one battleship. They're not in any formation I recognize."

If the Sifanis attack, all the Ellodian ships will be destroyed and most of the ground settlement as well. Kyran hopes no one dies today, but this show of force threatens imminent violence.

"Send the children with the key personnel to the sanctuary." A designated safe space has been built inside a nearby mountain and should survive any surface assault that isn't biological or nuclear. Knowing this moment might come, Kyran had insisted they prioritize its construction soon after solidifying their informal alliance with the other independent worlds.

"Already done, Advocate." Jivko is nothing if not proactive. "They're ten minutes from the tunnels now. Fighters are scrambling and awaiting your orders."

Kyran has never led a battle in her life. Protecting her people as best she can is now within her circle. One step at a time.

"How are the Sifanis advancing?"

More people swell into the room behind her. Since Kyran invited other planets and systems to form a coalition against Sifani rule, Ellod has hosted numerous conclaves of personnel from off-world. The greater numbers of people forced them to move the command center into a corner of the mess tent.

"They're not." Jivko doesn't seem to like it either. She raises her hand to the sensor tucked into her ear. "I've got a request for audio and visual communication."

Kyran steadies herself for the engagement. "Keep the fighters on the ground ready for launch and tell the ships in orbit to engage only if the Sifanis shoot first. Anyone who lights this fire without my command answers to me."

If any of us survive, she thinks.

"Understood, Advocate."

"Broadcast the feed." Whatever the Sifanis say, Kyran wants witnesses. If the Sifanis have come to destroy them, everyone in the coalition will know and take action.

Jivko rapidly keys in several commands and points to a mounted device, signaling its activation to Kyran.

"I am Kyran Loyal, Advocate of Ellod." Kyran stands before the relay sending audio and video to the Sifani contingent as well as the entire coalition. "State your intentions."

A screen beyond Jivko's station activates with an answering visual connection. Kyran gasps at the crisp, larger-than-life image and clenches her fists behind her back.

It's Davia.

Kyran's memories have done little justice to Davia's beauty. Her appearance is formal, with her hair swept back close to her head and her jawline emphasized by the high collar of her uniform. Davia is no longer hollow-cheeked; her skin is flawless, her brows delicate, her lips perfectly bowed.

The need spreading through Kyran overwhelms every other thought.

Davia's official presentation bears no resemblance to the passionate woman Kyran held in her arms. Kyran sees windswept hair, flushed cheeks, and lips swollen from endless kisses. She vibrates with want for what she does not have and cannot reach.

Kyran forces air into her lungs.

Davia recovers first from her surprise. "I am Emissary of High King Anin of the Exalted Realm of Sifani Prime. I seek an audience with your envoys."

Her voice is like a blow to Kyran's chest.

Davia is here. Davia is here . . . and speaking Ellodian. Despite Kyran never teaching her a word, Davia speaks the language of Kyran's people.

The swell in Kyran's heart at the knowledge Davia has learned Ellodian in the time they've been apart swiftly contracts as the words spoken finally register. Davia has come, but not for her. Instead, she is an arm of her brother's empire.

If the weapon of the king come to destroy them is wielded by the woman she loves, Kyran is doubly doomed.

She swallows the ache and focuses on the matter at hand, which is keeping this pregnant conflict from becoming a war. It takes her another moment to notice Davia has not identified herself by name or by relation to the throne.

"As Advocate, I speak for Ellod." Kyran is shocked her voice doesn't shake.

Davia furrows her brow. "Advocate?"

With everyone watching and listening in, what Kyran wants to say to Davia alone must be woven into the words appropriate for mass consumption.

"Though it is my right, I would not accept the title of queen." Kyran trusts Davia to understand. She tries to relax her shoulders as she fights the tension of the engagement, the multiple levels of implications within this conversation, and the marrow-deep ache of seeing Davia again, of being so close yet so far.

"Then, Advocate of Ellod, I will address you." Davia visibly draws her breath and exhales, and Kyran sees in that moment this exchange is equally difficult for Davia. Minute shifts of her expression reveal her distress, and her pause shows her discomfort.

"It is our understanding Ellod was the . . . instigator of a league of Sifani domains intending to reject the rule of the High King."

Her words are slow, measured even for Davia. Despite the elongated vowels and crisp consonants of Davia's enunciated and accented Ellodian, Kyran senses she too is attempting to communicate without inciting violence.

Relief mingles with her pain. Maybe their earlier connection will allow them to instill some peace between their peoples. Kyran will mourn the loss of the deeper relationship later, though she feels like she's bleeding.

"We were the first to suggest its formation, yes." She centers herself and forcibly loosens her tightly clasped hands behind her back. It is no small irony that the skills Davia taught her are the ones helping her navigate this tense confrontation. "The coalition contests the seizure of member lands—or in some cases, their complete destruction—by the former High King and Queen and their predecessors."

Singling out dead kings and the overthrown queen instead of the current monarch might give Davia room for compromise.

Yet Kyran is responsible for too much to yield, even before Davia. "I can only speak for what I know of the sentiments of the other members and can make no declarations on their behalf. As for Ellod, we are no longer a territory of Sifani Prime. We claim what is ours, no more and no less."

It's a weak statement for the magnitude of what they're demanding. She can't think through the tension to phrase it better. In any case, the deed is done. Ellod has excised itself from the empire. They will live or die as free Ellodians.

Davia arches an eyebrow. "Previously such insurrection would have been reason enough for immediate military engagement."

Benna moves into Kyran's peripheral vision. Kyran can't divide her attention because she's caught the key word. Davia has hinted at the possibility of a different response from the Sifani throne, and Kyran grabs it like a lifeline.

"We don't want war." She stops herself from saying Davia's

name. It's too personal—less a matter of revealing they know each other and more because it is a cherished treasure to be kept close. "We want our freedom, and we're prepared to discuss trade, provided it's fair, and we'll work with the rest of the coalition to ensure these matters are concluded as peacefully as possible unless your king decides to resist our independence."

She will fight if she must. A war would hurt Ellod badly. And the thought of leading her people against Davia's, of the two of them pitted against each other in battle again . . . it terrifies her, but Kyran will do what has to be done.

"While the High King rules over the domains in question," Davia says, "war will only destroy valuable resources."

Not a concession to independence—a hint Sifani Prime doesn't want to fight either.

They stare at each other across the connection, Davia's eyes flickering over Kyran intently.

"As Emissary, I would like to extend an invitation on behalf of the High King to representatives from your . . . coalition. A pair from each participating body." Davia's gaze intensifies. "Should Ellod agree to take part, perhaps you and another could accompany me now."

Kyran's knees tremble as she mentally translates the offer. By inviting two representatives, Davia has hidden her true intentions. After all this time, Davia has come for her.

Kyran cannot go.

Her nails bite into her palm as she collects herself. She is certain the king has made a legitimate invitation because she trusts Davia even if they have not spoken in months. Davia, who had left without a word to hide Kyran from Sifani troops, who had sent a message to enable her rescue from the moon—Davia would not allow harm to come to Kyran. No one would understand how or why Kyran believes that to be true.

"I will not send potential hostages who might be slaughtered at the new king's whim."

A flash of fire flares and disappears in Davia's eyes.

Kyran softens her tone, if not her words. "My people did not fare so well in the former queen's custody. I cannot allow any of my people to be put in such a dangerous position."

Understanding eases Davia's frown, and her sorrow matches Kyran's. Diplomacy must override their personal desires, no matter how much it hurts.

Davia's eyes glass over and clear so quickly Kyran wonders if it's a trick of the light. A steely countenance settles on Davia's face, and Kyran desperately tries to match it. The memories of who they were to each other will be only that, and she feels Davia pulling away.

A finality descends over their exchange, and Davia nods curtly. "I will convey your messages to the High King, and . . ."

The pause stretches long enough Kyran hears the rustling of movement nearby. She does not look away from the face she might not see again.

In the next breath, in slow, vivid, heart-stopping detail, Davia's jaw loosens, her serious demeanor fades, and her shoulders relax. Davia's expression eases into her true self, the one Kyran revered, the one Kyran saw every morning on the moon when she woke with Davia beside her.

The sentiments Davia cannot speak aloud brighten her eyes.

"You have my blade, Kyran Loyal," Davia says, her voice gentle and warm as sunlight.

Kyran bites her cheek, lets the pain stop the tears from forming. She can't speak. The screen darkens.

"The connection is terminated," Jivko says in confused surprise. "Their fighters are docking."

Kyran can only breathe in gasps.

"Stay on high alert." Her voice cracks. "No one comes back from the sanctuary until every last Sifani ship is gone."

"Yes, Advocate." Jivko turns away from her systems to peer at Kyran with worry. "Are you—"

Kyran doesn't stay to hear the question or to wait for Benna who is headed her way.

Instead, Kyran flees. She pushes her way past the first few people in her path, and halfway to the entrance the crowd parts for her to make her escape.

Outside, her vision blurs with the inevitable tears as she runs, and no one stops her. Back by the stream, she throws herself down next to the clearing. Kyran wants to step into its center, to draw the circle and find some measure of peace but she can't.

Davia came, and Kyran could not join her.

The last remnant of her hope breaks like a shattered rock and grinds itself to dust.

CHAPTER THIRTY-ONE

After directing the accompanying ships to resume course for the core systems, Davia instructs the crew to leave her undisturbed, and opens a communication channel to her brother.

For now, she sets her personal feelings aside to convey an update to the High King.

"You're sure?" Anin's voice is tinny over the less-than-optimal connection.

Anin does not usually require assurance, and Davia is asking a lot of him. The first days of his realm have been tumultuous and unprecedented, and Davia cannot blame him for his caution.

"Anin, I am certain. They do not want war; none of us do. They want their independence, but they would be foolish to sever themselves completely from the empire. Not one of those worlds can sustain itself indefinitely."

Ellod will hit a plateau with its development soon and need to restore trade off-world.

"Acknowledge them as independents, Anin, and offer amnesty for any previous damage to property or any nonviolent protests. Remind them violence will be met in kind if they build any armed force of their own."

"How does any of that help me?"

"Because you can also inform them they are now fiscally responsible for their own infrastructure, which means the royal coffers can stop bleeding. They do not have the technology we do and will need resources only Sifani Prime can provide. Trade with them at a fair price, and the supply delays throughout the realm will disappear, the margins will improve well enough to keep the court at bay, and everyone wins."

Davia prepares the killing blow. "This move will single-handedly halve the empire's debt in twelve years. What you lose in territory—most of which you were never going to be able to expand and develop in the next hundred years—you will gain in financial stability. If the court is smart, they will be richer for it sooner than they can imagine. And they will have their High King to thank."

More importantly, the atrocities will end. The contention between the independent worlds and the crown will be reduced to trade negotiations, which will no doubt continue to be heated if less volatile.

"Davia . . . I know you've said it doesn't matter to you, but you are as much a Sifane as I am. Perhaps we could . . . share the throne. Imagine what we could accomplish together. We could transform the empire."

"You have enough vision for both of us."

Fear clouds his eyes, and she knows the heart of it.

"You are not like them, Anin. Either of them. We are not our parents." Davia shakes her head, sad to refuse him and certain in her position. "And my place is not on a throne."

Resignation sets in his features. "You must visit me more often. I have enjoyed the time with you in person, and want it to be a more common occurrence."

Davia nods her head. "As my king requires."

Anin rolls his eyes and makes a rude gesture. For as serious as his life has been of late, he is more frivolous in private, and it gives Davia hope.

"And . . . Kyran?"

Davia shakes her head to stave off the conversation. She is not yet ready to speak of those details.

"What will you do now?"

Her circle has contracted now that the grand work is done. All the turmoil of the last year and a half has taken its toll. She needs to withdraw, to rejuvenate . . . to heal.

To mourn what has been lost.

"For now, I'm headed back to where it all began."

"Please take care. I know you are fully capable of looking after yourself, but a brother worries." He offers a wan smile and severs the connection.

Davia retreats into meditation until the tears take over. In private now, she lets them fall and does not fight the sobs when they come.

The confidence in Kyran's voice had flowed across the communication relay between them, and this version of Kyran had been even more captivating than the woman in Davia's memories. Viewed through the display, her vitality had been astounding. Kyran has recovered well from her ordeal, her features fuller, the lines of her muscles softer. Her life among her people is treating her well.

Davia is both pleased and heartbroken that Kyran now leads the Ellodians. Competence had flowed from Kyran in word and posture even though Davia's pain had been mirrored in Kyran's eyes.

Kyran is beyond reach for something as trivial as their previous relationship. Davia trained Kyran to stand firm, to yield to no one, to take solace in duty.

For the price of Davia's heart, Kyran has learned the lesson.

CHAPTER THIRTY-TWO

Rapidly approaching footsteps are Kyran's only warning. Benna isn't one to waste time.

"What the hell just happened?"

"Not now," Kyran stutters between sobs.

"Kyran—"

Kyran screams, though it comes out more like an angry wail. "Five minutes, Benna." She hangs her head, and her hair falls to cover her face—the only privacy she has to lament what she's lost.

"Go away and leave me alone." When the crying intensifies, she loses the ability to form words.

"Please, Kyran. I only want to help."

The shoulder-shaking sobs ease after a few moments. Kyran wipes away some of the endless tears. "You can't do anything."

Kyran has made her choice. Her heart is with Davia, but she can't leave Ellod now.

Benna sits in the dirt beside her, close enough to touch Kyran though she doesn't.

"Who was that woman?" Her tentative question is laced with worry.

If Kyran reveals all her truths, can Benna's judgment hurt much more than this? What's the point in keeping any of this to herself any longer? Would it make her feel better to say something out loud for once?

"Her name is Davia," Kyran says before Benna's impatience

becomes demanding. "She's the half sister of the High King."

Benna gasps while Kyran stares into the blurry dirt.

"We were marooned together. It was her ship you saw when you rescued me. "

Such simple words to describe their time that in no way encapsulates its meaning.

"She's who they were searching for," Benna says. "Because of her . . .all those months, the occupation . . ."

Kyran nods. None of that was Davia's fault. "I know what you're going to say, Benna, and believe me, at first . . . all I wanted to do was kill her. But she saved my life. Several times, in fact."

And gave her a purpose.

"I saved hers, too. We only had each other to rely on as we fought against all the ways that place tried to kill us."

"Does she think you owe her something now?"

Kyran can't blame Benna for her suspicion.

"No, not at all. You're missing the point. Don't you see? I wouldn't be alive if it weren't for her. And she didn't just save my life. She saved me. She gave me hope, Benna." So many broken places inside Kyran had been healed while they'd lived and hunted and sparred and . . .

And loved.

Kyran closes her eyes against the onslaught of memories.

"I do owe her something. It's not like you think." Benna will only ever care about one thing. "She will not ask or expect me to do anything to betray Ellod. You wondered why their people left and never came back? She's the one who ended the occupation."

One detail comes to mind, and she raises her head to look Benna in the eye. "She sent you the coordinates to find me."

Benna frowns at this. She's looking for a trap when there isn't one.

"What did it mean when she said you had her—her blade?" Benna's hesitant but urgent need for answers grates on Kyran's already abraded emotions. She'll persist until Kyran gives in.

The tears quicken, constant in their flow. "It means she . . ."

Kyran rocks back and forth, the distraught energy within

her screaming to be dispelled. Speaking it aloud feels wrong. The truth isn't for anyone's ears but hers.

"She loves you," Benna says, astonished. "And you . . ."

Kyran can't say that either. Those words are for Davia.

But Davia is gone.

"You—you fell in love with a Sifani royal?" Benna's palpable outrage is edged with horror and something like pity. "After all they've done to our people? Kyran, how could you?"

Benna's attack snaps Kyran out of her grief and ignites her temper.

"I have given Ellod what was asked of me, everything I can without losing myself." *And now, the last piece of me is gone.* "My parents are gone. The rest of our family, gone. For months, I thought I'd lost you. So many people . . . forgive me, I have lost count."

It's not fair, she knows. Every one of their people has been through hell. No one remains unscathed, and before she puts on a brave face and steps forward once more as a shield between her people and the High King's empire, she claims a moment to be selfish.

"We've all made sacrifices, Benna." Kyran wipes her cheek and it's immediately wet again. "I am not special in this, and deserve no different treatment, but . . ."

The sobs cut into her words. "Before Ellod needs me again, can't you give me a minute to say goodbye? Even if she's never going to hear it?"

Because Kyran hadn't said anything. Davia had spoken of her love in a way only Kyran would understand, and Kyran had said nothing back.

Kyran hides her face again. She doesn't care about Benna's disapproval because she's too crucified by her own.

To her surprise, Benna stays beside her without saying a word, and though she is not the person Kyran craves more than air or sunlight, at least Kyran isn't alone.

CHAPTER THIRTY-THREE

Every time Davia touches her blade, she wonders what Kyran might be doing.

She had not anticipated such a side effect. Whether Davia has presented her blade to Kyran's hands or not, her heart has been given to someone who is nowhere near her.

Near the center of *Fidelity* is a hexagonal chamber, a sacred space for her meditations and martial forms. An altar in honor of her teachers is bolted on one bulkhead, and two others hold her training weapons.

Davia mounts her short sword, the exalted space not for the weapon itself but for what it represents.

For Kyran.

In the same system as Duveri is an uninhabitable world named Tannus. Robotic systems mine its rock and ore under remote supervision from the station above. For centuries, Venu Pakrim Mins have obtained their weapons from the forge on the station, which constructs the best in the empire.

Davia spends some time with the craftsmen, and more in meditation to determine what weapon suits the next part of her personal journey.

The sword she chooses is longer than the one she has carried for most of her adult life. The blade is matte charcoal gray, sleek and elegant and deadly, its inky appearance belying its sharpness. It is also something to focus on, to take her mind off the restlessness with no other outlet.

It affects her gait and changes the way she moves, and she will adapt to this as she has to all the changes in her life. She tools a scabbard to strap to her back, and while her former blade never felt wrong, this one is right in a different way.

The first time she slides it over her skin, the cut is deeper than anticipated, and that too seems fitting. She raises the blade to her own highest worth again.

While Kyran has not been cast aside, Davia remembers who she is alone.

"Thank you for doing this, Iza. The Mins assigned by the Jeweled Circle would do their duty, but—"

"You'll feel better if it's me." Izabel finishes Davia's sentence with a wry smile. Izabel now leads a collective of administrators untangling Ethelyn's web of clandestine adoptions.

Through the window, afternoon storms pound rain onto Montalans' streets.

Izabel gazes around the room as her smile fades. "So many memories here. It will be strange to think of someone else living in this space."

Davia has kept an apartment near the monastery for years, and today is her last day. She is leaving the furniture for the next tenant, and her other possessions have been transported to *Fidelity*.

Izabel arches one eyebrow and sets aside her sentimentality to Davia's relief. "I understand the Jeweled Circle has rescinded their offer of a seat on the Consortium."

"My proximity to the throne is now an issue as opposed to a benefit." Davia rolls her eyes and counts on her fingers in demonstration. "I have repeatedly rejected their invitations, have proved how far I am willing to persevere in righting injustice, and would never make a proposal that did not benefit all involved. And yet Min Estebin told me with some humor several of the other Mins are actually concerned I might claim the crown and use the monastery as my personal army."

"How would that work?"

"I have no idea, but . . . it does not matter now."

"Rumors abound you've withdrawn your name from the lecture circuit postings," Izabel says. "So what's next?"

Davia is weary of a question for which she has no answer. "This is what I am doing today. Tomorrow is . . . beyond the circle."

When Izabel offers a parting embrace, she seems to understand.

Two days later, Davia undocks from the station above Duveri, her only planned destination the next set of wormhole coordinates.

CHAPTER THIRTY-FOUR

While Ellod and the rest of the coalition await the High King's response, Kyran turns to duty to save her sanity.

"We need fabricators, not orbital weapons," Kyran says, fanning the perspiration from her neck with a waving hand. The day's heat is oppressive in the main tent. "After we get the central power station up and running, we can utilize those same systems for weapons later. Offer them some of the ore in trade."

They've spent decades in space, scrambling for resources. Now is the time to build their own.

"Yes, Advocate." Jivko turns to her console and delivers Kyran's request to one of their trading partners.

As Advocate, Kyran governs by providing the strategy of what must be done and leaves the tactics of how to those better suited. She reminds them she doesn't have all the answers, and together they can solve any problem.

The colony on Ellod has stabilized, and more of their people arrive weekly from across the empire. The population has doubled, and at the current rate of arrivals, will double again before the end of the year.

If Kyran is burying herself in work so she doesn't think about Davia, so be it. It is not simple, it is not easy, and when she lets down her guard, the pain scratches inside her like a wild thing trying to escape. Davia is outside the circle for now. Kyran will not accept the distance between them as permanent. If she's learned anything over the last year, it's how quickly her circumstances can change.

She also refuses to believe she found such love only for it to be taken from her forever.

Ellod, however, is within her circle of influence, and she devotes herself like never before. With so much to do, early mornings and late nights are guaranteed. Venu Pakrim keeps her centered, the work keeps her focused, and time passes faster when she doesn't stop to think.

When she sleeps, she doesn't dream.

If Benna notices any change, that the heart of Kyran is missing in all she does, she says nothing. She has not asked Kyran anything else about Davia, and Kyran is grateful.

Kyran has nothing more to say.

The late summer harvest comes with no response from Sifani Prime. The Old King would have squashed the hint of rebellion long before it could take root. High Queen Ethelyn would have invaded by now and decimated their forces, no matter what the cost to her own troops.

High King Anin hasn't sent so much as a missive since Davia and her ships came and left. Benna has been on high alert for weeks and it's starting to make Kyran itch.

This evening, after the sunset kim venu and a quick bite to eat, Kyran lends a hand at the landing field where Fillip is supervising the construction of a permanent hangar bay. The structure is an attractive combination of natural resources from the planet and scavenged materials from the fleet.

Kyran plans to work until she gets tired, and the ache doesn't stab as deeply on evenings like this. Twilight paints brilliant shades of red, gold, and purple across the sky, and the nearby fields and meadows offer a clear vista all the way to a mountain range. The broad hangar doors are open despite the cooler air, and the view has everyone in high spirits.

She likes it here more than most other places in the

settlement. The open landscape is freeing. She doesn't feel trapped on Ellod, only . . . incomplete. Nothing can be done about that yet.

Once again, she pushes her thoughts aside to focus on her work.

Benna appears, her collar loose and her sleeves rolled up despite the chill. She holds a portable beverage container by her side and wears a hesitant smile.

Sometimes Kyran misses their old relationship, back before they'd found Ellod. This distance between them is unnatural and tense, and Kyran isn't sure how to change that without giving up personal ground or somehow insulting Benna's experience and leadership.

"The first barrel brewed on Ellod was tapped today." Benna unscrews the lid and offers the container to Kyran. "First sip goes to you. No one else knows it's done yet."

Benna wiggles her eyebrows and Kyran laughs.

"I'm honored." Kyran doesn't mention she hopes it's not a bad batch.

The brew is chilled, light, and flavorful, fruit forward with no bitter aftertaste. It's perfect, and Kyran is proud of another instance of what her people have made, another testament to their resilience.

She passes the container back to Benna, who sips and hums in appreciation.

They stand side by side gazing at the sky while passing the ale back and forth. It's mild enough not to alter their sensibilities much, but Kyran drinks sparingly. Benna doesn't make conversation and the silence isn't weighted by anything. It's a welcome change.

Twilight turns to dusk and Kyran debates returning to her work or ending the evening early for once.

A new figure appears in the hangar door, one of the systems technicians, who searches around quickly. When he sees Kyran and Benna, he changes course and rushes towards them.

"Which of us do you think he wants?" Benna asks.

"Definitely you. I'm busy." Kyran leans against a stack of crates and raises the container to her lips for another sip of cool ale.

"Advocate." When he comes to a stop in front of them, he tilts his head in deference. "There's a private high-priority message for you. You must come to the command tent immediately."

Kyran squelches the thought of Davia when it forms. Hope is a difficult habit for her to break, and she has to remind herself constantly that it was her choice.

"Which member of the coalition is it?"

"No, it's—it's the High King. He's asking for you."

CHAPTER THIRTY-FIVE

The command tent staff clusters near the entrance with apprehensive and guarded expressions in the glow of the evening lamps.

Jivko steps outside the command tent as Kyran arrives.

"The channel is open and awaiting your acknowledgment. I've cleared the rooms and will be monitoring the connection from the annex." Awed by the royal request though professional as always, Jivko has once again anticipated Kyran's needs. "Switch over to the secondary channel if you need me."

Kyran offers a reassuring glance to all present and a nod to Benna who's joined the small crowd, then enters the command tent and closes the entrance behind her.

Across the room near the tables the council uses for its gatherings sits the command array. The larger display is dark, and the High King's connection is live on a smaller screen. Kyran breathes deeply as she sits down and enables her own video feed.

High King Anin is a young king and a man in his prime. His hair is trimmed close to his head, and a full, neat mustache and beard frame his face. His pale eyes are intense and intelligent.

"Advocate Kyran Loyal," he says in Sifani as if asking for confirmation.

Kyran swallows against her nervousness. "I am." She responds in Sifani and doesn't address him by title. It's a dangerous risk, but she has claimed Ellod's independence and cannot afford to acknowledge his rule, even in greeting.

Yet Kyran is desperate not to misstep. With a word, he can order the destruction of dozens of planets, and rain fire and desolation on Ellod and everything they have worked to accomplish.

He could also recognize the coalition's independence. His initiation of this private communication must signify something.

Though it might be perceived as weakness, she waits for him to phrase a question.

The High King tilts his head in hesitation. "I have been assured you would be receptive to this unprecedented direct conversation."

He can only mean Davia.

He continues. "This discourse would best progress if you'll assure me this is a private channel reserved for only the two of us."

In answer, Kyran keys in a command at her station leaving his line open so he can hear. "Jivko, please confirm this connection is secure from any and all external feeds and isolate it from Ellodian lines as well."

"Yes, Advocate."

A moment passes while Kyran holds the High King's gaze in the feed.

"Secured and encrypted," Jivko says. "I suggest you switch to implant for audio. I'm severing my link now."

An orange indicator goes dark, and only one light remains on the system. Kyran takes an audio implant from its designated storage on the console and tucks it in her ear.

"This is a confirmed private channel and, on my honor, restricted to the two of us."

His expression loses a modicum of tension. How interesting that he trusts her word.

"I will address the most significant issue first," the High King says.

She steels herself, preparing for angry threats or, worse, the exorbitant price he will exact from the people of Ellod in response to her declaration. The distance between them shrinks with the severity of his gaze, as if they're both in the same room instead of light-years apart.

When he speaks again, his tone is grave. "Allow me to convey my deepest sorrow and regret at the unjust execution of your father, Rudd Loyal, and your mother, Althea Loyal, along with their . . . confederates."

His words slam into her chest with explosive power, stealing her breath. No concession has ever been stated by Sifani Prime.

"For their crimes," he says, "they deserved a fair trial. I doubt you will be moved by the immeasurable depth of my mother's grief. It is the only explanation I can offer."

The new king appears sincere. He might also be a good actor. Kyran chooses to believe him. He raises his head, his regard steady. "As monarch of Sifani Prime, I recognize both the injustice and the incalculable loss you have suffered."

It's far too late, but it has been offered. If this is his way of leveling the field of their interaction, so be it.

"More so," he says. "I want to assure you personally that those methods of securing Sifani Prime are no longer permissible and are in fact intolerable. I don't expect you to believe me, and I intend to have my actions speak for themselves. Which is another reason for this conversation."

She nods, feeling like a toy puppet. The fear of inciting war keeps her silent.

A sound like the tapping of a finger comes across the channel. He arches an eyebrow—so reminiscent of Davia.

"This discussion will be more productive if you stop worrying about saying the wrong thing."

"Can you blame me?" She surprises herself with her candor.

"No, but . . ." To her surprise, he shakes his head and becomes less a king and more a man before her. "I chose this private conversation for two reasons. One, I've already mentioned, and the other . . . since you declined the invitation to come to Meteus, I had hoped this method might provide a more direct and personal discourse."

Another unprecedented concession.

Will it cost much more to take him at his word? Whether she makes a mistake by saying the wrong thing or insults him by saying nothing, the result will be the same.

The truth, then.

"I wanted to go. My role here necessitated a different approach."

The pain of Davia's leaving washes over her again.

"Sometimes duty answers for us, and so you understand my position. As a new king, I must be seen to have steady hands and a firm grip, and rebellion has now grown to sedition. I sympathize with all you have endured, but if I publicly acknowledge your independence, I risk further insurrection in the empire."

"Your empire has terrorized millions." She regrets her words. They're true, but Kyran wishes she'd found a less volatile way to state them. "All for the misfortune of standing in its path."

He frowns. "I would have Sifani Prime put its despotic rule in the past and move into a brighter future. I will not speak to the pending changes in policy after the . . . previous monarchy's missteps, but . . . I will ensure they are implemented. My most-trusted advisor will no doubt ensure I suffer the consequences should I fail."

Despite the private connection, they're dancing around the only common ground they might have. Kyran grows weary of political fencing, of speaking about Davia in euphemisms.

"Your sister is formidable."

He takes her measure, and she does not drop her eyes. Kyran will never be ashamed of her love for Davia, and she does not care if he sees.

"At her suggestion," he says, "I offer a possible proposal for how we might move forward. Ellod and several other planets in your coalition have resources of value to Sifani Prime. Previously the crown would have borne the cost of their collection and distribution. As acknowledged independents, however, those costs would fall to you. I would publicly sever all support of your infrastructure in penalty for rejecting the benevolent hand of the empire, but offer trade at reasonable rates in private reparations.

This grants me political advantage, discouraging further sedition, while solidifying your independence."

Kyran is shocked at such a mutually beneficial proposition. "I can make no promises. It does merit a deeper discussion."

Though Kyran never relaxes, her fear eases over the course of their discussion. She's surprised by the concessions he's willing to make. How much did Davia push him?

Two hours later, as she tries to stretch one leg without it being visible on the video feed, the High King takes a deep breath and straightens in his seat.

"I will make a public pronouncement to the imperial court next month," he says. "For now, I recognize the declaration of your independence. Sifani Prime will initiate commerce negotiations with Ellod as a test case for the rest of your coalition."

No small measure of relief surges through her. There will be no war.

"I want to be clear, Advocate Loyal. These . . . concessions on my part are not because of my sister's attachment to you, or because you saved her life."

His face softens. "Or at least, not only because of that. I am, however, grateful to you. You may never know how much she means to me."

Kyran wonders if her feelings are plain on her face. "I understand."

"Sifani Prime was built by the great men and women of my family, and our origins are not pristine. While I believe we have a destiny, we also have a lot to answer for."

Kyran's actions have responded to that particular issue, so she makes no comment.

"My sister agrees," he says. "I asked her to rule beside me, to keep me honest if you will, but a life on the throne holds no appeal for her. She renounced all claim to it before she left."

Kyran wants to ask. She burns with the need of it, and only her dedication to duty keeps her from inquiring about Davia's whereabouts.

He seems to see right through her. "Perhaps she's not the only one who would rather be elsewhere."

"No," Kyran says. "I don't wish to walk away from what we have built. I want to secure it without bloodshed so I'm grateful we can move forward peacefully, but . . ."

He is Davia's brother, but he is also the High King, and she does not know him.

"My path and your sister's may cross again." Kyran will share no more with him.

"She told me she was returning to where it all began," he says to Kyran's surprise. "I'd imagine she's at the monastery."

Kyran's hope and longing wrestle for dominance before she pushes them to the side. The High King stares, and she wonders what he sees.

She cannot thank him for his concessions to Ellodian self-rule lest it be mistaken for obeisance. She does finally nod in deference to his rank.

"We will speak soon, I am sure," he says, and sounds optimistic.

Kyran finishes the conversation with plans for future engagement. She quickly updates the anxious crowd outside with a simple "we've won," inciting a celebration lasting two full days and nights before anyone thinks about getting back to work. Although the people of Ellod have achieved a decades-long goal, she is distracted.

One minor detail is singularly important and of immeasurable magnitude.

Davia has renounced any claim to the throne and has ventured off alone.

CHAPTER THIRTY-SIX

The blade mounted on the bulkhead has become distracting.

Three times a day, Davia feels its presence as she performs the kim venu, disquieting her mind. She has begun to use the excuse of being off-ship to perform the ritual elsewhere, which is foolish. The blade was hers for years, yet now it is a foreign entity.

She must move beyond this diversion, and nowhere on the ship does the blade service. She refuses to put it in storage.

The answer does not come until her travels lead her to Iniskeppa, a world on the border between the core systems and the outer territories.

She has spent several days exploring the planet, sampling the cuisine and an abundance of new experiences. While she visits a mountain range along the planet's equator, Davia's interest is captured by a tourist advertisement of its impressive snow-covered crags. The mountain peaks extend far past the dark tree line, reaching for the sky, and adventurers require supplemental equipment to survive the climb.

Davia chooses a lower altitude day hike through the trees, one taxing her endurance. The elevation gain is as refreshing as it is challenging, and the way the air clears her head is welcome.

At the top of the trail sits a handful of stalls offering simple fare and a few wares aiming to eke more coin from travelers. Tucked into a hollow between viewing platforms over a high mountain lake, one vendor's table draws her attention.

The vendor is an older man, twice Davia's age if she were to guess. His hands are gnarled by a lifetime of craft, his skin aged by years in the elements. He stands when she approaches and greets her with a smile more from his eyes than his lips.

"Welcome, Duveri Min. I hope your day is a good one."

"It is, thank you." Davia spares him a glance, and then her eyes are drawn back to his merchandise. He sells only staffs, each a different shade of gray or black with some minor variation in length and thickness, and all exquisitely carved.

She is gratified he allows her to shop without interruption. He makes no pitch and offers no information. She does not know exactly what will meet her needs and is glad to be left alone while she decides.

The answer to her unspoken, unformed question is tucked inside one of the stands towards the back of his stall. The staff is as tall as Kyran in her memory, as thick as the wrist above the hands she can recall when she closes her eyes. It is dark gray, smooth as skin, unvarnished and not as ornate as the others, but no less complete.

"This one," she says. "And I will require a custom carving."

Fillip's normally reserved face breaks into a smile. "I motion we adjourn."

Kyran stays silent as several other Ellodian councilors sound their agreement. Over the comm relays, members of the newly formed Independent Planetary Parliament add their comments before the session ends.

Embraces, handshakes, and back pats spread around the room. Benna's regency ended with Kyran claiming her birthright, and Kyran has now formally dissolved the monarchy. She remains Advocate at Benna's insistence, retaining a permanent vote along with a singular veto right she intends to never use.

Ellod is officially governed by an elected council, and in the hands of the people.

"Keg's tapped," Lora calls from the kitchen area, and a small cheer answers in kind.

After everyone has a full cup, Kyran excuses herself from a conversation with Benna and Fillip about the latest trade proposals from the High King's court. She stands before the council table and raises one hand. The room quiets.

"Let me say a few words and you can get back to this fantastic Ellodian ale."

"Make them brief," Benna says to good-natured laughter from several others.

Kyran glares without true heat. She clears her throat more from nerves than need.

"We've come so far, my friends. Let us not only celebrate what we've accomplished, but also offer veneration to what it cost us."

She doesn't mention their names out loud, those who died before their people achieved this long-improbable reality. Around her, she sees the memories of others on the faces of everyone present, and amid the smiles are a few tears.

"It was my parents' wish the throne of Ellod would usher in an interplanetary alliance of independents."

Kyran raises her eyebrows. "Of course, I made a few changes."

Warm laughter sends their love back to her. Benna has proud tears in her eyes, and Kyran nods in her direction.

"What we build will become the history of our people." Kyran lifts her cup of ale aloft and everyone follows. "To Althea and Rudd Loyal. May we always remember them and keep them in our hearts."

Ellod is a beautiful planet, rich in resources and possibilities. For such opulence, Davia might forgive the piracy involved to claim it if doing so had not cost so many lives.

After arriving in the system undetected—a deactivated transponder and hidden propulsion render her ship a ghost in the void—she hopes to present herself to the Ellodian authorities and request an audience with their Advocate. In preparation for such an appeal, she decides to first assess the likelihood of a nonviolent welcome.

Surveilling the comms proves to be Davia's undoing.

Kyran's voice on one of the open frequency bands fills the cargo bay. ". . . for your help. The new medical center is better equipped to support the settlement thanks to you."

"Maybe next time you can part with some Ellodian ale in trade," a man says. He must be the operator of the transport leaving the planet.

Davia is frozen, waiting for the response.

"I'm afraid we haven't brewed enough yet," Kyran says, a smile in her voice. "Safe travels."

The conversation ends when the transport operator signs off.

Davia lingers in orbit and does not initiate a channel. Instead, she listens to the Ellodian comms, hoping to hear Kyran's voice again.

In time, she reaches a new conclusion.

Davia loves Kyran too much to interfere in her new life, and her own inertia must stop.

When her former path no longer felt complete, she had found the strength to resign her posts, end the research suspended by her isolation, and put all those known yet unsatisfying aspects of her life behind her to venture alone back into the stars.

Now, her nebulous path has led her to the elbow of this system, shadow-stalking her former lover—a label piercing her heart anew—while she makes no progress.

This is no longer about what is in or outside the circle. There is no circle here at all.

Davia craves Kyran by her side, but Kyran's place is with her people, and Davia's . . . lies somewhere else, beyond her brother's rule, beyond the duties of Duveri. Perhaps a journey to the outer planets, to learn more of what lies beyond the empire, may hold some answers.

First, she will say goodbye the only way she can.

Late morning sunlight warms the hangar bay. In recent weeks, Kyran has spent most of her time here. The sound of the ships landing or launching from the attached field is a soothing balm, or a portent of things to come.

When Kyran started at first light, she thought it might take longer to load the stacks of crated provisions and supplies. The small frigate is designed for a four-person crew and suitable for long-range missions. Its actual crew is only one, and Kyran is almost finished securing her gear.

Despite the cool crisp air, she wipes the first drops of perspiration from her forehead with her sleeve and unzips her flight suit to her waist, leaving her in an undershirt.

A shadow blocks the light. Benna leans against the cargo bay door, arms crossed over her chest. "When will you be back?"

Kyran locks another compartment. "Before the planting season."

She rests her hands on her hips and looks everywhere but in Benna's direction. She's postponed this particular conversation, fearing it would be difficult.

"I love Ellod, Benna. And while I fought it for a long time, I am not shying away from my duty, but . . . there's this part of me that—"

Benna surprises her by laughing.

"You don't have to explain love to me, Kyran. I mean, of course I'd prefer you find a nice Ellodian, maybe raise a few kids here at home, but . . ." She shrugs her shoulder. "I can't have everything."

Though Benna's eyes are sad and uneasy, they hold no judgment.

"I'll check in so you don't worry," Kyran says.

"Where will you go?"

Kyran secures a few more containers in the cargo bay. She won't need some of them unless she decides to camp in the wilderness on any of the planets she might visit. After being marooned without them, she's made them requisite for her journey.

"To Duveri." Kyran tamps down the hope rising within her.

Benna steps closer, offers a hug, and when Kyran nods, she gingerly wraps her arms around Kyran's shoulders.

That won't do.

Kyran squeezes back until Benna grunts. They're both laughing, the chasm between them gone.

Her standard day is at its end, and normally Davia would retire for the night, but having decided what to do, she might change her mind if she sleeps on it, and that cannot happen.

She bypasses the asteroid field altogether, adding hours to her journey. A scan of molecular anomalies leads to her former ship faster than searching the database for the original coordinates. She lowers *Fidelity* beyond a bluff near the crash site, leaving the refraction panels active. Nerves twist her stomach, though her hands are steady as she lands.

The slant of morning light throws long shadows across the sand as Davia disembarks and hikes to the canyon.

She stares at the wreckage. That she survived the battle was a miracle, and to have lived for so many months with so few resources—it defies her understanding in retrospect, even if her presence is proof of having lived through it.

Their projects and constructs appear derelict and sad now, but each task had kept them sane, given them purpose, and staved off despair.

The wind and sand, rain and meteors have reclaimed much of the space. To her surprise, an addition has been made since her rescue.

A ring of stones in the sand.

Joy and grief battle anew, both bringing more tears as she strides towards the permanent marker. She misses Kyran so much—and now Davia has something to commemorate what happened here, and how it changed her.

She steps inside the circle.

Kyran's voyage to Duveri will take about twelve days. Finding Davia once she arrives will be another challenge. Here and now, beginning the journey is what's within the circle.

Anticipation quickens Kyran's blood, and she is also excited by the prospect of being back in space. She has missed its quiet dark and the peace of its stars.

Yet once Kyran leaves Ellod's atmosphere, the pull she feels—like a fear to be faced, or a final task to be completed—is not toward Duveri. Davia may have traveled to the monastery to begin again, but for Kyran, her new life began much closer.

Her previous eagerness morphs into no small amount of trepidation as she approaches the asteroid belt. Thoughts of the crash make her hands tremble at the controls. She reduces speed though she's in no danger. This time, her ship's instruments are in prime condition and the frigate is far sturdier than a badly damaged one-person fighter.

In what feels like no time at all, she's flying above the ground, veering toward the old canyon. Some of the sensor data is inconsistent—listing two ships on the ground instead of one—most likely the result of the magnetic interference from the orbital body itself.

She lands her ship near the stone wall Davia built. When she steps through the frigate's boarding door, the scent of the wind evokes the first memories—of the days after the crash when she was terrified and desperate, wounded, and alone. Now she appreciates the stark beauty of this place—the reds and deeper brown strands within the sienna of the banded rock walls.

Armed much the way she was when she was stranded, with her pulse pistol and her dagger, Kyran approaches the canyon. Sand has accumulated in the corners and crevices of the rocks and swallowed the part of the ship once only half buried. More cooled meteors are scattered across the ground. The wind has knocked a few items from the table under the wing. Otherwise, everything is the same if somehow smaller.

She walks toward the sand-covered firepit, and when she turns toward the ritual space—where Davia knelt alone until Kyran joined her, where Kyran knelt after Davia had gone—Kyran freezes, every muscle locked.

A second circle of rocks has been paired with the one she left.

That's not the only change. At the western-most point of Davia's circle, one fist-sized rock has been removed, and in its place a spear has been mounted, one Kyran has never seen before.

She reaches to touch it, only then realizing she's traversed the distance. The shaft is constructed of wood not from this moon. Kyran gasps at the words carved in both Sifani and Ellodian near the spearpoint.

My heart is this blade, offered true and without shame despite its flaws.

The sleek dark blade affixed to the end of the spear is as familiar as her own. It's from Davia's sword, her proclamation made substantive and left here. Davia has been here and judging by the state of the stones and the spear and the lack of sand near them, not that long ago.

Why hadn't she contacted Kyran? Why come all this way only to return to this place? The ache in Kyran's chest wars with anger at missed opportunity, at paths never crossing at the right time or under the right circumstances, and Kyran is tired of it.

An itch between her shoulder blades crawls up the back of her neck until she interprets its meaning.

Someone is watching her. She whirls around, hands falling to her weapons.

On the bluff of the canyon wall, Davia stands motionless.

Dressed in black, armed with a pulse pistol holstered outside one thigh and a new, longer sword rising from behind one shoulder, Davia exudes danger. Her long hair is tied back from her face and falls freely down her back, her arms bent with her hands resting at her waist.

Once, Kyran had thought such presentation combative—ruthless, arrogant, and bloodthirsty. Now she knows better.

Davia is magnificent.

The surroundings, or maybe Davia's attire, prompt Kyran to speak Sifani. "I—I didn't see a ship," she says by way of greeting. It's not at all what she wants to say.

Davia's gaze is steady, her face blank as she responds in her own language. "I have a cloaking feature." She jumps from the bluff onto the sand and walks toward Kyran.

"Benna . . . my cousin." Kyran speaks again without thought. "She's alive."

Davia stops, shocked. She recovers quickly. "For your sake more than my own . . . it is good to know she survived."

They gaze at one another until Davia's earlier words get through Kyran's dazed state.

Cloaking feature? "How long have you been in this system?" Kyran asks.

At this, Davia's eyes drop for a moment as she takes another few steps forward. "Not long."

It is the first vague response Kyran has ever heard from Davia.

"Why didn't you send word?" Kyran doesn't mean for it to sound like an accusation.

Davia stops again, still too far away. "I could ask the same of you, though I am certain of the answer."

It wasn't time yet; there was work to be done. The challenging parts are finished now.

Davia arches an eyebrow, and Kyran's heart stutters in response. "It took far longer than I had hoped to convince my brother to accept the coalition of independents. Repeated appeals to the royal purse were required."

Kyran wants to smile. She's hurt, yes, that Davia has been so close without her knowledge, but it feels too good to hear Davia's brevity and crisp wit.

Davia frowns, trepidation all over her face when Kyran doesn't move. "Is there something more you need to hear, Kyran Loyal?" she asks in Sifani-accented Ellodian.

Hearing Davia speak her language and her name snaps Kyran from her stupor. The proof is all around her in so many ways. Davia is here. Davia stands waiting for Kyran to welcome her. Davia's blade has been offered to Kyran.

Davia has given everything she is and all Kyran has to do . . .

By the time she finally steps in Davia's direction, Davia has rushed forward and crashes into her arms. The strength Kyran remembers is there, and Davia feels more substantial now. This woman is like the one Kyran first saw in this very place in what seems so long ago—strong, vibrant, powerful—and so different because this Davia is hers.

When Kyran loosens her embrace, she can't wait anymore. "Davia," she whispers before their lips touch.

Davia's hand clutches the back of Kyran's neck and boldly holds her fast, not that Kyran would go anywhere. Her kiss feels desperate, consuming, like she fears Kyran will float away if not held down.

Kyran doesn't stop until she's had her fill. Finally, though, she has things to say.

"I wanted to come with you." Kyran fights her tears. They block her view of Davia's face. "To be with you, but I . . . I—"

"I understand duty, Kyran, and why you could not come. It was only my hope you might."

Kyran rests her forehead on Davia's. "I missed you." She breathes in Davia's scent, gives in, and lets the tears well in her eyes.

"I am sorry it took me so long to stand up to the queen," Davia says, her eyes uneasy.

Kyran doesn't want to tally points for Davia's action or inaction.

"What you've done for Ellod, Davia . . . I never expected you to—"

"I did. You showed me what the cost of her rule was to

everyone else, and I could not stand by and let it continue." Davia draws in a deep breath and exhales. "I would never have been able to do that had I not met you."

"And you taught me how to do what needed to be done. I didn't know how angry I was, but I learned how to use it to help my people, to be better, to be stronger. Now Ellod is free, and its people govern themselves."

"Are you still Advocate?"

"Yes, though I've dissolved the monarchy and transferred governance to the council. They wouldn't accept absolute abdication, like yours."

"I do not want you to misunderstand or think less of me." Davia frowns and rests her palms against Kyran's chest. "This was not some ploy to garner your favor. Despite the depth of my feelings for you, I did not renounce the throne for you."

"Nor I mine for you, but now, neither of us is as . . . duty-bound as we were."

The weight of their words sits between them, and it isn't uncomfortable.

Davia casts a quick glance around the canyon. "Why are you here now?"

"I . . . I guess I came to say goodbye before I went to the monastery to look for you." At Davia's inquisitive expression, Kyran brushes her lips across Davia's again. "Your brother said you were going back to where it all began."

Davia shakes her head and holds Kyran's face with her cool hands. "I came to begin anew, and I thought I would have to leave you behind once again. All I want is you, my sunlight."

Kyran closes her eyes and savors the moment's sweetness. The power of Davia's words sears her, brands her with permanence. Will there ever be a time Davia's influence doesn't forever change her?

She hopes not.

"I love you, Davia. I had to come find you."

Davia smiles and her eyes gleam with tears.

Kyran squeezes her closer. "I thought it might take a bit

longer, though. What happens now since I've found you already?"

"Do you still wish to go to Duveri?"

"Yes, absolutely yes, and . . ." Kyran's shyness wars with her elation. "I want to show you my world."

"I can think of nothing I want more." Davia pauses in thought. "We have one too many ships."

Kyran grins. "Mine is loaded with the fresh bounty of a free Ellod."

"*Fidelity* is larger with better tech." Davia's eyes dance with what can only be happiness and a touch of engineering superiority. "We can move your supplies to my ship and return yours to your fleet. Ellod first, then Duveri, and then . . . perhaps beyond them both."

An adventure for the two of them.

Kyran squeezes Davia in her arms. "I just packed the whole thing up a few hours ago."

"That sounds suspiciously like a complaint," Davia says, a wry twist to her lips.

"I wouldn't dream of it, Min Davia." Kyran pulls away and lifts the spear from the circle, measuring its heft with a gentle shake. "I will treasure this as much as I treasure what it represents, my love."

Davia grasps her other hand and weaves their fingers together. "Come. The stars are waiting for us."

ACKNOWLEDGMENTS

What started as an homage to all the retro sci-fi films and novels that captivated my early years now has a place of its own.

Thanks to my publisher, Bywater Books, for believing in me and my work. Salem West endured countless inquiries and offered her encouragement and support along with every response.

Kit Haggard, editor extraordinaire, broke my brain in all the best ways. Her feedback was spot-on, of course, but more importantly, she identified opportunities in this story I had never considered. Davia Sifane's journey is one of the many results. Thanks, Kit, for helping me expand this universe far beyond Ellod.

Ann McMan's superpowers are legendary at this point, and this cover still stunned me. It's so close to the one I envisioned; I wonder what else she knows about me that I haven't told her yet.

This story has evolved over several incarnations and a few folks have been with me from the beginning. Quinn Clarkson has been involved since the second day of its inception. Terri Furuya and Shawn Marie Bryan both endured multiple unpolished versions. Heather Flournoy helped me wrestle the tale into proper form and is a personal constant upon whom I increasingly rely. Anna Burke has been a champion throughout the story's journey, as has K. Aten. Many thanks to Amy Harley and Renae Standen for beta reading.

Kate Dilworth, Bruce Wyman, Meredith Doench, and MB Austin saved the day with their proofreading skills, and have my sincere gratitude.

I hope you all enjoy the final product.

My two fathers are long dead, but each in their way contributed to my love of science fiction. While not my first published novel, this is my first full-length sci-fi work. They probably wouldn't have read it (or would have at least skipped *those scenes*), but I think they'd be proud.

To those who have supported my every creative endeavor, to those who introduce my work to all who might read it, to those who helped me along the way and yet I've somehow neglected to name you here—thank you.

Lastly and in no way least, I offer my eternal gratitude to the 1,647 (and counting) readers who invested their most valuable resource in the original version of this story. Every comment, every thumbs-up, every kudo meant more to me than I can possibly express, so I hope this extended version of the tale is proper thanks.

ABOUT THE AUTHOR

Virginia Black likes strong whiskey, loud music, and writing, though not necessarily in that order. When not penning sci-fi and dark speculative fiction, she is almost always reading. Born in California—where even the green is brown—Virginia escaped to the verdant gardens and rain showers of the Pacific Northwest. She lives with her wife of more than twenty years and their savagely witty teenage daughter.

Virginia's debut novel, *Consecrated Ground*, published in 2023 and her short story, "Ravenous" was included in the Bywater Books anthology, *Soul Food Stories: An Otherworldly Feast for the Living, the Dead, and Those Who Have Yet to Decide*, which also published in 2023.

Twitter | @virginiablk517
Instagram | @virginiablackwrites
Facebook | facebook.com/virginiablackwrites/
Bluesky | @virginiablack.bsky.social
Website | http://virginiablackwrites.com/

Bywater Books believes that all people have the right to read or not read what they want—and that we are all entitled to make those choices ourselves. But to ensure these freedoms, books and information must remain accessible. Any effort to eliminate or restrict these rights stands in opposition to freedom of choice. Please join with us by opposing book bans and censorship of the LGBTQ+ community.

At Bywater Books, we are *all* stories.

We are committed to bringing the best of contemporary literature to an expanding community of readers. Our editorial team is dedicated to finding and developing outstanding writers who create books you won't want to put down.

For more information about Bywater Books, our authors, and our titles, please visit our website.

www.bywaterbooks.com

www.ingramcontent.com/pod-product-compliance
Lightning Source LLC
Jackson TN
JSHW080106141224
75386JS00028B/844

* 9 7 8 1 6 1 2 9 4 2 7 9 7 *